I0694976

STORM AND FLAME

Enchanted I

MALLORY WANLESS

Cover design by GetCovers

First edition

ISBN:

Paperback 979-8-9855733-0-5
Ebook 979-8-9855733-1-2

Library of Congress Control Number: 2022906893

CONTENT WARNING

This story mentions incidents of child abuse, sexual assault,
and birth trauma.
May not be suitable for some readers.

Also by Mallory Wanless

The *turmio* trilogy:
Storm and Flame: Enchanted I
Blood and Destiny: Enchanted II
Reign and Ruin: Enchanted III

Enchanted Standalones:
Reclaiming the Frost: Enchanted IV

Vexia Standalone Novellas:
Of Poison and Passion

Coming soon:
Enchanted V
Enchanted VI

To my amazing husband, who has been my biggest supporter. This book would not be out in the world without him.

And to my wonderful children. If not for them, this book would have either never been written or been published years ago.

Pronunciation Guide

Characters:
Elena: eh-LAY-nah
Agon: A-gone
Quinn: qu-IN
Lyra: LIE-rah
Madame LaBelle: ma-DAM la-BELL
Zied: ZED
Fàidh: FAY-d
Roska: ROSS-kah
Demoni: de-MON-ee

Places:
Andover: ann-DOVER
Nexton: NEX-ton
Cyra: sigh-RAH

1

ELENA

"**C**OME ON. JUST WORK, dammit," Elena muttered to herself, trying for the millionth time to cast her spell.

Agon had stretched his lithe, weasel-like body across a long, skinny patch of sunlight on the floor of the testing room. He'd spent the morning basking in the warmth of the sun-drenched stone and flicking his fluffy blue-black tail back and forth. As her closest, and arguably only, friend, Agon knew nothing he could say would make her feel better. She was in a mood, and the best thing he could do was to leave her be.

Sparks flared and quickly sputtered out from Elena's fingertips.

"Dammit. Why can't I get this stupid spell right?" It was a rhetorical question, but Elena was so frustrated by her own ineptitude that she would have traded everything she owned to successfully complete a spell on the first try.

Elena was easily the worst enchantress in her class, probably the whole school. The other students mocked her mercilessly.

It didn't help that her mother, Madame LaBelle, was the most famous enchantress in the whole country, possibly the world, and the headmistress of their school. She could turn a seed into a centuries-old tree with the flick of her wrist. Elena could grow a seed into a sapling with twenty minutes of chanting, flicking, waving, and praying. Maybe. On a good day.

Madame LaBelle was notorious for her skills with magic as much as her beauty. Unfortunately for Elena, she inherited her looks from her father. At least, she assumed that's where she got her flat hair and dull brown eyes. She'd never actually met him. In Waverly, as far as enchantresses were concerned, men served one purpose: impregnating women. The men were used and released of all parental rights, whether they liked it or not. Most men didn't even know the woman they had lain with was an enchantress, much less that they had fathered a child as a re-sult. The women opted to disguise themselves—bar wenches, visitors lost in the big city, damsels in need of aid on the side of the road, etc.—just to get what they needed and be gone before the man even knew her name.

It was crass and cowardly, but Elena had been raised to believe it was for the best. Men weren't capable of raising children, especially magical ones, and an enchantress always gave birth to another enchantress. Never in the history of the world, had an enchantress given birth to a non-magical child.

Or a boy, for that matter. Enchantress beget enchantress. End of story.

Elena dreamed of love and happy endings when she was younger. All the girls did, but their time at Harbor Ridge taught them that magic was their top priority, followed closely by their loyalty to the school and Madame LaBelle. Elena always felt that it was a tad hypocritical how often her mother preached about loyalty to their family—the school and their classmates—when she never paid any attention to her own flesh and blood. What sort of mother neglects her own child to favor those who are more adept at magic? *Not a good one,* Elena mused glumly.

Agon had been with her since before she was born, like all familiars. They were born together and stayed attached for an "unusually long time," according to her mother. Typically, familiars disconnected from the baby's umbilical cord within a few days before settling into their permanent animal form. Agon and Elena stayed connected for two weeks, all the while Agon remained a blob encased in the placenta. Her mother had many specialists, including a Therionology Enchantress, or an animal enchantress, come and inspect Agon and try to coax him into taking any form at all. Nothing worked. Baby Elena just spent her days cuddling "this disgusting blob of goo" and sleeping. Madame LaBelle often liked to remind Elena of how unusual that was, and how that should have been a sign that her daughter was going to be different, and not in a good way.

Agon did eventually develop into an animal; however, he didn't change into anything anyone had ever seen before. When she was young, Elena overheard one of the scholars reminiscing with another about how they'd managed to identify Agon as a *Raju*. Madame LaBelle had tasked all of the scholars in the Therionology department to scour all the history books and tomes to identify him. Agon was the only known *Raju* in ages, and Madame LaBelle hated it. *Rajus* were blue-furred, weasel-like creatures that had lightning abilities. Another frustrating hiccup, as far as Madame LaBelle was concerned. Familiars weren't supposed to have magic of their own; they were just meant to be guides to help the enchantress learn to control her powers. Elena knew they were unique, and she knew that her mother despised her for it. Not only did she look nothing like her gorgeous and flawless mother, but she was as inept at magic as she was clumsy. Not to mention her familiar was a troublesome weasel with issues controlling magic he shouldn't have even had. Elena tried very hard in her lessons to improve her control and help Agon to control himself, but it never seemed good enough.

Harbor Ridge was set back in the heart of the aptly named Dark Woods. According to legend, the school was originally built as a safe harbor for magical beings who were being hunted and persecuted throughout the country. The king of Waverly took pity on the enchantresses and gave them the land along the mountain ridge to build a sanctuary. Thus, Harbor Ridge was created. A shelter for all enchantresses on the ridge of a mountain to train, educate, and live without fear. The school itself was an ominous castle made of black obsidian; the stone so dark you could almost feel it sucking the light from the sky. Four immense towers stood at the cardinal points and served as the dormitories for the girls. Four girls to a room, four rooms to a floor, four floors to a tower. There was magic in the number and the balance it created. Without that balance things would come to a grinding halt, according to school rumor. The legend said that one year, a girl in the north tower couldn't handle the pressure and jumped from her window. The instant her heart stopped beating, the whole northern tower started to tilt and pull away from the castle. According to the stories, the headmistress at the time had to admit some less desirable girl from the nearest village just to keep the school from literally falling apart.

Elena never fully believed the legend, simply because she could never see her mother admitting any student unless they had impeccable credentials and at least ten relatives who were once prolific students at Harbor Ridge, on top of passing the incredibly strenuous entrance exam. She truly believed that her mother wouldn't have admitted her if that had been an option.

However, it would have been disastrous for the daughter of the headmistress to not go to Harbor Ridge, too much of a scandal for her mother to bear.

This was a day unlike any other. It marked Elena's sixteenth birthday, a very special birthday. At Harbor Ridge, an enchantress' sixteenth birthday was the day she took her specialty test to determine which division of magic she would be best suited for. The test was always different, based on the enchantress, the season, the time of day, even her lunar cycle. There would be no way to prepare because there would be no way to know what your test would be.

When Elena had walked into her testing hall earlier that morning, she was surprised to see that the room was utterly empty. No alchemy supplies. No seeds meant for her to grow into beautiful trees. No fire or water to highlight her elemental skills. Nothing. Not even a table or chairs. Agon had been nestled around her neck, his preferred spot, and he, too, was awkwardly quiet. There should have been someone in the room; the tests were always different, but there was always someone there to administer them.

"Maybe we're just early, Agon," she had whispered as she'd crept into the middle of the room, further into the empty expanse. The room was eerily still. It felt like a violation to be there, much less making any noise above a hushed tone.

"Maybe they forgot," Agon replied, in an equally quiet, albeit more condescending, voice. She could feel the nervousness coursing through his veins, both as his heart pounded around her neck and through the magic that bound them.

Standing in the middle of the empty room, she had decided to wait. It was supposed to be her big day, and it was impossible to think her mother simply forgot. Elena convinced herself that waiting was merely a part of the test. Assessing her patience and perseverance. She would stay put until someone showed up to evaluate her skills and place her in a specialty. This was her day, dammit. She'd spent the day watching the sun pass through the windows, from one side of the room, up and over to the other side, repeatedly trying and failing to accomplish even the simplest of spells. Maybe she'd finally get that damned spell right before someone arrived to test her.

"It's been hours," Agon whined, "can we please just go find someone? Your mother. I'm sure she'll have a good reason for all this. I'm bored, and I want a snack."

"Familiars don't need food or sleep to survive, Agon. You know that." Elena was bored too, but she was far too stubborn to give up now. She estimated that they were about an hour from sunset, meaning everyone was sitting down to supper in the Great Hall. They'd forgotten about her. She had waited all day, and her own mother had forgotten about her birthday, the biggest birthday that an enchantress ever had at Harbor Ridge. The only one that muxing mattered, and her damned mother had forgotten her. Elena realized that this shouldn't be so surprising; her mother never paid much attention to her before, so why would this change anything?

"I didn't say I need to eat, only that I want a snack. I'm feeling peckish." Agon was lounging in the last rays of sunlight on the floor a few feet from where she sat. He was, of course, not really peckish at all, but he could feel how hungry she was, and he was hoping to motivate her to feed herself. Agon was a very attentive familiar, always making sure she took care of herself even when she didn't want to. She was certain that he would go and fetch her food himself if he could venture more than twenty paces from her. That was the thing about being magically tethered: there was an unseeable force that physically kept them together. There were rumors that the wizards and enchantresses of old could travel miles apart from their familiars, but they were just rumors. No enchantress could really do that. They'd die. You cannot be separated from your soul.

"I know what you're doing," Elena muttered, shifting in her seated position on the floor. "Fine, we'll wait five more minutes. Then we'll go find her and see what sort of excuse she musters."

"Let's swing by the kitchens first and grab a quick snack. I can feel your stomach rumbling through the stone in the floors. This is what you get for skipping breakfast." Agon played the part of the fretful parent with practiced ease. Elena truly believed he had happily jumped into the maternal role hours after her birth when it had been clear her own mother wouldn't. She suspected that was about thirty seconds after Madame LaBelle realized just how "different" her daughter and Agon were. Madame LaBelle hated when things were out of sorts, and everything about the two of them was subpar in her eyes.

"Will that make you happy? If we stop and grab a roll, will you please shut up about food for a while?"

"Absolutely!" He was already on his feet and getting a running start so he could jump onto her shoulders and settle back onto his perch.

"You are a very frustrating creature, you know that?" she mumbled as he landed perfectly, the result of years of practice, and snuggled her ear. His way of saying *yes, but you love me anyway*, and she did. He was the only one who ever bothered to make sure she was ok, and he went to great lengths to help her find happiness in this dreadful place.

The trip to the headmistress' office was an uneventful one, with only a quick pit stop for a couple of dinner rolls in the kitchen before rushing up the four flights of stairs to reach her mother's tower. Much to her surprise, the door was wide open and her mother was waiting for her. Sitting behind her imposing ebony desk, her mother looked almost regal, especially with her familiar, a snowy lion named Zeid, lazing to her right.

"Elena, please come in. Shut the door." It wasn't a request; nothing ever was with Madame LaBelle. She was cold and distant, but that was her way with Elena.

"Today was meant to be your testing day. You failed. Unfortunately, you have been expelled from Harbor Ridge and must leave immediately."

Elena didn't move. She just stood there as if someone had cast a spell and frozen her in place.

"Wha—how? What are you saying?" she stammered, and she stumbled to the closest chair.

"You never showed for your evaluation. That is unacceptable. You have until the morning to pack your things and leave. If you are still here at first light, you will be forcibly removed." No sooner had she finished the words did she go back to the paperwork on her desk. Madame LaBelle, her *mother*, had evicted her from the only home she'd ever known and she hadn't even batted an eye.

"How can you do this to me? I'm your *muxing* daughter! I waited all day in that room. No one ever showed up to test me. I waited!" Rage flowing through her veins like molten lava, lighting a fire within her. Agon jumped down from her neck and onto her mother's desk, small blue sparks flicking off the end of his tail as he swished it back and forth.

"You will not use that sort of foul language in my presence. Get control of your familiar, child. You are my daughter. That is the only reason you have lasted this long. You don't belong here. We both know it. It's time for you to go." While her mother never moved, Zeid rose slowly and powerfully to his feet, sending the message, *Go now or there will be painful consequences.*

"I can't believe you're doing this. I mean, I knew you were disappointed in me, but I never thought you hated me. How can you be so heartless?" Elena knew if they remained in this room, it was very likely that there would be blood, she just wasn't sure whose. But she needed answers. She *deserved* answers. "What did I do that justifies expelling me from my home? Don't give me that nonsense about how I didn't show up. I was there at dawn."

"I am under no obligation to explain myself to you, child. You've only survived this long because you carry my blood. We both know you don't belong here." Her mother's tone was cool. Distant. Bored, even.

Bored? She's imploding my entire life, and she's muxing bored?!

Sparks flashed off the tip of Agon's tail, and he stood on her mother's stack of papers, forcing her attention to them rather than the work she clearly felt was more important than her flesh and blood.

"What did I ever do to make you hate me this much?" Elena's voice was a hushed, heartbroken whisper. All of her rage had instantly drained from her body.

For a split second, she thought she saw a flash of guilt on her mother's face, but it disappeared in a blink of an eye replaced by her practiced enchantress mask, cool detachment.

Madame LaBelle gestured to Agon. "You must learn to control your familiar." She rose from her throne-like chair and turned her back on her daughter. "You will be gone by first light. If you cause a scene, the guards will remove you by force."

Elena snatched Agon off the headmistress' desk and stormed out, leaving the only family she'd known in her wake.

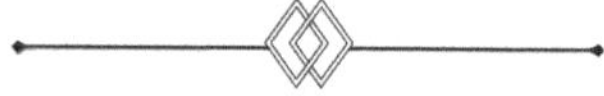

Elena threw herself onto her bed, curled up around her down feather pillow, and cried. Agon wiggled under her arms and tried his best to comfort her, rubbing his velvety blue nose against her cheek and licking her tears away.

"How could she...? Why? I just don't understand." She choked out the words once her eyes had run out of tears. "How can she be so callous? And what about the girls? The tower will be out of balance and surely start to crumble as soon as I leave, won't it? That's what the legend and rumors all say."

"I don't know, El, but I imagine her Holier-Than-Thou-Ness will have found a way to maintain the balance. She's too calculating to do something like this without a fool-proof plan." Agon wiped the last of her tears away with his fluffy tail.

"I must be missing something. I was told to report to the exam room this morning, at first light. We were there! We waited all day and no one came to test me! We were there." Elena sighed, devastation weighing on her like a thick blanket, making it nearly impossible for her to take a deep breath.

It just didn't make sense. It was unlike her mother to be so unreasonable. She had always had exceedingly high expectations for Elena, and Elena had never felt like she could truly reach her mother's goals for her, but expulsion? Why would Madame LaBelle make up an excuse to expel her only child, then promptly evict her like it was nothing? Like Elena was nothing, just some failed enchantress who couldn't be taught and must therefore be amputated like a gangrenous limb, for fear that she might infect the others.

"How serious do you think she was about having us 'forcibly removed' at first light?" Agon questioned gently.

"Knowing her? Very. Madame LaBelle never makes empty threats," Elena grumbled. Slowly, she sat up in her bed. "I don't know how to pack our stuff. It's not like we've traveled a lot before. Maybe we can stuff it all into the pillowcase?"

As she went through her wardrobe, Elena tried to ignore the reality of her situation. She packed her few belongings into her pillowcase, a few dresses, a spare pair of boots, and a woolen coat, made her bed one last time, and walked out of her room.

Elena was grateful that the other girls were still at dinner. No one had ever been expelled before. No one even knew that was possible. She didn't know how to explain what had happened.

They passed through the kitchens and filled the pillowcase with as much as they could, said a quick goodbye to the cooks, and left.

With Agon perched atop her left shoulder, Elena hiked the pillowcase on her right and started down the path, away from the school, into the Dark Woods and the unknown.

2

QUINN

WHEN YOU GROW UP in an orphanage, you learn to read people pretty quickly. When you grow up in an orphanage run by an abusive drunk and his neglectful wife, you learn that everyone is full of shyt and you have to fend for yourself if you want to survive. The former enabled Quinn to do the latter. Reading people helped him find good marks, then he and Lyra would rob them blind. Lyra was quick and clever, like most foxes, but she was special. She could start fires with the flick of her tail, which came in very handy when you needed to distract a mark to pickpocket them, or on cold nights when you didn't have an actual roof or walls to protect you from the harsh frost seasons. He'd learned long ago that they had to take care of themselves. That meant doing whatever it took to survive.

Q didn't like looting corpses, but he wasn't above it either; sometimes they had the best shyt. When he saw her lying there half-curled against the cold, on the side of the road just outside the Dark Woods, he couldn't pass up the golden opportunity.

She had a whole bag of who-knows-what lying next to her. It could just be food, but it could be decent enough stuff to sell or use themselves. Even if it was food, he and Lyra weren't exactly feasting these days. Besides, she was dead. What did a dead girl need with whatever was in that bag?

"Lyra, you know the drill," he whispered. As a fox, she was innately adept at sneaking, which was why she always made the initial approach. They'd tried other ways when they first started out on their own, but this was by far the most effective. Q sat back, partially hidden behind an old oak tree, and waited.

As Lyra crept closer, he could feel her heart rate slow and her senses heighten. She was inches from the corpse when he felt a violent shock, as though he'd been struck by lightning. He cried out, as did Lyra, before nearly blacking out. Q pulled himself from behind the tree, barely able to crawl to his knees before a second, more powerful blast struck them and he keeled over completely.

Quinn awoke to find himself bound to the oak he'd been using as shelter by some sort of invisible force. Lyra appeared to be unconscious still and was being kept under a small cage that looked like it was made entirely of branches. Almost like the trees themselves had turned on him and Lyra and were holding them prisoner.

"Lyra," he hissed as he tried to wriggle free from his invisible binds. "Lyra, wake up! What the hells happened? We need to get out of here."

"She can't hear you, and the more you struggle, the tighter the binds will get." It was a girl. A GIRL!?! How the hells had that girl gotten the drop on him and Lyra like that? What was that shock? She was hiding close, by the sound of it, but it was too dark to see anything.

"Who the mux are you? Why are you holding us? What the hells did you do?!" He was scared, but more importantly, he was livid. This should never have happened to him. He was better than this, dammit.

"Why were you sneaking up on us? What do you want?" Her voice was shaky and coming from behind him now, to the left, but there was something else, an animal by the sound of its light steps, closer to Lyra. He could almost make out the shape of it. Whatever it was, it was small and nimble.

"We thought you might be dead. We were checking to see if you needed help. Can you let us go now?" He kept fidgeting with his binds but she was telling the truth, the more he moved, the tighter they became. When he started losing feeling in his fingers, he finally gave up on freeing himself.

"Liar! You wanted to hurt me, rape me, kill us, and steal what little we have!"

Q heard the charge before he saw the flash of blue light or felt the shock.

"*Muuuuuuuux*! Stop doing that! Fine, we were going to rob you, but only because we thought you were already dead. We're not killers." He must've been seeing things, or maybe he hurt his head with all the electrocution, but it looked like the shocks were actually lightning bolts coming off that small creature over by Lyra. But that was impossible, right? There was no such thing as an electric animal. Everyone knew that magical animals died out eons ago. Although, Lyra's fire-starting would probably be considered magic...

"You were going to rob my corpse?" Her question interrupted his thoughts. "And you think that's somehow supposed to make me comfortable enough to let you go?" She had moved again. Closer still, but now she was more to the right, like she was trying to get a better look at him without letting him do the same.

"Listen, lady, we aren't going to hurt you. We're just trying to make a living here. What are you doing sleeping on the side of the road like that anyway? You could get hurt or killed." He left the *idiot* implied since she clearly already knew she'd screwed up. Only a complete moron slept on the side of the road. If you must camp out while traveling, you do it further into the woods for protection from the elements and shady people looking for trouble.

"Trust me," she replied, "this wasn't my first choice. This wasn't my choice at all." The sadness and despair in her voice were palpable. He was starting to feel sorry for her until he remembered that she was currently holding them prisoner.

"If you let us go, I promise we won't hurt you. Maybe we can even help you. Our place is close by. It's nothing special, but it's warm and safe, and we can feed you for the night. This is a one-night-only kinda offer though. You can't get comfortable with us." While he wasn't thrilled about the idea of anyone seeing where he and Lyra took shelter every night—security risk, and all that—he needed to do something to get her to release them, and he was starting to feel bad for her. She seemed genuinely scared and alone. That was a feeling he'd known all too well.

For an agonizing few seconds there were no sounds, like she was weighing her options and trying to decide if he was being serious or trying to trick her. Then he heard the rustle of leaves to his left, and she stepped out of the shadows and onto the road before him. She wasn't what he expected, although he didn't really know what he thought she would look like. She spoke with the presence and authority of someone who had experienced a great deal, but she had the face of an innocent little girl.

"Gods, you're just a kid," he muttered, more to himself than anything.

Indignant and offended, she puffed up her chest, straightened her back, and said, "I'm not a child. I'm old enough to know how things work, and at sixteen, I'm considered an adult enchantress."

Enchantress? Holy mux. That explained the invisible binds and tree-root cage, but it opened up so many new questions. He'd never met an enchantress before, although he'd heard they were beautiful beyond measure and brilliant.

"Beyond measure" was an exaggeration. Sure, she's pretty, but physically, she's nothing special, he thought to himself. Even as he thought it, he knew it was a lie. Her hair was the color of fallen pine needles that blanketed the forest floor. In contrast to her pale pink skin, her eyes were the color of fresh, wild honey. She was pretty enough, but there was something about her, he couldn't quite place it, that drew him in. He had to force himself to look away. She was mesmerizing. Enchanting.

"Why would you help me? You were about to rob my dead body. Now you're tied to a tree, and I'm supposed to believe you've had a change of heart and want to feed and shelter us for the night?" She was, understandably, doubtful of his motives, but how could he explain that he wanted to help because she reminded him of himself many years ago when he and Lyra were first thrust into the world to fend for themselves? He didn't want to show any weakness, and he was pretty sure she wouldn't believe him anyway.

"Look, it's your choice, but if you don't and leave us trapped like this? None of us will survive the night." It was an exaggeration. They'd probably be fine out in the open for one night, but he wasn't interested in risking it when his home was so close by. "I've already told you I have no desire to hurt you. I'd also like to point out that you and your friend have been the only ones inflicting pain here tonight." That got her attention. She'd been pacing between Q and Lyra, but she stopped dead in her tracks at his words.

"Holy Mother, you're right. Agon, how could we have been so cruel? Protecting ourselves is one thing, but we crossed a line." She was speaking to the electric weasel creature that was standing guard over Lyra. Based on what Q knew about enchantresses, he decided that the weasel must be her familiar. "I'm so sorry," she said waving her hand back and forth several times. It seemed to take her a few tries, but eventually, he felt his hands release from the invisible binds, and the cage over Lyra melted back into the forest floor. He took his time rising to his feet, rubbing his wrists to try and get the blood circulating properly again. Slowly, with his eyes locked on her, he made his way to Lyra. Her heart was racing, and he wanted to position himself between Lyra and the girl, just in case. Lyra didn't take too kindly to being imprisoned.

"We're ok, girl, just stay calm," Quinn spoke to Lyra as he held eye contact with the girl. "Everything is fine. It turns out that the body wasn't dead, just tired and homeless. They're going to stay the night with us now."

Have you lost what little sense you had?! They locked us up and electrified us. A lot. And you want to take them home like a couple of lost puppies? Did you bump your head in between all those lightning bolts? Her voice practically reverberated through his mind. Their connection enabled them to share thoughts, as well as their feelings. At that moment, Q could feel the rage and confusion coursing through her veins, but he desperately needed her to calm down. That girl had already proven she and her familiar, Agon, were a force to be reckoned with; and he could tell they desperately needed help. The best way to prove that he wasn't a threat to her was to open himself up to another attack. He turned his back on the girl and knelt down to look Lyra in the eye.

"I know what happened, and you don't get to be snippy with me. I felt those shocks just as much as you. They are on edge because this isn't their home, and they don't know who to trust." He knelt closer, held Lyra's stare, and added mentally, *We know what that feels like.*

As he sat back, he spoke louder to ensure that the enchantress would hear him, "We snuck up on them, remember? They were just defending themselves. I've offered to let them stay the night, one night, and we can take them into town in the morning."

Lyra shifted uneasily, glancing over his shoulder at the girl, then over her shoulder at the electric weasel still positioned behind her on the edge of the road. He could feel her weighing their options, but he knew she'd see he was right and concede.

I don't like it, and I don't trust them, she grumbled.

"Trust me." Q had seen the fear in the girl's eyes. The desperation. The need for some sense of safety or security. He recognized it because he'd had that same look for moons. He wished someone had offered them even a modicum of help in those first few moons, but no one had. Not until they'd snuck into that inn's kitchen to steal some food and found Amelia. He refused to make this girl go through all of that, especially when he and Lyra were fully capable of helping. Amelia taught them better than that. Lyra could feel his determination as intensely as he could feel her doubt, but she trusted him and gave him a slight nod before relaxing her stance. Q had a feeling she wouldn't get any sleep tonight, that she'd opt to keep watch instead, but that was fine.

When he turned back to the girl, he noticed that her weasel had moved and was now wrapped around her neck. She was looking at him oddly, studying him and Lyra as though she were trying to make sense of them. Q realized a little too late that she only heard his part of the conversation. Lyra hadn't spoken a word aloud. This girl probably thought he was in-sane. Would she follow an apparent crazy guy into a makeshift house in the woods?

Q stood unmoving from his spot on the road between Lyra and the enchantress. He studied her and realized she seemed to be having a similar discussion with her familiar, attempting to get the weasel to trust her as well. It was clear that he was no more thrilled about the plan than Lyra was, but both had grudgingly conceded. For the time being, at least.

"We live just over that rise, by a small creek. You can follow me." Q pointed north-east of their location and started walk-ing in the direction of their home. Lyra ran a few paces ahead. She was distancing herself because she was pouting, but she stayed close enough that she could jump to his aid if she felt it was necessary.

"Thank you for helping us," the girl said as she followed him into the woods. "I'm Elena, by the way."

"Quinn."

3

ELENA

ELENA KNEW IT WASN'T smart or rational to trust a boy she just met. Agon certainly didn't trust him, but Quinn seemed sincere, and she didn't really have a lot of other options. She'd proven that she was capable of defending herself if attacked, so she was pretty sure he wouldn't try anything. Elena could hear the voices of the guards from Harbor Ridge telling her that she was making a bad decision in trusting any male, but where else would they sleep tonight? Her intuition told her that she could trust him, and she'd never been wrong when she followed her intuition.

Elena had studied him while he'd been unconscious. The boy looked to be about her age, maybe a cycle older. He was a bit grungy, dirt smeared on his forehead and both of his hands, but his skin was a soft olive color. Elena knew that following a stranger back to his home in the woods was risky at best but she didn't have a lot of other options. Plus, he seemed like he was also a formidable opponent. She felt confident in the belief that they wouldn't be attacked by any outside forces. Although she wondered a little at his sanity considering he'd just had a very vocal and one-sided conversation with his fox-dog, in which he had seemed to be waiting and responding as though the animal was talking to him. One night and they'd be headed into town and off on the next step in finding a new life. A life outside the school, the only home she'd ever known.

No, she thought, *stop that right now. Self-pity won't accomplish anything.* Elena walked a few paces behind Quinn with Agon curled protectively around her neck, head up and fully alert. He wasn't happy with her, but he saw the logic in her choice and begrudgingly agreed. Quinn had said his home was close by, but it felt like they'd been walking for a while.

"I thought you said it was close. Close would've been a five to ten-minute walk. We have been going for nearly an hour." She was anxious. In reality, she had no idea how long they'd actually been walking but it was definitely more than five minutes.

"See that creek over there?" He stopped walking and pointed ahead of them and to the east a bit.

"No, not really. I think I can hear it though." It was much too dark to see, especially through all the trees but if she listened closely, Elena was pretty sure she could hear the babble of water slowly flowing over rocks and brushing against low hanging limbs.

"We live right next to that creek. We're close, I promise. Just a bit farther, and we'll be home." Quinn began walking in the direction he'd been pointing, veering slightly more to the east.

"Why do you live out here, so far from town? Don't you need people? For food? Supplies? Companionship?" Elena didn't understand his isolationist lifestyle. At Harbor Ridge, you were never alone. She'd always shared a bedroom with at least three other girls, and there were people everywhere she went. All meals were served in the great hall, and everyone ate together. Time was spent in class, the library, or your room, all of which were always filled with people. The thought of being alone terrified her, and here he was, clearly intent on having a great deal of space between him and anyone else. "Don't you get lonely?"

"No. People annoy me. I prefer the companionship of Lyra and the quiet peace of the woods." He didn't say any more until they got to the creek. "Here we are."

It was dark, and all Elena could see were dense woods and the small creek. "What do you mean? You just live on the creekside? I thought you said you had shelter. An actual home. This isn't any safer than where we were."

Quinn just chuckled and started rustling around in some bushes beside the water. He pulled back a branch and revealed a decent-sized hut hidden behind—or maybe within?—the thicket. His fox, Lyra, ran in first and seconds later there was a fire burning in the stone circle at the center of the space. The hut was surprisingly roomy and cozy, with plenty of room for a large cooking fire. An opening in the center of the roof allowed the smoke from the fire to escape, and a pallet made of furs near the back served as his bed.

"This is... really nice." She tried not to sound as shocked as she felt but failed miserably. "How did you find this place? It's the perfect hideout!" As she said it, she realized that was exactly what it was. A hideout. *Who was he hiding from?* she wondered. Elena thought better of voicing that one. She was curious to know more about this strange boy, but she feared what she might learn. Harbor Ridge always looked down on magept, those who were magically inept, and made them seem ignorant, selfish, and ultimately, conniving cheats. She knew that was probably an inaccurate representation of non-magical humanity as a whole, but weren't all stereotypes rooted in some level of truth?

"It's a nice little place. Safe from the weather and prying eyes. We've been here for nearly a full solar cycle now, and it suits our purposes. Freshwater right outside, plenty of game to hunt, and food to gather. We can live very happily here for some time. To answer your questions from before, I don't need the town or its people because we're perfectly capable of taking care of ourselves out here. We do go into town, rarely, to trade and stock up on the few things we can't find or make on our own, but I don't like the crowds, and they aren't overly fond of us either."

He walked over to the fire and started unloading things from pockets she hadn't noticed he had. A hunting knife as big as her forearm, some rope, a rabbit carcass, berries, something green that she couldn't see clearly enough to identify, a large waterskin, and two dented metal flasks. He took his cloak off and hung it on a small branch from one of the trees he used to make the walls of his hut and reached out his hand to take hers.

Elena, not comfortable enough to disrobe in the slightest, gently shook her head and wandered over to the fire instead. She analyzed their new temporary travel companions. Quinn picked up his hunting knife along with a large, flat stone, rubbed some sort of oily bar onto the face of the stone, and began slowly slide the blade across the whetstone. The steady, repetitive motion, and the sound of the blade on the stone seemed like an almost meditative habit for him. He kept his focus on the knife, giving Elena a chance to study his face further, drawing her attention to the long, thick, blond eyelashes that curtained his forest green eyes. She tried to be subtle in her observations of him, but he caught her staring when he pushed his blond hair from his brow as he finished working with the knife. Quinn tried—and failed—to hide a chuckle as he turned to the fire, placing a dented tin pail on a hook near the fire.

Elena's focus shifted to the flames. *How had Lyra started that fire?* There were so many things she didn't know about this boy and his rust-colored fox. What was she thinking coming back here with them?

Agon, still perched around her shoulders, nuzzled her ear and sent his thoughts into her mind. *There's something amiss with that fox. She's not what she appears.* His words carried a suspicion that she shared. Elena just nodded. There wasn't enough room in this hut for her to voice her response without being overheard, and she wasn't sure how to respond. She was equally intrigued about Lyra.

Elena decided that conversation was the best way to learn anything about anyone, and sitting here in silence would just make everyone more tense and solve nothing.

"How long have you been living on your own? You said you've only been here for a cycle, right? Where were you before this? Do you have any family nearby?"

"You sure do ask a lot of questions," he replied as he began to skin the rabbit.

"I suppose. Questions are a great way to get to know someone." The sounds of the skin being removed from the rabbit's flesh made her nauseated, but she knew that showing weakness wouldn't do her any good. Instead, she decided to talk about herself and try to get him to open up some. "My mother always told me I ask too many questions and I'm too nosey, but how else will we learn if we don't have the courage to ask?"

"Your mom sounds sweet." The sarcasm in his statement was clear, as well as the hint of jealousy and possibly sadness.

"She is a very busy woman. Having a child wasn't really a priority for her. Raising a child was simply too much work for her, on top of running the school and advising the King. She didn't have the patience or tolerance for children. It always amused me that she was the one running the school. You'd think it would be someone who actually liked children, wouldn't you?" Elena knew she was telling too much about herself, but she couldn't help it. She was a nervous talker.

Quinn dropped the knife and the half-skinned rabbit carcass, turning toward her abruptly, and blurted, "Wait, your mother is *the* enchantress? The one who basically runs this whole damn country? What the hells are you doing sleeping on the side of the road? You're practically royalty. If people knew who you were, you could be in a lot of danger. You shouldn't be all by yourself."

"Don't yell at me. I didn't choose to be out there. If it were up to me, I'd still be at Harbor Ridge with my friends, well, classmates, and the people I cared about. My mother kicked me out. She sent me away. I didn't *have* any other options." Elena's eyes filled with tears, but she refused to let herself cry in front of this boy. He didn't know her. He didn't understand how she was feeling or what she'd been through. "I appreciate your willingness to help us, but if it's going to be a night of you chastising me, Agon and I will find somewhere else to sleep."

"I'm sorry." Quinn looked her in the eyes when he spoke, most likely to make sure she knew he meant every word. "I shouldn't have yelled at you. It's very risky to be out on your own regardless of who you are, especially if you're someone important. I didn't mean to snap at you. I was just shocked that they would let you out of the safety and security of that fortress of a school so carelessly. Please, stay. Stay as long as you'd like."

Elena nodded in acknowledgment of his words. She didn't trust her voice enough to respond without crying, and she *really* didn't want to let him see her tears.

4
QUINN

Q UINN HAD CROSSED A line. He'd overreacted and lashed out at her and instantly felt guilty for it. Hells, he'd made her cry. She was too proud to show it, but he'd seen the tears welling in her eyes when he'd snapped at her, and he'd heard her quietly sobbing on the floor with her back to him. After he apologized, she'd said nothing else to him. Quinn had tried to make small talk, though he was pretty bad at it. She was obviously not interested in talking anymore so they quickly switched to tense silence. He made a small stew with some of the rabbit that he'd caught earlier in the day and some vegetables from the small garden he maintained just outside his hut. She'd eaten her bowl of stew in silence, then curled up on the floor with her back to him, wrapping her body around her familiar.

Logically, Q knew that he wasn't actually the source of her tears. He was just the trigger that forced her to deal with all the shyt she'd been through in the last day or so, causing her to face the fact that she was now alone and on her own. Logically, he knew it, but logic was never his strong suit. The second he'd seen the tears in her eyes, Q realized that he would protect her until his last breath. He would never let anything or anyone cause her pain as long as he was around.

The problem was that he had no way to explain this feeling to her, and she would likely think he was insane if he tried.

Q grabbed his only bucket and stepped outside to get some water for the morning and a bit of fresh air with Lyra quick on his heels.

"I know what you're thinking, and you're out of your mind. You have no ties to this girl. No obligations. No reason to risk your well-being and the life we've built here to help her. She's no one to us, and she's a big deal to a lot of people. She could very well get us killed." Always the voice of reason, Lyra made good points, but Quinn wasn't interested.

"If you know what I'm thinking and feeling, then you already know that nothing you say will change my mind or my plans. You feel it too, I know you do. Something is pulling us to them. Something strong. Something magical. Her familiar has magic. Don't you think that's a little weird? He does *and* you do. The only two familiars in at least a thousand cycles with magic. You might want to ignore them and send them on their way, but you can't ignore the fact that there is something different here. They aren't just a couple of wayward travelers. I know you can feel it."

Quinn wasn't a big believer in anything, but he always trusted his instincts, and they hadn't failed him yet. Something inside of him was telling him they needed to stay close to Elena, at least for the time being, and he wasn't about to start ignoring that feeling now. Lyra didn't have to be happy about it, she just needed to get on board.

"So what's your plan, then? Stick to her like a shadow?" Snarky and patronizing. Lyra's version of concession. The closest thing he'd get to her admitting he was right.

"I'm not sure yet. I don't have a long-term plan. Tonight, we'll keep them safe and give her a chance to rest and process all the shyt she's been through in the last day or so. Tomorrow, we'll feed them breakfast and take them into town, as promised. That's all I've got so far." He rinsed out the old bucket he'd used to cook their stew, then refilled it with water from the river.

"I know this is weird," he said, turning back to Lyra. "It's weird for me too, but I've never felt this intensity or attraction toward another human being. Ever." Q paused for a moment, internally debating his use of the word attraction. It wasn't like he wanted to be *with* her physically, but he felt an undeniable urge that he was meant to be *near* her. He shook his head as if to rid himself of the thought and continued, "I'm not going to simply let that go because it's weird. We need to figure out why we feel this connection to them. Something big is coming. You can feel it too. Something changed inside of us when we met them. We need to see this through, Lyra." He was practically begging her. He wanted her support. He could do whatever he wanted and drag her along with him as the human in their dynamic that was always his option, but he preferred for them to work as a team, and he would need her by his side if—or more likely *when*—shyt went sideways.

Quinn barely slept all night; he kept thinking of all the ways this day could go wrong and all the people who would love to get their hands on The Enchantress' daughter. He didn't consider himself to be a bad guy, but his time as a thief had allowed him access to many of the same circles as people of questionable morals. In the early cycles of their time on their own, Q and Lyra had built some pretty profitable relationships with those who made a living trading other people's property, or lives, for gold, silver, gems, etc. If any one of them found out who she was, they'd pounce, and Elena would get seriously hurt, or even killed. Slavers would be thrilled to have such a high-value trade. His fellow thieves would kidnap her for ransom since her mother was the richest woman in the world, and she was having a not-so-private affair with the King, the richest man in the world. They would settle for nothing less than their weight in gold and have no qualms about sending parts of Elena home to prove their point. Not to mention the creeps who would keep her for their own twisted, personal pleasure... The thought of someone using her in such a way made Q's skin crawl and his blood boil.

No. No one would touch Elena.

He'd come up with a few plans to keep her safe, including refusing to let her leave his hut, but the only prudent, viable option was lying. Lie about who she was. Lie about who her mother was. Lie about being able to do any magic at all. Magical types tended to be unwelcome anyway. The Enchantress and her King had been taxing the towns and villages into poverty for cycles and funneling that money into their precious school. Villagers resented magic because it had cost many of them everything. Sometimes literally. Elena would be safer if she agreed to not do any magic and tell everyone she was just a poor girl looking for a new life. It was relatable and realistic. She might even make some friends and be happy here, as long as no one knew who she really was.

Q was pretty sure she'd object to his plan, but he was hopeful that she'd go along with it once he explained what was at stake. Elena woke up in high spirits, and he didn't want to push, but he also knew the best option for her was to stay isolated and away from any potential threats.

"Do you want to go into town today? You can stay here as long as you'd like. I'm not rushing you if you want to stay here and get used to life outside that school first. Stay here for a few days, maybe a week, then I can take you to town." He tried to sound as casual as possible as they ate a simple breakfast of wild berries and oats he'd purchased in town the week before.

She popped a couple of berries into her mouth while she considered his offer.

"No, I think I should get out there and start building my new life. I can't hide out here forever. I need to figure out what I'm going to do. Thank you, but I think it's time."

"Well, I'm not rushing you, but if you're sure you want to go today then there are some things you need to know." Q looked her in the eye to make sure she knew he was serious, "You can't be yourself out there. You have to be a normal, poor, homeless human. No magic. No school. Absolutely no fancy, famous mom. Those things will get you killed, or worse."

She balked at his words. Elena said nothing, but her face told him that she didn't believe him. She had no reason to and he knew that—they'd only just met yesterday—but he desperately needed her to trust him.

"I know this sounds crazy, but the people around here don't like magical folks, and your mother has made life especially difficult for those who live near the school. If you want to travel farther south, across the river to a big city like Cyra, you might get away with being mildly enchanted. But here? Here people will see you as a threat, and they will do everything they can to get you out of their lives. Not to mention those who would try to make a profit from you, selling you to the highest bidder or ransoming you back to your mother."

"She wouldn't pay." Her words were hollow, but there was no doubt in them.

"Maybe, maybe not. That won't stop them from sending her little pieces of you to get their message across. A finger. A toe. An ear. Until she pays or they kill you. The safest option is for you to be someone else. Elena: a girl in search of a new life after losing her home in another town. Haravel, maybe. Work out whatever details you want, but remember them. Personally, I prefer to leave as much to the imagination as possible. Keeps me from having to remember all the lies."

He watched her face, studying the way she chewed on her lip while she tried to process his words and determine what she was going to do. He desperately hoped she'd change her mind and choose to stay with him, but he knew that wasn't likely. Not to mention it was completely insane for him to want this girl to stay. Personal attachments made people weak. They created unnecessary vulnerability, and he needed to be free of such entanglements if he and Lyra were going to survive.

Still, he could feel his chest tightening at the mere thought of her leaving him. *What the mux?*

"Perhaps you're right," she replied after what seemed like an eternity.

"You want to stay here for a while longer? I think that's the best course. I know it's awkward, but—"

"What? Oh, no." Elena cut him off. "I think you're right about lying. For now, anyway. I don't want undue attention, and I need to figure out who I am outside of the school. What better way to do that than to make up an entirely new story?"

Lyra spoke up without hesitation, "Well then, let's get going. Get you two off to start your new life."

Elena jumped at her words, and her eyes widened more than he thought possible. Q realized a moment too late that Elena's reaction had nothing to do with the harshness of Lyra's words and everything to do with the fact that Lyra had spoken at all. He glared over his shoulder at Lyra where she lay by the fire. She could feel his tension, yet she was unfazed. Lyra had just tipped their hand, revealing herself to be more than a mere fox, and she didn't seem to care at all. More like she was beyond eager to free herself of these untrustworthy strangers. She was more than happy to send them out into the world, regardless of what could happen to them. It was equally clear that Agon was on the same page as Lyra. At her words, he'd quickly jumped back to his perch around Elena's shoulders and started practically pulling her toward the hut opening.

"Yes, we should really get a move on. We need to find somewhere to get settled. The sooner the better," Agon said. He seemed as anxious to get out of their home as Lyra was for them to leave. Quinn was surprised to hear the weasel speak. He'd known that the creature was Elena's familiar, but he had incredibly limited experience with familiars, and it still shocked him to hear Agon speak.

Quinn released a tense breath he hadn't realized he'd been holding. This girl needed his protection, just like those kids at the orphanage had. Q decided in that moment that he would escort her to Andover. It was the safest town he knew and one where everyone knew him. No one would mess with her and she'd be safe. Regardless, he wasn't about to let her out of his sight until he knew she was safe and settled in town. Maybe not even then.

5
ELENA

LYRA HAD SPOKEN. IT wasn't supposed to be possible, but clearly, the gods had something unexpected planned for them all. Elena spent the morning in silence, pondering the ramifications of all that she'd learned about this strange boy and his fox. Elena desperately wanted to ignore the glaring truths before her, simply because her life was already far too complicated to add this boy and his fox to the mix.

Once they finished breakfast, Elena took it upon herself to clean their dishes—wooden bowls carved from thick tree limbs—as a thank you for Quinn's kindness. Agon had been pushing her to leave the hut since they'd awoken at dawn. She understood his eagerness to get farther from Harbor Ridge, and it was very clear that he didn't trust Quinn or Lyra, but Elena was admittedly very nervous about going into a new town filled with people who didn't know her and would—apparently—try to hurt her if they knew who she was.

She was comfortable with Quinn. There was something about him that felt familiar and safe. Elena couldn't explain it; she knew it was foolish to trust a complete stranger but she trusted her intuition, and it hadn't misled her yet. If her gut told her he was a friend, then she accepted him as such. Agon was a little harder to convince, but he'd seen her intuition proven true time and again. She knew he'd come around sooner or later.

Elena returned to the hut with freshly cleaned bowls and placed them on a makeshift shelf along the far wall of the hovel. She then collected her pillowcase of meager possessions and followed Quinn through the woods and back to the path that would take them into town. Elena's mind was reeling after the revelations Quinn had forced her to confront last night. Homeless, and now she had to live a lie or risk being kidnapped, tortured, murdered, or sold into Gods-only-know what kind of hells-ish life. She wasn't sure how she'd ever manage to survive on her own. Quinn had made it seem like everyone would be out to get her for one reason or another.

It will all be ok. We'll be ok. We always are, Agon's voice echoed in her head. One of the many benefits of having a familiar was the connection they shared. A shared soul. Shared feelings. They could communicate without saying a word. That connection had gotten her through many frustrating classes at Harbor Ridge when she could feel all the other girls, even the teachers, silently judging her and her inability to master the simplest spells.

We've always been sheltered and protected. We have literally no idea how to take care of ourselves. She didn't want to sound as harsh and snarky as she did, but her nerves were fried. She hadn't slept well in Quinn's home. Despite her peppy and chipper outward appearance her mind was racing, and Elena was struggling to complete any single thought. They were all a jumble of half-processed plans, ideas, and realizations.

"Watch your head," Quinn said as he tried to move a low-hanging branch from their path.

Elena nodded her thanks though she didn't say a word to him, too engrossed in her conversation with Agon and anxious about what they were walking into.

You are strong and capable. We will find a way and things will all work out. Agon nudged her cheek with his nose from his spot on her shoulder, trying to emphasize his thoughts in her mind.

I guess we don't have any other choice. Mother made sure of that. In less than a day, her entire world had turned upside down and left her feeling completely disconnected and un-moored from the world. Elena had no plan, no idea what to expect from the world she'd been so unceremoniously dumped into. The only thing she did know was that her feet hurt, she was tired, and she desperately wanted a hot bath.

Andover. The word "town" was generous. The entire place consisted of about a dozen buildings, including an inn with a rather large pub and stable, a small market where the locals sold their wares, a blacksmith who—according to Quinn—was mated to the town seamstress, and a handful of small homes that encircled the fountain and well at the center of town. The entire town and all of her residents could have comfortably fit in the Great Hall at Harbor Ridge and there still would have been plenty of room for all the students.

"This is… quaint," Elena announced as they crossed the stone bridge into the heart of the town. "You might have mentioned it was such a modest place. I'm not sure how to blend in here. I'm used to hiding amongst the crowd. Everyone here is already staring and pointing. What am I supposed to do now?"

Q just kept walking. This was, after all, his town, and these were his people. He walked straight to the inn and let himself in, holding the door for Lyra, as well as Elena and Agon.

"Did you get your backstory yet?" he asked as he casually placed his hand on her shoulder. Agon snapped at Quinn's hand where it rested near his head. Elena started to move away when he leaned in and whispered, "These people know me and most of them even trust me. The quickest way for them to accept you is to be seen with me."

This town trusts a thief more than magic? What kind of crazy, backward world is this? She didn't like the idea of being associated with a thief, but she decided to trust his judgment and see how far it would take her in this town. Plus, even though she would never have admitted it to him, she took comfort in the feel of his hand on her shoulder and his voice in her ear.

Agon shifted his position on her shoulders, bringing her focus back to the situation at hand. He could feel her unexpected warmth toward Quinn, and he didn't approve. He would have some words for her when they were settled and alone again.

Quinn guided Elena and Agon to the bar while Lyra skirted along the floor, sniffing and inspecting seemingly at random.

"Good mornin', Amelia! How's Marty doing?" Quinn was casual and friendly. This was not the same guy she'd met last night. Elena followed a few steps behind and watched him work.

"Good morning, darlin'. Marty's doing just fine, thanks for asking. Still grumpy about the changing seasons, but he'll survive. He always does. It was so kind of you to bring him that special soup. What can I do for you today?" Amelia appeared to be a bit older than Elena's mother, maybe in her early forties. Her graying maple brown hair was tied in a tight knot on the top of her head, and her face was littered with freckles. She was about the same height as Elena but considerably heavier. She looked like she would be a very comforting and affectionate mother. That thought instantly sent a shock of pain through Elena's chest.

"I'd like you to meet Elena. I found her lost in the Dark Woods last night, and I was hoping you could help her get settled. She lost her home and most of her belongings in Haravel, and she could use a fresh start." Quinn took Elena by the hand and pulled her out from behind him.

"Oh, you poor dear! I'm sure we can find a nice place for you here. Are you planning to stay long?"

Elena froze. She had no idea. She hadn't thought that far ahead. She still had no plan.

The tears came suddenly, without warning, and without a foreseeable end. Amelia came rushing around the bar and scooped her into her arms.

"Hush now, sweet girl. Everything will be ok. You can stay here at the inn for as long as you need. We have plenty of space. And we can find you a job if you wish. It will be ok, don't you worry. Everything will work out just fine." Amelia hugged her close, rubbing her back and shushing her quietly while Elena unleashed all of her fears through her tears. Agon moved from his perch on her shoulder to cuddle her neck tightly and cleaned her tears as best he could.

Elena had no idea how long they stood like that, but when she finally regained control of herself, she felt like a foolish child. She didn't know this woman, yet she had bawled into her blouse hysterically.

"Oh my," she sniffed as she wiped her face and took a step back, "I'm so sorry. I don't know what came over me. That was incredibly inappropriate of me, and a terrible first impression. Please forgive me."

"Darling child, you have been through an ordeal. You have nothing to apologize for. I'm just glad you're here now. Safe and sound." Amelia offered her a handkerchief and gave her shoulder one last squeeze. "You can always talk to me if you want. I'm a bartender and I've raised five babes over the years. I'm a great listener, and I offer perfect advice."

Amelia winked to Quinn at that last remark. He'd been standing behind Elena, watching her emotional meltdown unfold. Elena couldn't tell if he was embarrassed for her, or *of* her, but his cheeks were bright red and he seemed to be avoiding making eye contact with her.

Elena smiled at Amelia as she accepted the handkerchief. "You are too kind. I don't know what came over me. I'm not usually this emotional, I promise. I would very much like to repay your kindness. Is there any work you need help with around the inn? I'm not very adept at cooking or cleaning, but I'm a quick study."

"Don't worry, darlin'. I'm sure we can find something for you here. There's always something that needs doing. But first, let's get you settled, all right?" Amelia took Elena by the hand and led her towards a hall and, presumably, the rooms.

6

QUINN

*M*UX. WATCHING ELENA BREAK down like that had been torture. All he'd wanted to do was wrap her in his arms, kiss her forehead, and tell her everything would be ok. He would make everything ok for her. What the actual hells was going on with him?

"Thank the Mother that's over. I thought we'd be stuck with them forever. The way you're behaving around her isn't normal." Lyra was pacing in front of him, flicking her tail so anxiously that sparks were starting to fly. "We should go now."

He knew she was right, but Q couldn't seem to convince his body to move. He needed to make sure Elena settled in and that she'd be all right here. He didn't want to leave without saying goodbye. Which was stupid. He didn't know this girl. Why did he care so much?

Rationally they should leave, but he had never been a very rational person, so he wasn't surprised when his feet carried him to the bar rather than the door. He took up residence on the last barstool positioning himself with his back against the wall, facing the hall that Elena had disappeared down with Amelia. Q couldn't leave until he knew, without a doubt, that she would be safe and happy here.

"You see what's happening here, don't you." It wasn't a question, and Lyra's tone suggested disdain and disgust. He didn't answer. Quinn knew he didn't need to; she was going to say her piece regardless of his response, so he said nothing and waited.

"You're falling for her. The whole helpless, damsel-in-distress thing is working on you. It's such a cliché." Lyra jumped onto the barstool next to him and got comfortable. She knew they were going to be waiting here for a while. She had sensed his feelings, of course, and knew there was no point in trying to convince him to leave. He'd made up his mind. They weren't leaving until he knew Elena was ok.

When Amelia came back, she was alone. Quinn nearly jumped out of his seat the moment he saw her, but he managed to contain himself as she walked over to him. Lyra rolled her eyes, her ears twitched ever so slightly, expressing her annoyance with him. Quinn waited until Amelia was clearing a table near him before he spoke to her. "How's everything going, Amelia?" He prayed to the Mother that his voice came out more nonchalant than he felt. He desperately wanted to know how Elena was doing. Was she ok? Would she be happy here? Was she going to stay? Was she going to stay in character and keep her true identity hidden? Was she going to miss him?

He nearly kicked himself over that last thought, but it wouldn't stop bouncing around in his head. He wanted her to feel the connection he inexplicably felt to her.

"Honey, just ask what you really wanna know. You're practically vibrating." Amelia didn't even look up from the table as she collected the dirty dishes and balanced them on a large tray on her way back to the kitchen.

Mux, how does she always know? Quinn shuffled his feet, then grabbed the remainder of the dishes from the table and followed her to the back.

"Is she ok? Did she say anything else? Tell you what happened to her? Who she is? Where she's going?" Quinn put his dishes onto the counter next to the sink and started pumping the water from the small kitchen water pump until the sink was about half full. Amelia scraped leftover food off the plates into the large barrel by the sink, smiling up at him.

"You silly, sweet boy. You really care about her. You just met her and you are already so invested. I love it, baby. I haven't seen you care for someone like this before. You must really fancy her." She shook her head, shooed him away from the sink, and handed him a towel. "I'll wash, you dry, and we'll talk."

When Q first left the orphanage—or rather after that hells-hole burned to the ground—Amelia had taken him in. She was the only mother figure he'd ever had, and she could read him like a book. She'd gotten him out of trouble more times than he could count, given him a real job, and helped him turn his life around. She would be very disappointed to learn how he'd actually met Elena; attempting to loot her body. *But,* he reasoned, *looting a corpse is a victimless crime. I didn't kill anyone. It isn't any worse than when a vulture picks a body clean.* He knew that logic wouldn't fly with Amelia, so he didn't bring it up, and he prayed Elena would leave that part out as well. Q hated disappointing Amelia. He'd happily take a thousand beatings from that drunk bastard who'd run the orphanage rather than see the look on Amelia's face when he'd let her down.

"Is she ok?" Q asked again as she handed him a freshly cleaned plate.

"She will be," Amelia replied. "The poor girl claims she has no idea what happened to her before you found her. She says she doesn't remember anything before the Dark Woods. I imagine she's not being completely honest, but there's no reason to push her on the subject. She'll talk when she's ready; just like you did."

Amelia was right, as always. It had taken him nearly a solar cycle to open up and tell Amelia the whole story about what had happened in that orphanage. That was the only time he'd ever seen her so livid, heartbroken, and proud all at once. She hated the way those people had treated Q and the other orphans, and while she said she didn't agree with how he'd handled it, she'd been very proud of him for standing up and protecting the others. He couldn't expect Elena to open up to anyone right now. For all he knew, everything she'd told him had been a lie. He took her at her word because he felt tied to her, and he always trusted his gut feelings.

"Try not to worry too much, baby. I'll take good care of her. And it's not like you're leaving her. You live close enough to come visit every day. Or you could move back in here. We always have room for you, and Marty would love to have you back. He asks about you often." Amelia continued washing and handing him dishes to dry.

"I'm sorry I haven't been to visit lately. Do you mind if I stay the night? Just to make sure she's settled and feeling comfortable?" Q could feel Lyra glaring at the back of his head, but he shrugged it off. She knew how he was feeling, and despite her misgivings, he knew she would relax once they knew Elena was happy here at the inn and not coming back to their hut any time soon.

"Baby, you know you can stay here whenever you like. You don't have to ask." Amelia handed him the last dish. "You found her last night?" Amelia asked pensively.

"Yeah, she was trying to sleep on the side of the road." Quinn finished drying the last plate and put it away.

"Interesting," she murmured.

"How so?" Q pressed. She had his full attention.

"Well, last night was a Black Moon. You know what they say about Black Moons, don't you?"

Quinn shrugged. He tried to recall childhood memories, knowing that she'd mentioned something about the different phases meaning different things in the past, but he drew a blank.

Amelia swatted his arm with a damp towel. "Gods, it's like you only listen when it's about hunting or gossip," she teased. "The Black Moon is an auspicious time. It's a time for new beginnings, making changes, and renewal. It's just interesting that you happened to make a new friend, someone you clearly care greatly for, on such a magical night."

Amelia made a plate of chicken, roasted vegetables, and a thick slice of warm bread for him and Lyra. Then she set them up at the bar before grabbing a fresh ale for Q as well as some warm buttermilk for Lyra. Amelia knew them both so well. Lyra didn't have to say a word, but Amelia could tell that she wasn't thrilled about Q's attachment to Elena. Warm buttermilk was Lyra's weakness, it was like catnip and liquor rolled into one, and she loved it. Lyra gave Amelia a soft lick on her face while she was setting Lyra's place. Amelia ruffled her fur in return. Amelia was always the only person that Lyra would allow to touch her. It was a sign of complete trust and loyalty. Lyra didn't trust often or easily, but Amelia was special.

7

ELENA

"S HE SEEMS NICE," AGON commented in reference to Amelia. "I liked her. I know we just met her, but she seems like a really good person. No familiar, which is weird. But maybe that's normal? Do magepts have familiars?" Elena had no idea. They never talked about non-magical people at school, other than to discuss breeding with the males to carry on their magical bloodlines.

"I guess not. I mean, it makes sense, right? You are supposed to help me focus and channel my magic. A person who doesn't have magic doesn't really have a use for a familiar," Elena reasoned aloud. Logically that explanation made sense, but then it opened up new questions about Quinn and Lyra. If she was his familiar, then what was he? There weren't supposed to be any male enchantresses. That's what the school taught them. Males were too weak to handle magic and therefore died before birth. Every time. But Lyra spoke. Traditionally, foxes didn't speak. Then there was the question of how she managed to start that fire last night. There was definitely something unique about the pair of them, but Elena wasn't sure she had the mental capacity to dissect that at this moment. She had spent the last several minutes embarrassingly bawling her eyes out on the shoulder of a woman she'd *just* met. She needed to focus on one thing at a time, and that was not going to be Quinn or Lyra.

Elena unpacked the few things they owned from her now-filthy pillowcase and put her clothes away in the wardrobe next to the window. She entertained the idea of trying to use some simple spells to remove the dirt from the pillowcase and erase the stains but thought better of it. Even if she could actually get the spells to work—which was un-likely—she worried that someone might see or hear her casting and mark her as an enchantress. According to Quinn, being an enchantress was the worst thing she could openly be in this town. Elena didn't fully understand why the magept would hate her so much simply for having magic, but she thought it best to defer to Quinn. She tossed the pillowcase into the wardrobe, resolving to wash it herself, once she learned how.

There was a small table next to the bed, a bedpan under the table, and an extra quilt in the wardrobe for cold nights. There was no fireplace in the room, but a bed warmer was stored under the bed. On colder nights, the warmer would be filled with bricks heated most likely by the kitchen fires and used to heat the bed and room to a more comfortable temperature. It wasn't as nice as the dormitory she shared with her roommates back at Harbor Ridge, but it was far more welcoming than that oppressive, pitch-black castle on the mountainside. Elena had been in the room for a matter of moments and already felt more at home here than she'd ever felt at the school with her mother and all of her so-called friends.

It was still light out when Elena finished unpacking and getting settled in the room. The unexpectedly loud rumble of her stomach reminded her that she hadn't eaten since breakfast, so Elena and Agon decided to head back out into the dining hall to find something to eat.

"We need to find a way to repay Amelia for her kindness. I know she said we could stay here as long as we need, but we can't stay here for free. We need to pay our way. We're on our own now, and we need to act like it." Elena opened the door at the foot of the bed, and Agon jumped down from the window sill to follow her out of their room.

The dining hall was still fairly empty when she and Agon entered. Quinn and Lyra were having a meal at the bar and chatting with Amelia. Elena sat down on the barstool next to Lyra and smiled cautiously at her. The fox made no effort to hide her feelings about them, nor did she attempt to disguise her distrust of Elena and Agon. Elena was optimistic that she could change Lyra's mind once she got to know them. It was potentially a foolish endeavor, but once Elena committed to something, she had to see it through. Befriending Lyra had become a top priority for her, although she wasn't sure why. It was very likely that she would never see Quinn or Lyra again, but Elena found it unbearable to be so openly disliked by someone who didn't even know her. She was convinced that she would eventually win the fox over, and maybe then she would uncover the mystery of Lyra and Quinn.

"Good evening, everyone. I'm so sorry and embarrassed about my outburst earlier. I think I'm just tired." Elena tried to sound casual, knowing that she'd made a complete fool of herself. She shouldn't have lost control of her emotions like that. That was Enchantress 101: Keep your emotions in check. Always. Her mother would have lectured her for hours about it.

"I already told you, love, you've nothing to apologize for." Amelia patted her arm and then disappeared to the kitchen for a moment before reappearing with a heaping plate of food. "Here you are, sweetheart. I imagine you must be famished. Quinn is resourceful, but he doesn't put a lot of energy into creating a full meal." She grinned at him and patted his arm with a maternal love that was nearly tangible. It made Elena's heart break a little. No one had ever looked at her that way.

"I can cook. I just have better things to do with my time. Besides, I fed her last night *and* this morning. That's more hospitality than I've ever offered any human being." Quinn looked very proud of himself at this announcement. Lyra's sidelong glare at Elena and Agon was filled with annoyance.

"Yes, Q, and I'm sure the stew was delicious, but this girl needs a little more than some carrots, rabbit, and water. She's been through quite the ordeal. She needs sustenance."

Elena had a great deal of mixed feelings at seeing the playful interaction between Quinn and Amelia. It was clear that they loved each other very much, and Elena really enjoyed seeing someone poke fun at Quinn and watching his face turn red. However, their banter and closeness were a harsh reminder of what Elena had never had: a mother who genuinely cared for her. More tears threatened so she tried to distract herself by focusing on the pile of food in front of her. Roast lamb, a chicken breast smothered in some sort of garlic butter sauce, mashed potatoes, caramelized carrots, green beans, two fresh rolls with melted butter, a tankard of cider, and a second tankard of ale. There was also a smaller second plate with a chicken leg, some green beans and carrots, a roll, and a warm bowl of milk.

"I know familiars don't need to eat to survive," Amelia whispered conspiratorially to Agon, "but I also know that you *like* to eat, and Lyra here loves warm milk with a dash of cinnamon. If you don't like it, I can always get you something else. Give it a try and tell me what you think."

Amelia was a gift from the Mother Goddess. There was no question about it. Somehow, she knew the truth about

Elena and Agon—or at least that Elena had some level of magic that granted her a familiar—but she was still kind. She didn't comment on the obvious lie about Elena's origins and her reasons for being currently homeless. She knew Elena had magic, which Quinn had said would be a death sentence if the wrong people found out. Amelia knew and didn't seem to care at all. At that moment, Elena loved her, and she could sense that Agon felt the same way.

In an effort to keep herself from breaking down, yet again, Elena decided to get right to the point.

"I want to repay you for your kindness. I don't have any money, but I'm a hard worker, and I don't want to take charity. I can clean the rooms or wait on your customers. I can't cook very well, but I can learn. Please, tell me how I can earn my place here."

"I appreciate that you are so willing to work, darlin'. I could use some help cleaning the rooms between guests, and I can always use an extra hand during dinner. It seems like no one in town likes to cook their own food these days. Good for business, but hard on my old bones." Amelia rubbed her hands together as though trying to massage the pain away. "I want you to take some time to adjust to your new surroundings and get to know the townsfolk a little first. After that, I'll start you at breakfast, since that's the slowest time for us, and it will give you plenty of time to learn the routine and get to know the regulars."

"That sounds wonderful." Elena beamed as she took a bite of her chicken. Everything was going to be ok. They were going to be ok.

The next few weeks flew by in a blur of new experiences, sights, sounds, and smells. Elena had never been around men before. There were a couple of eunuchs that worked at Harbor Ridge, but they were rarely allowed to come near the girls, and they were never permitted to be in the same room as the students without an instructor present. Just in case. Men could not be trusted. The instructors preached daily that men only wanted one thing from the girls, and they would do anything to get it. Eunuchs were safer but still untrustworthy. Naturally, it took some getting used to when it came to being in a town with a population made up of more men than women or children. Harbor Ridge was very clear that men used and abused women as if it were their life's calling, and no girl was safe on her own. It took nearly three weeks for Elena to gain the confidence to leave the inn and go around the town by herself. Q, as she had started to call him, came to visit every other day, and he always offered to give her the grand tour of their quaint little hamlet, but she always declined. It was scary, and she didn't know how she would handle it without magic—not that hers had ever been terribly reliable. She didn't want to go out at all.

"We can't just hide in here forever, you know." Agon lounged in his favorite spot in their room, high on the windowsill, basking in the morning sun and watching the townsfolk going about their morning routines.

"I know... I'm just not sure I'm ready. That's all." They'd had the same conversation every morning for the last week. Agon was eager to get out and see everything. He was far more adventurous than she'd ever been, and being forced to stay inside made him stir-crazy.

"Let's just go down to the fountain. It's just a few steps outside of the inn, and it will give us a chance to talk to people in a very open and simple setting. Everyone goes there, every morning! It wouldn't be odd or unusual for us to go as well. Besides, if I spend one more day locked in this room, I'm going to start throwing my poop. Is that what you want, Elena? A poop-hurling familiar?"

He was trying to make her laugh and help her relax. Elena couldn't help picturing him throwing his poop. The idea was just so ridiculous. Agon hated getting mud on his paws. Poop? Ha! That would be one of the most entertaining things she'd ever witnessed. Not to mention, what with him rarely eating anything, he didn't really have any poop to throw. It was an empty threat, but one meant to amuse her and possibly boost her confidence just enough to go outside.

"That does sound tempting... I imagine it would be pretty hilarious, actually." Elena prodded him and laughed. "All right, fine. But just to the fountain, and we come right back if any man makes a move toward us."

Elena grabbed her cloak on their way out. It had started to get cooler out in the evenings, and the sun hadn't risen high enough to warm the town yet that morning. The cloak also provided a bit more camouflage for them, as Agon could wrap himself around her neck and when she put the hood on, he was nearly invisible. If he kept still enough, he could even pass for a scarf.

In their weeks at the inn, Elena had met many of the townsfolk as they came in for meals in the dining hall. Everyone she'd met seemed very kind, and she genuinely liked them all, but seeing people in the inn and seeing them out on the street felt very different. Distrust of people—especially men—had been ingrained in her from birth. It was a hard behavior to overcome.

It was a lovely day, despite the chill in the air. The fountain was more than "a few steps" from the inn, as it was the center of town, but it was still close enough to the inn that Elena felt they could easily retreat if needed.

For a hamlet, there seemed to be quite a few people living in town. Quinn explained once that there was a pretty large farming community around the town, so many people lived in town and worked on the farms just outside of it. There were also quite a few migrant workers who lived on the farm properties and came to Amelia's to eat. Elena had seen many of those men, and they had always made her feel uncomfortable. The way they stared was almost predatory, and they were always unclean. She hated when they came into the inn. They would come in packs of five to seven filthy, sweaty, smelly men, take up two or three tables, and make a huge mess. Somehow, their food ended up everywhere. The tabletops, the chairs, the floor, their hair, their shirts, and once they even got mashed potatoes on the ceiling. They drank too much ale and usually had to be asked to leave. On the mashed potato night, the town blacksmith and Quinn had to forcibly remove one of the men because he was belligerent and grabbed a girl as she walked by. They were everything Harbor Ridge warned her about.

Aside from those men, the rest of the townsfolk seemed like good, hard-working people. It was late enough in the morning that most of the men had gone off to hunt, farm, or work their wares. The only people at the fountain were women and small children. Amelia mentioned once that the town had its own little schoolhouse and the older kids would spend a few hours there every day before going to learn the family trade. Elena loved that even in such a little country hamlet, the children were taught to read and write. Harbor Ridge might have been a magic school, but students couldn't learn magic until they could read and write.

The women at the fountain socialized and washed their laundry. It was their daily ritual. Elena thought it was lovely. She smiled meekly at the women and was immediately waved over by one of the younger women. She appeared to be just a couple of years older than Elena.

"Good morn'!" She said in a cheerful voice. "I'm Nikki," she continued, "and this is Marie, Seraphina, Viktoria, Hazel, Willow, and Isela. Come sit! You're new here, right? I've seen you around the inn before. Elena, isn't it? It's nice to see you're venturing out into the town."

Well, she's definitely a morning person, Elena thought to herself. She could almost feel Agon cringe at Nikki's overly perky attitude. "Uh, yes, my name is Elena. We just arrived a few weeks ago. From Haravel."

"We?" one of the other girls asked, eyebrows raised.

Mux. "Um, yes, my... pet, Agon and I. We were living in Haravel with my parents, but they passed away. We came here looking for work. Amelia was kind enough to offer us a place to live and give me a job in the dining hall while I figure out our next move." She hoped the lie would be simple enough that she wouldn't forget anything, but substantial enough that the women wouldn't question it.

"Oh, you poor dear!" one of the women exclaimed. Willow. Elena was pretty sure that woman's name was Willow.

"Amelia is so kind. She's always willing to take care of those in need," another said.

"Just like she did with that Quinn." There was disgust in the woman's voice.

"Viktoria, be nice," Nikki chastised. "Amelia did a wonderful thing, taking him in when he had nowhere else to go."

"You're too young to remember *why* he had nowhere else to go, but I remember," Viktoria continued. "He killed those people!"

Some of the girls gasped. Agon tightened around Elena's neck, and she heard his voice in her mind. *I knew there was something wrong with him.*

"He didn't kill them for sport," Seraphina spoke up. "They were terrible people. You must remember how many kids they had in that so-called home. At least ten kids at all times, and they were always bruised or broken. They sent those kids out to work the fields, then beat them when the harvest wasn't enough to quench their thirst for ale and smokes. Those people you're referring to were horrible, and they didn't deserve to live."

"They didn't deserve to be burned alive either!" Viktoria seemed to be taking the conversation very personally.

"I heard he killed them and then burned the house down and took all the kids to Amelia's," Hazel added quietly. "That doesn't make killing ok, but at least he was doing it for good reasons."

"Good reasons? Are there any good reasons for killing people?" Viktoria snapped. Elena was stunned. She had learned more about Quinn in the last few minutes than she had in the last few weeks. Abusive parents, or foster parents, that he killed and saved other kids from. It sounded plausible. In her limited experience, Quinn had seemed to have a very strong protective instinct.

"Ladies, ladies, please. We didn't invite Elena over just to spread gossip from nearly a decade ago. Let's all take a deep breath and get to know our new friend, shall we?" Even though Nikki was one of the youngest women there, it was pretty obvious that she was in charge.

"Umf. Little love," Nikki said, rubbing her slightly swollen belly. She was sitting on a short stool on the ground with laundry in a scrubbing bucket between her legs. Elena had missed the subtle bulge of her belly. "Mummy's trying to visit with her friends. Kindly stop kicking my insides, dear." And with that, the conversation turned to babies, pregnancies, labor, breastfeeding, and Elena quietly settled down on the ground, leaning back against the fountain while she processed all this new information.

Elena and Agon spent the rest of the morning listening to the women talk about their lives, brag, and complain about their kids and husbands. Hazel announced that she and her husband were trying for another baby after their youngest—of three—started walking the week before. The ladies were all very excited by this news.

Elena couldn't help feeling a twinge of jealousy for the simplicity of their lives. The bond, the closeness and love of their family and friends. Elena had no idea what that felt like, but she hoped she might finally find out.

8
QUINN

QUINN WALKED INTO THE inn and scanned the room. As a mostly reformed thief, being aware of his surroundings and the people in them was second nature. Developing that sense of spatial awareness had been vital for survival for many cycles. If you ran into someone you recently robbed, it was pretty much guaranteed that it would end badly for you. Despite having given up on his criminal past, he kept his mind and senses sharp. Better to be paranoid than dead.

Elena was behind the bar, casually chatting with Amelia, so Q and Lyra sat down on a couple of empty barstools and waited.

"I'm so glad you ventured out today! That's great progress. I am sorry that you had to meet Viktoria. She's as rotten as those parents of hers. The whole lot of them are just wretched humans."

It was a little shocking to hear Amelia talk so negatively about anyone in town. Amelia loved everyone and was always kind, regardless of a person's situation. It was one of the things he loved most about her. It was also the thing that baffled him the most. *Viktoria... Why does that name sound familiar...?*

"She didn't say much after Nikki shut her down," Elena replied, tossing a not-so-subtle glance at Quinn. "I like Nikki. She seems like a really sweet person. She was very kind and welcoming to me." Elena was beaming. She'd finally left the inn, and it had gone well, he noted.

Quinn couldn't help but feel a little disappointed that she didn't let him take her around and introduce her to everyone, but he was happy that she felt confident enough to go out and meet people on her own. Lyra flicked her tail at him, and he felt a small spark of heat on his thigh.

"What?" he muttered to her. He was allowed to have feelings. He was allowed to care for this girl. He didn't need to justify himself to Lyra. Of course, he didn't need to express all of this to her. She could sense how he was feeling, and she knew he was being emotional again. As far as Lyra was concerned, emotions were unnecessary tethers that held you back and got you caught up in other people's messes. Q didn't wholly disagree with her, but he also knew that if they hadn't developed relationships with other people and created emotional attachments, they would have been dead a long time ago. Amelia was a perfect example of emotional entanglements that proved well worth their while. Lyra couldn't disagree with that but she often, more like daily, tried to convince him that his attachment to Elena and Agon was unhealthy and would be their doom.

"You're just being dramatic," he would say to her every time she tried to convince him to cut ties with Elena. "Elena isn't evil. She's a lost girl who needs our help. I don't know if you remember, but we help people in need." That statement would always abruptly end their fight. She remembered. She remembered that steaming pile of horseshyt masquerading as a man and his cruel, vindictive wife. The people who were supposed to raise and protect them. Q didn't like to think about it too much, the thoughts just made him mad, and Lyra had a tendency to catch things on fire when he dwelled too much on that part of their past.

It didn't matter anymore, anyway. They'd taken care of things. They'd taken care of those kids and those monsters in that hells-of-an-orphanage. It was done.

Elena enthusiastically placed a large mug of ale in front of him, and a warm bowl of milk with cinnamon in front of Lyra, shaking him out of the dark abyss he'd been spiraling down into and bringing him back to the present.

"Good day, you two! Did you hear? We had an adventure today, and I met lots of new people! It was so exhilarating!" Her smile and excitement were contagious.

"I heard. That's wonderful. Where did you go?"

"Just to the fountain, but all the ladies were there with their little kids, and we got to chatting. I feel like a magept!" She was so giddy, and he couldn't help but smile up at her. She was bouncing around behind the bar, practically dancing. It was adorable.

Adorable? Really? Lyra scoffed in his mind. He chose to ignore her.

"Wait... you feel like a what?"

"A magept. A normie. You know, a non-magical person." She handed him a plate with scrambled eggs, toast, and four slices of bacon. Elena placed a second plate in front of Lyra with four slices of bacon as well. Lyra might not like Elena, but Q could tell that Elena was trying to win her heart through food. He could also feel that Lyra was warming to her, despite her endless protests to the contrary. A few more visits with bacon and Elena would be Lyra's new best friend.

"I've never heard that before. Sounds a little insulting," Q said before taking a bite of his toast and smirking at her.

"Oh, does it? I'm sorry. I didn't realize. That's just what we've always called them at Harbor—"

Quinn choked on his eggs trying to cut her off before she finished that sentence.

"Hey!" he whispered loudly, "You can't talk about that, remember? It's not safe." He was struggling to catch his breath. "I think I inhaled my eggs..."

"Dear Goddess, are you ok? Here," she handed him a glass of water. "Drink this and try to take deep breaths. I'm sorry. I forgot. I was just so excited, I didn't think." Her face fell as she handed him a tall glass of water. Q instantly felt miserable. Elena looked so disheartened. He'd put that look on her face.

"No, it's ok. I didn't mean to jump at you like that. I'm sorry." He took a few deep breaths and took her hand in his. "It's ok. Really. Did you have fun? Did Agon go with you? How did that work?"

"He hung around my neck. With my cloak on, he easily passes for an animal pelt scarf."

"Hey! I heard that! I'm no one's scarf," Agon muttered, jumping onto the bar with an indignant look on his face. Q chuckled to himself. A moon ago, he never would have imagined reading the facial expressions of a weasel.

Agon slunk over to Lyra and twitched his nose in hello. She flicked her ears in return and pushed a slice of bacon over to him from her plate.

"Don't look now," Elena leaned across the bar, grabbed his arm, and whispered playfully, "but I think Lyra might not hate us anymore."

9

ELENA

SINCE THEIR FIRST ADVENTURE out to the fountain, Elena and Agon started making daily trips outside the inn, exploring the town. The weather was getting colder as the harvest season was ending, but the town fountain was still the center of the morning for most of the townsfolk. Elena and Agon spent the first week visiting with the girls at the fountain. Elena learned more about the ladies and their lives.

Viktoria revealed herself to be a cold and cruel woman. She had one daughter and her parenting style made Madame LaBelle seem warm and affectionate. Viktoria was not suited for motherhood, Elena decided, and she felt terrible for her daughter. She did get the sense, based on stories from the other ladies, that Viktoria's husband was a very kind and loving father. Elena hoped his affection and paternal joy balanced out Viktoria's aversion to parenting. Unlike the other women, Viktoria was the breadwinner in her family, and she was quick to brag about that fact to the other girls. Thankfully, her role as the town's literal bread-maker meant she wasn't available to socialize at the fountain as often. She ran the bakery six days out of the week. The shops and trades closed their doors on Moon's Day, the Mother Goddess' day, to honor Her.

Elena originally envied these women and their friendships, but over the weeks, she began to cultivate her own close friendships with them. She felt an especially strong bond with Nikki, who was only three cycles older than Elena. The more time she spent with these women, the more connected and comfortable she felt in Andover. Maybe Andover would really become her home.

She and Agon explored all of the shops in town, wandered around the blacksmith's forge, and they even spent some time in the tannery. Watching these men toil over furnaces and boiling pots of melted metals as they turned ugly hunks of stone and minerals into beautiful and functional pieces was mesmerizing, and Elena would have happily spent all day every day watching them work. The men didn't seem to notice her presence most days; they were doing hard, dangerous work, and they needed to focus. On rare occasions, the blacksmith would nod her way, but he was often far too busy to spare her a moment's notice. It was a perfect situation for Elena; she could build her confidence and comfort level around men without having them pay any attention to her.

She started helping Amelia by serving breakfast at the inn. Amelia had been right, of course, as breakfast was the slowest part of the day. Lunch was pretty heavy and dinner was usually a shyt show. The only people that came to breakfast were young, unmarried men who wanted coffee, eggs, and bacon before heading off to a long day in the fields. The men made Elena a little nervous at first, but after the first few mornings serving them, she realized that they weren't interested in her, just eating and getting to work.

Q still came by every other day, usually around lunchtime, to check in on her and get some free food from Amelia. Lyra was finally warming to Elena. She'd let go of her dislike for Agon weeks ago, after the bacon sharing event, but it took a while longer for her to accept that Elena was, in fact, just a girl and not some sort of chaos demon hells-bent on ruining their life.

They'd created a very comfortable routine for themselves and, some days, Elena thought it seemed crazy to think that only a few short moons ago she'd been kicked out of her home and left to fend for herself. She was really proud of how she and Agon had managed to carve out this little life for themselves. Granted, none of this would have been possible without the help of Quinn, Lyra, and Amelia. She made a point to thank them both, often.

"You have to stop that," Quinn said one day. "I'm happy you're doing so well, but I can't take any credit for it, and you should really stop giving it to me. You did this, El."

El. He called her El. This started around the same time she started serving breakfast a few weeks back. He just said it once, casually, and it stuck. She loved that he felt comfortable with her and gave her a nickname. When she was at Harbor Ridge, the other girls were distant and formal with her because they knew who her mother was and didn't want to risk any disrespect. Q knew her. He didn't care about who her mother was; he just liked her.

"Stop thanking you for saving my life? Not likely, Q. In fact, I might just start thanking you more!" She smiled before ducking back into the kitchen to grab the plates for the blacksmith and his apprentice.

When she came back out, a large group of migrant field workers had taken over three of the tables and were loudly demanding breakfast.

"I'll be right with you." Elena tried to sound confident and casual, but they made her very uncomfortable. It was the same rowdy bunch that had been physically removed from the inn after groping another waitress a few moons back.

Q seemed to recognize them too and stood, presumably to address them and the potential situation, but Elena caught his eye and shook her head to deter him. She needed to be able to handle these types of men on her own. She couldn't rely on Quinn to save her. That was not his job.

Elena delivered the fresh plates of bacon, sausage, and eggs—sunny side up—to the blacksmith and his apprentice, took a deep breath, and headed over to the tables of rough, bordering on aggressive, men.

Agon didn't stay with her when she was waiting tables. Amelia expressed concern that customers might have questions about a weasel around their food and even though she knew he was cleaner than most of the men that came in the dining hall, she had suggested that it might be best if he spent his time in the kitchen with her. Agon had begrudgingly conceded. This meant that Elena was very much on her own, as Amelia was busy cooking up a storm, preparing for lunch and dinner.

"What can I get for you all this morning?" Elena asked, charcoal stick and pad poised in her shaking hands.

The leader of the pack took a full minute, looking her up and down, inspecting her, and making Elena wish she could curl up into a ball and disappear.

"Hm... how bout some of that sweet ass?" His cronies burst into fits of maniacal laughter. Elena felt her face flush and her skin instantly dampen with nervous sweat.

She didn't know what to say, so she turned to walk away, but the brutish pig grabbed her arm and pulled her back. She lost her balance and nearly landed in his lap, catching herself on the table just in time.

"Aw, come on, babe. I need a little pick-me-up this mornin'." His grip on her arm tightened. Elena felt cold and terrified. Her body froze. This was what the school had always warned them would happen. *Men only want one thing*, they'd say, and now this filthy piece of human garbage was going to take that thing, and there was nothing she could do about it.

He pulled her down, onto his lap, and his friends crowded in closely. She felt hands on her body: her face, her neck, her arms, her legs. There were hands on her breasts, fighting with the fabric to gain access to her skin. She wanted to scream, but no sound came out. This was it. They were going to take what they wanted and leave her a broken mess.

Suddenly, she heard a series of screams. The first was filled with rage and fueled by fire, both metaphorically and literally. The second was the scream of the man who had pulled her into his lap. Elena felt his hands release her as he wailed in agony. The side of his face was on fire, melting before her eyes as Elena scrambled to get away. Within seconds, the rest of the gang of molesters were screaming in pain and climbing over each other to escape the fray.

As quickly as it began, it was over. She was unscathed and completely detached from the remaining chaos that surrounded her.

Elena felt a new pair of hands gently but firmly grasp her shoulders and steer her towards her room. She felt the warmth of Agon's fur wrap tightly around her neck. He was saying something, but the words didn't register in her mind. Her eyes were unfocused as she was guided to her room. A disembodied hand opened the door and a furry orange blur brushed past her and onto her bed. The hands on her shoulders led her into the room, turned her, and carefully nudged her to a seated position on the edge of the bed.

Someone knelt in front of her.

Quinn. It was Quinn.

His face filled her field of vision, but her mind barely acknowledged his presence. He was saying something. Elena could see his mouth moving, but she couldn't comprehend his words.

There was a ringing in her ears. She felt disconnected from her body, from her mind. She was aware of where she was and who she was with, but it felt as though she were watching herself from above rather than actually having lived through that experience. Everything felt wrong and loud, dirty and distant.

Elena could hear her mother's voice in her mind. Telling her how useless she was and how much of a disappointment she'd been. Turns out, her mother was right. Elena was a useless enchantress who couldn't even protect herself when she had desperately needed to. She had needed to be rescued. Again. By Quinn. Again.

She wanted to curl up into a ball on her bed and sleep for the rest of time, but she didn't seem to have any control over her body. She couldn't make herself move. Hells, she couldn't even make her mind pay attention to Q and whatever words of comfort or sympathy he was likely offering her. She was just a useless girl like her mother had always told her.

10
QUINN

OW HAD HE LET that happen? Why had he brought her here? Why hadn't he kicked those filthy bastards out the second he saw them? Why hadn't he protected her?

She looked like a ghost. Pale, oblivious, completely disconnected from the world. She wasn't responding to his questions or Agon's words.

Thankfully, Agon informed Q that he could feel her emotions and knew she was still aware, but it seemed that she had pulled herself into an internal lockbox. Q knew that feeling. He used to lock his mental awareness away in a steel box whenever his foster parents decided he needed "discipline." It was his preferred survival technique, and it was clearly the only thing keeping Elena from going off the deep end.

"Maybe you should lay down for a little while, El," Quinn suggested, knowing that she wasn't fully aware of his words. He guided her to a horizontal position on her bed, covered her with the blanket from the wardrobe, and took a seat in the chair by her window. Elena curled into the fetal position, with

Agon around her neck, and Lyra curled up at the bend in her knees.

How could I let this happen?

Amelia quietly crept into Elena's room. Quinn wasn't sure how long he'd been sitting there, waiting for Elena to wake up. It could have been minutes or days.

"How's she doing, love?" Amelia inquired, adjusting the blanket over Elena's shoulders, pausing to brush some hair away from her face, before looking over at Q.

He was the picture of self-loathing and shame. Amelia knelt in front of him and took his hands in hers

"Quinn. Look at me. This is *not* your fault. You saved her from those sick bastards. You are a good man and you did everything right. You protected her. You didn't do *anything* wrong." Amelia was so steadfast and sure, he almost believed her.

"I shouldn't have let her serve them. I shouldn't have let them sit down. I shouldn't have—" she cut him off before he could finish his downward spiral.

"No. You will not blame yourself because some pieces of shyt tried to hurt our girl." That caught his attention. Amelia never swore. He wasn't even going to let himself think about the "our girl" part of her statement.

"I should have protected her better." The tears filled his eyes. Lyra lifted her soft, white head and locked eyes with him. She didn't say a word, but he knew what she was thinking: *Shut the hells up. We saved her. She's safe and will remain that way as long as we draw breath.* The wave of love and protective energy that radiated off of her was nearly tangible and completely unexpected.

"Well, that's a surprising change of heart, Lyra. I never thought you'd ever like someone else, much less feel this protective of them. I'm impressed." Q's voice was gruff and raw with emotions, but teasing Lyra helped lighten the mood a little and helped to get him out of his own head.

"Shut it. I know where you sleep, Q," Lyra said with a smirk before snuggling her head back onto Elena's knee.

Amelia squeezed his hands and kissed his forehead. "She will be all right, sweetheart. She's been through an ordeal, and she will need time to process that, but we will be here for her in whatever way she needs. For now, we just have to wait and give her space to breathe."

11
ELENA

WHEN ELENA WOKE, IT was dark outside. Agon was comfortably draped across her neck, as per usual. Elena was surprised to find Lyra had curled herself into a warm little ball in the curve of her knees. Q was asleep in her chair by the window, covered with a blanket that Elena didn't recognize. Amelia must have brought it in at some point in the night, along with the pillow that was supporting Quinn's head in a more comfortable position, propped against the high back of the chair.

Elena gently shifted Agon onto her pillow and slowly rolled over, trying not to wake everyone. She desperately needed a drink of water, and she wanted to change out of her ruined dress. She was going to have to burn this dress. Which was a pity because she didn't have many dresses to begin with, but she knew she would never be able to look at it again, much less wear it.

She had almost made it out from under the blanket and Lyra when she heard Q groan and yawn from his station in the chair.

"Hey," he said quietly, "you're awake. Are you ok? Do you need anything?"

Elena knew he was concerned; worry and anxiety were practically dripping off him. She didn't want to lie, but she didn't really know what to say. She decided bluntness would be good. Her brain wasn't exactly functioning at a high level, anyway.

"I'm not sure how I feel. I would like a drink of water and to burn this dress." Elena's directness must have taken him by surprise because Quinn just looked at her like he was trying to solve a very challenging riddle.

"Um... well I can get the water, and I'm sure Lyra would be more than happy to help with the dress burning if you'd like." At the mention of her name Lyra stood up and stretched her legs before sitting back down, prim and proper, at the foot of the bed.

"What does that mean? How can she help me burn my dress?"

"I'll let her explain while I get some water and food. I'll be back in a few." And with that, Quinn left. He had a mission, and he seemed highly motivated to complete it. Elena smiled privately at his enthusiasm. He was probably just thrilled to have something to do, somewhere to focus his energy.

Lyra stood and stretched a second time, ending with a rather loud yawn then she hopped off the bed and dragged the bed warmer out from underneath Elena's mattress.

"If you would be so kind as to drop the offending garments in here, I can help you dispose of them." All business, but none of the callousness or coldness that Elena usually experienced when it came to conversations with Lyra.

Elena glanced at Agon, who had curled into a little ball on her pillow, still warm from where her head had just been. He lifted his head and eyed Lyra before turning to Elena and twitching his head from side to side. He had no idea what Lyra was talking about. They were both fairly certain that foxes, even talking foxes, couldn't start fires.

"Humor me," Lyra said. She was trying to be patient with them, but it was very apparent that she was eager to get this done.

Elena removed her corrupted dress and undergarments, dropped them in the bed warmer, and dressed in clean, unaffected undergarments and a nightgown. Lyra rearranged the dress to ensure that all of the cloth was in the bed warmer, then turned her back to them. She flicked her tail back and forth a few times, building speed and what appeared to be smoke. On her final tail swish, a flame burst on the tip of her tail.

Elena jumped backward, landing roughly on her bed. Agon hissed and pounced into Elena's lap, hair standing on end as he eyed Lyra's tail suspiciously.

"What in the hells did you do?!" Elena was amazed. Lyra had magic. That wasn't supposed to be possible. "How did you do that?"

Lyra sat calmly next to the flaming dress and twitched her ears.

"I don't understand your question. What do you mean 'how'? How did Agon manage to electrify Q and me? It's magic, Elena. I don't know how it works, it just does."

Elena got up from the bed and opened the window to let the smoke out. Her dress was quickly engulfed in Lyra's magical flames and the room filled with smoke.

"That's amazing. What are you? You clearly aren't a typical woodland fox; foxes don't usually start fires with their *tails*. Foxes don't usually start fires at all." To say Elena was intrigued would have been the understatement of the century. Magical animals were supposed to all be extinct. Agon was the only exception anyone at Harbor Ridge had ever known.

"I don't know what I am. Quinn's the only person who knows about my fiery capabilities. Well, and Amelia. She knows but she's never actually seen it. You are the first person I've ever shown, besides Q." Lyra flicked her tail in front of her, wrapped it around her front paws, and began licking the singed hair clean. As she licked the black soot off, it was clear that the hair itself was completely unharmed.

"Lyra, you are amazing," Agon whispered in a hushed tone. Even Agon was riveted by her magic. If she could have blushed, Lyra certainly would have. They spent the remainder of the time waiting for Q to return with a snack, in silence. As they watched the dress burn to ash, Elena pondered all the things that had dramatically changed over the course of the last day.

12
QUINN

Quinn couldn't help but blame himself for what had happened to Elena. He didn't say anything to Elena about it, but he did move back in with Amelia the next day. Q wanted to be close by to protect her. He felt compelled to keep her safe. Lyra didn't even complain about the move, although that could have been because Amelia spoiled her with warm cinnamon buttermilk at every meal. She had a seat permanently reserved next to the hearth in Amelia's rooms upstairs, above the inn and dining hall. Not to mention an actual bed to sleep in, rather than a nest of leaves and pine needles that she'd made for herself in their hut.

Elena never commented on their relocation either, but he had a feeling that she enjoyed seeing them every day. Lyra and Agon were quickly becoming friends, and Elena smiled every time he walked into the room. The feeling was mutual.

Every morning, the four of them would go for a walk down to the fountain to collect fresh water and check in with Elena's new friends. Viktoria didn't hide her disgust at Quinn's presence, and he still hadn't discovered why she hated him so, but the rest of the girls were kind and welcoming. Nikki was Q's favorite. She was spunky and direct. No bullshyt. No gossip or ridiculous drama. She said what was on her mind and never tried to sugarcoat anything. She didn't come to the fountain as often. Elena said she was due to have her baby any day and was probably staying close to home just in case.

The piece of shyt who had initiated the attack on Elena hadn't been back to the inn, but Quinn had spoken with some of the other men in town and learned that he was still working at a local farm. That information was what solidified Q's plans to stay close by, indefinitely. He didn't want that bastard to try anything for a second time.

A few weeks after he'd moved back in, Quinn and Elena headed down to the fountain only to find the typically casual group of ladies were all upset and anxious.

"What's going on?" Q asked Seraphina.

"Oh, Quinn, it's awful. Nikki has been in labor since yesterday morn and the babe isn't coming. If she can't get the baby out soon, they'll both die!" Seraphina sobbed and covered her face with a damp handkerchief.

Hazel nodded, rubbing Seraphina's back consolingly. "It's true. The midwife is at a loss. It seems the baby is stuck somehow, and nothing they're doing is helping."

"I was with her all night." Willow looked like she was fighting back tears. "Nikki is so exhausted. I don't know how much longer she can go on like this."

"Oh, my Goddess. We have to help her!" Elena looked equally terrified and determined. "Is she still at home or did they move her?"

"She's still home, dear, but I doubt there's anything you can do. Leave it to the experts. They've been birthing babies for much longer than you." Viktoria scoffed. Clearly, she wasn't as affected as her friends.

Heartless bitch, Quinn thought.

"I can try. I was trained to be a doula when I was younger. Maybe there is something I can do. If nothing else, I would like to go visit and sit with her for a while." Elena was unfazed by Viktoria's condescension. Q loved that about her.

No. Not love. Quinn mentally corrected himself. No love here, nope. Never gonna happen.

"A doula? You? You're just a child," Viktoria scoffed.

"It was… the family business," Elena replied quickly.

Quinn wondered if that was standard practice at the school. He didn't imagine they'd let outsiders assist in the births of their precious enchantresses.

"I'm sure she'd appreciate the visit, Elena," Willow replied, ignoring Viktoria as well. "I'll go with you. I haven't been to see her today. We can bring some fresh drinking water too."

Q took the bucket from Willow's hand, filled it with water from the small well beside the fountain, and the girls led the way to Nikki's.

When they arrived, the house was solemn. Three men were sitting outside, one Q recognized as Nikki's husband, Elias, the other two he didn't know, but the older man looked like Elias so Quinn assumed that was probably his dad.

"How's she doing, Elias?" Willow gave him a tight, comforting hug and offered a nod to the other men.

"The midwives left. They said there's nothing they can do, and they were needed at another home in town." Elias looked so dejected and broken. "They said it's just a matter of time now."

"Can I see her?" Elena asked barely above a whisper, eyes downcast.

"Of course," Elias opened the door for her. "I know she'll be happy to see you. I'll wait out here."

Quinn thought it was a little odd that he didn't want to be with his wife, but maybe he just wanted to give Elena some privacy with her friend before she passed unto the fade.

"I'll wait out here. Take as long as you like." Quinn squeezed Elena's hand, then he and Lyra walked over to a bench near the side of the house, to sit and wait with the other men. He knew this was going to be a hard day for Elena. He'd buried friends before. It never got easier, and he was going to support her in any way he could.

13
ELENA

T HE HOUSE WAS DARK but warm, with a fire crackling softly in the hearth on the back wall of their home. It was a large, open cabin. No walls to separate the rooms, so one fireplace worked well to keep the whole place comfortable. Their bed was set off to the left side of the home as Elena walked through the door. A table and four chairs were under the window directly to the right of the front door. There was a second, smaller table next to the bed that held an oil lamp and a cooking spit across the hearth. As she crept quietly into the center of the room, Elena, with Agon on her shoulder, realized this was the first time she'd been inside Nikki's home. It was surprisingly quaint and lovely. Small, but cozy. Love lived here.

Nikki was on the bed in her dressing gown. She looked pale and there was a sheen of sweat all over her body. Her swollen belly was rock hard, and Nikki was moaning through the contraction. She was exhausted. Nikki opened her eyes as Elena and Willow crossed the room and stood at her bedside, but it was unclear as to whether or not she could see them or knew they were there.

Willow dropped to her knees and carefully rested her hands on Nikki's forehead and belly.

"Oh Goddess, bless her. Bring her into your arms and welcome Nikki and this sweet baby unto the fade. Ease their suffering and bring them home to you, please." Willow prayed quietly but as Elena listened to her words, she felt a rage she didn't know or understand rising up inside of her.

"She's not dead! Why are you treating her like she's already gone? She's right here! She doesn't need to be taken, she *is* home. She needs our help!" Elena tried to contain her outrage, but the idea of giving up on her first and closest female friend just wasn't acceptable.

"Elena, please calm down," Willow replied, looking equally outraged. "I'm not condemning her to death. Death already has her. I'm asking the Goddess to have mercy and release her from this torture."

The calm resignation in her voice broke Elena.

"I'm sorry." Elena placed her hands on Willow's shoulders, rubbing her gently as she attempted to feed a calming spell into her friend. "I didn't mean to snap at you." Elena didn't want to upset her friend, but she needed to help Nikki, and she wasn't going to be able to do that with Willow there. "Can you please give me a few moments alone with her? I would like to say my goodbyes and pray with her for a little while."

Elena's sudden change in demeanor didn't seem to register with Willow. She merely nodded, gave Elena a quick, gentle hug, and left the house without another word.

When she was certain Willow wasn't coming back, Agon hopped down and gently padded across the bed to sit by Nikki's head, while Elena climbed onto the bed next to Nikki and repositioned her from the fetal position on her side to laying on her back, head resting on the pillows, legs bent at the knee.

"Nikki, I'd like to check on your baby. Is that ok?"

Nikki's eyes fluttered, and she looked frantically around the room.

"Elena? Elena, is that you?"

"Yes, Nikki, it's me. I'd like to check on the baby. I have been trained to help in births, and I'd like to try and help you bring this beautiful babe into the world if you'd let me."

"Hannah. Her name is Hannah. Please, help us." Tears streamed down her pain-stricken face as she pleaded with Elena.

"Try to relax. I'm going to check your progress and see if I can determine why Hannah isn't making her way out." Elena pushed Nikki's gown up, over her belly, and began feeling around her stomach, trying to determine where the baby was and what might be holding her up.

"Nikki, I'm going to check inside you now. This will probably hurt a little, but I'll be as quick and painless as possible." Elena's small hands were considered a blessing in her doula classes and one of the few things that granted her favor with the teachers at Harbor Ridge. She'd apprenticed in a handful of births before she'd been kicked out of the school, and she felt confident enough in her skills to help Nikki and her baby.

"Ok, Nikki, I think I know what's wrong. It feels like Hannah's shoulder is caught on your pelvic bone. I can help her, but it's going to be very uncomfortable. I'll time it between contractions. We should have her out and in your arms in a matter of minutes. I want to warn you though," Elena paused as a contraction hit Nikki. She cried out and clutched fistfuls of the sheets in her hands, straining to find relief from the pain. Elena tried to coach her to take deep breaths through the pain and massaged Nikki's swollen and solid belly until the contraction passed.

"Will she be ok? Will my baby be ok, Elena?" Nikki's face was colorless and the stress of this labor was written on her tear-stained face.

"I don't know, Nikki. I don't know if she's been able to breathe this whole time or not. I don't know how she's doing, but I do know that if we don't get her out of you, you will both die." Elena didn't like being so brutal and blunt, but they didn't have any time to spare for niceties.

Nikki nodded. Her fearful face took on a countenance of tense resolve as she braced herself for the next contraction.

"When this one passes, I'll try and reposition her. We should be able to get her out with the next contraction, ok?" What Elena didn't tell Nikki was that she was casting spells to ease pain, soften bones to make them more malleable, and a third to ever-so-slightly shrink the baby's head just long enough to get her through the birth canal.

Like clockwork, the contraction ended and Elena got to work. She wasn't an excellent enchantress, but she always managed to make things work when it was absolutely necessary. Her teachers referred to her as a "clutchantress" because she was useless in peaceful circumstances, but she always came through "in the clutch." Elena had no idea what that meant, except to know that when it really mattered, her magic never failed.

Right now, it *really* mattered. She finished casting, and Nikki visibly relaxed.

"What did you —" but before Nikki could even ask, Elena demanded that she push with all her might. Having been in labor for nearly two days, Nikki didn't have a lot of energy left, but she had just enough to give one big push.

Elena saw the head and grasped it. Gently, but firmly, Elena pulled the baby while Nikki drained every last ounce of energy she had.

"She's out!" Elena cheered. She held Hannah up and bundled her in a blanket that Agon had dragged across the bed from a stack that had clearly been left there by the midwives. She was a sickening shade of gray and not breathing.

"Where is she? Is my baby ok?" Nikki panted and strained to see her newborn.

Elena put her ear to the baby's chest. Agon stood by the babe's head, licking her face and nudging her with his nose. She wasn't breathing, but Elena heard a very faint heartbeat. Quicker than she'd ever been able to do anything, Elena cast a recovery spell and pressed it into Hannah's chest.

"Breathe," Elena muttered. She cast a second recovery spell and pressed it onto the baby's lips. "You can do this. Just breathe."

Nikki whimpered beside Elena. She knew something was wrong, and she feared the worst.

It felt like an age had passed, but in reality, it was probably only a few heartbeats before Hannah let out the most magnificent and heart-swelling wail of a newborn babe.

Nikki cried and Elena gently rested the baby on her mother's breast. Elena took a moment to cast one last spell, a healing spell to aid in quick recovery for Nikki and to minimize any serious damage that this lengthy birth had caused. Elena took the towels that lay next to the bed, collected the placenta, and gently patted the blood away, trying to clean Nikki up as thoroughly and carefully as she could. She used one of the clean towels to dry the sweat from her own body. Elena hadn't used that much magic in a while. Her body had lost its tolerance for magical fatigue and she was a bit drained.

"You did it, Nikki. You made a human and brought her into the world. You are amazing." Elena beamed down at her friend. "I'll go get Elias."

Nikki grabbed Elena's hand as she was getting out of the bed. "I don't know how you did it, but I know you saved us. Thank you. Thank you for everything."

Elena just smiled. There were no words. Besides, if she said anything, she would certainly start to cry.

Elena stepped outside and gave Elias the good news. He was so ecstatic; he hugged Elena so tightly she thought she might pass out. It was easily the best day of her life. If only her mother could have seen her, maybe Madame LaBelle would have finally been proud of her only daughter.

She shook the thought from her mind. No point dwelling on a woman who didn't appreciate her own child when Elena had just saved the life of a dear friend and *her* child. Elena felt a bolt of heat rush through her. She had called on her magic, and it had answered. Elena basked in the warmth of the sun on her face and the heat of victory within her.

Elena, with Agon around her neck for warmth to brace against the chilled winds, went back to visit Nikki a few days later, fully expecting to find her in bed, baby beside her, resting and recuperating. Instead, Nikki was standing over the cooking spit, roasting a rabbit with her sweet little Hannah wrapped up and tied snuggly to Nikki's chest.

"Well, this is unexpected," Elena exclaimed from the doorway. "Shouldn't you be in bed?"

"Elena!" Nikki rushed over and gave Elena a hug that rivaled the hug she'd received from Elias on her previous visit to their home. "What are you doing here? Do you want to hold Hannah? Everyone does. That's why they come to visit me these days. No one wants to see me anymore. I've been replaced by a babe." She rolled her eyes in mock offense but it was clear she was loving every second of it.

"You look amazing. And of course, I want to hold that sweet little angel!" Elena carefully took the baby from her friend and sat down in one of the wooden chairs at the table. "I'm surprised you're not still in bed. You went through quite the ordeal. You need more rest, Nikki."

"Are you kidding? I feel amazing, plus Elias is a great man and a phenomenal hunter, but he can't cook to save his life. If I leave the food to him, we'll be eating raw rabbit and squirrel for weeks. No, thank you."

"Ha! That's so mean, Nikki. Hilarious, but mean. It's a good thing he has you then." Elena laughed and snuggled the tiny, soft, and warm baby girl in her arms. Suddenly, she was struck by a thought. "Hey, Nikki, how did you know she was going to be a girl? You were so certain. How?"

"I just had a feeling." Nikki winked. "No, actually, please don't tell Elias or the girls. They won't approve, and I don't need that drama. Swear to the Mother, and I'll tell you a secret."

Intrigued, Elena said, "Of course, I swear to the Mother Goddess. I won't tell a soul."

Nikki sat down on the chair next to Elena, leaned in, and whispered conspiratorially, "I saw a witch."

Elena sat, stunned. She must have misheard her. Witches don't exist. They were supposed to be wiped out decades ago. Witches had been labeled evil, untrustworthy agents from hells, and were all executed under the command of King Oron in the Age of Blood. She felt Agon tense against her skin. The idea of witches obviously made him as uncomfortable as it made her.

"Um, Nikki, I think you were tricked. Witches are gone. They were all killed ages ago."

"I thought so too, but this woman was the real thing, Elena. She knew things that she couldn't possibly know. About me, Elias, our friends. She warned me that bringing Hannah into the world would be hard and potentially impossible, but that I could do it if I had the right help. She said that this little girl would be worth the work and trials, I just needed to make sure I had the right people by my bedside. I thought she meant the midwives, but now I know she meant you." Nikki reached out and took Elena's hand in her own, gazing lovingly down at her perfect little girl. "We wouldn't be here if it weren't for you, Elena. I know that, and I will make sure she knows it too. Auntie Elena saved both of our lives. You are already famous in our family."

"Famous? That's crazy. I just did what I was trained—"

"Stop. You *saved our lives.* Don't try and act like that's not a big deal." Nikki locked eyes with her for the longest moment of her life. Elena felt Agon tense around her neck. "Thank you." She added with a gentle squeeze of Elena's hands.

"I'm just happy I was able to help. Really. You're the first friend I made in this town. I certainly am not going to give that up without a fight." Elena smiled and felt tears threaten. She decided to change the topic to something less emotional.

While Nikki busied herself around the cooking fire, sharing the latest gossip, Elena looked down at the perfect little bundle wrapped snuggly in her arms. This little girl wouldn't have survived without Elena. It was a crazy thought, but she knew it was the truth.

Do you think the woman she saw was really a witch? Agon asked.

I don't know. Harbor Ridge said that all the witches were dead, but maybe they were wrong. They were clearly wrong about men not being capable of magic. Elena mentally replied. It was an intriguing idea. Witches. They were said to be incredibly powerful, with magical familiars and access to magic that enchantresses weren't privy to. Elena couldn't help but hope that this witch was real and she might one day get to meet her.

14
QUINN

“I DON’T UNDERSTAND. YOU did what?” She did *what?!* Q didn’t mean to sound so pissed, but he was pretty damn unhappy. “I can’t believe you used,” he glanced around to make sure no one was listening to their conversation at the bar, “*magic* on Nikki and the baby. Are you insane? Have you lost your damn mind?! What if she saw you? What if she said something to Elias or any of those girls? Elena, that was the dumbest, most reckless thing—”

“What was I supposed to do?” Elena hissed back angrily “They were going to die! Was I just supposed to stand there and do nothing? Is that what you would have done?”

No. Of course not. He was incapable of standing by and doing nothing when he knew he could help someone in need. It was his weakness and downfall more often than not. But he certainly wasn’t going to say that now.

“You could have been exposed. Keeping your magic a secret is the safest way to survive out here.” Damn it all to hells, why didn’t she get that?

"I don't think everyone is as anti-magic as you think they are. Amelia knows about Agon and me. She didn't care at all." Elena scratched behind Agon's tiny blue ear.

"Amelia is… different. You have to know that by now. She's not the standard. She's like us."

"Like us? What does that mean?"

Mux, I thought she would have told you by now. At the very least, I thought you would have put the pieces together at this point. You've been living here for moons. It wasn't his secret to tell. If Amelia hadn't told Elena about her 'skills' or introduced her to Marty yet, then it wasn't his place to out her.

"I just mean she's nice. Open-minded. She doesn't judge people until she gets to know them. She judges based on actions and behaviors, not biology." He hoped that would be a good enough explanation.

"I get it. I'm sorry I upset you, but I'm not sorry for what I did. There's no way I was going to let them die if I could do something about it." Elena looked genuinely offended that he'd come down so hard on her, but he understood her side of things too. He would have done the same thing, but he'd never tell her that.

Quinn smiled and offered Elena his cinnamon buttered roll. "Truce?"

"Sure," she replied, accepting the fresh roll and taking a big bite.

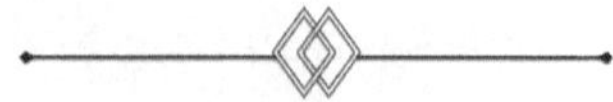

The frost season came in hard and fast making Quinn grateful to be living back at the inn rather than in his hut. The makeshift home was nice enough. It was good for keeping out the rain—not to mention unwanted guests—but it did little for keeping warmth in. His bed at Amelia's was always warm and welcoming. Not to mention his cooking skills left much to be desired. He could cook to keep himself alive, but Amelia's cooking kept people happy.

It had been a full season since the incident with the would-be rapist and his gang. Quinn kept an eye out and regularly asked around but no one had seen or heard about them in weeks. There had been a rumor floating around town for a few weeks after the attack that the leader was pissed and looking for revenge after Lyra had severely burned his neck and face. Q had been on high alert for a while after that, but they never showed their faces in town again, and the harvest season was over. Presumably, that meant they'd moved on to the next seasonal job in another town. Migrant workers did, after all, migrate to find work.

Quinn took this time to do all the handyman projects that Amelia had on her to-do list. Amelia had been married before, but Herb passed long before Quinn had come into her life, and she had been left to run the inn on her own. They'd never had any children of their own, which Q assumed was why she'd always been so willing to help anyone in need. She had so much love to give but she was incapable of having kids herself, so over the years she'd taken in anyone who needed her.

Amelia would never ask for help but she and Quinn had established an unspoken agreement many years ago. If something needed to be fixed, Q would do it. She never had to ask, she simply needed to mention that something wasn't working the way it should. He wasn't always able to fix what was broken, but he always tried to do his best for her. The things he couldn't fix himself, he found others to complete the work in exchange for fresh meat or a day's labor. He loved her like a mother. He'd never knew the woman who had given birth to him, but he knew what love was and how it was supposed to be as a result of his relationship with Amelia.

Most recently, Amelia had commented that there was a leak over the stove that was making it especially challenging to cook meals while raining. Q had chosen to patch the leak that morning, after the breakfast rush, while things were slow and Amelia didn't need the space yet. Lyra was napping on the floor in front of the kitchen hearth completely oblivious to his grunts and struggles with the thatching. They were both oblivious to the pack of hungry wolves that walked into the dining hall, hunting for their prey.

15
ELENA

ELENA WAS WORKING THE late morning crowd by herself. It was the slowest time of the day, after breakfast and before lunch. This was the time to clean the tables and floors, refill the salt shakers on the tables, and thoroughly scrub down the bar.

Agon used this time to nap on the windowsill of their bedroom. He liked the peace, and she was enjoying having time alone. She loved Agon more than anything, they shared a soul after all, but everyone needs a break from their soulmate every now and then.

Elena was struggling to open the lid to the salt barrel in the storeroom when she heard a grunt behind her. She turned around quickly, realizing she was no longer alone.

Blocking the doorway was the same burly, scruffy, filthy man that had attacked her before. He looked different now though; the skin on his neck and the left side of his face had been severely warped and damaged, like the sun-damaged leather she'd see the town tanner try to repair. The smell of sweat and manure radiated off of him, and when he smiled Elena could see he was missing several teeth. It was the smile of pure evil.

"Remember me, pretty?" His breath reeked of ale. "I look a li'l differen' now, right?" He gestured to his neck and arms. "This is all yer fault, bitch."

He stepped closer, and she could see he was not alone. Her blood run cold. Elena looked frantically around the room for a way out, but there was only one door, and it was blocked by his cronies, three equally disgusting men, who hooted with laughter.

He grabbed her arm roughly and knocked her into several barrels of flour.

"I ask'd you a quesshun," he grumbled, slurring his words, although Elena couldn't tell if that was a result of his drunken state or the anger rapidly boiling to the surface.

Before she knew what was happening, his comrades rushed into the room. One barricaded the door with a couple of barrels of ale as the other two rushed to grab her arms. They backed her into the flour barrels until she fell backward on top of them. The men held tight, gripping her by her arms so she couldn't get back up. When she tried to scream, the third man covered her mouth with his grimy hands. The burned, drunk leader positioned himself between her legs and started to shove her skirt up and out of his way.

Elena could hear her blood pounding in her head. She was scared, terrified. These men were going to hurt her, rape her, and almost certainly kill her. She was alone. No one knew where she was, and no one was going to come to her rescue this time. Elena closed her eyes, feeling the heat of their predatory gazes all over her body lighting a fire of fear within her, and cried.

Without warning, Elena felt the heat within her shift from the mere fire of terror to electricity coursing through her body, as sure as if Agon had shocked her himself. The shock grew and she heard someone scream. It was her. She screamed, but it wasn't a cry of fear or pain. This scream was guttural, filled with rage and anguish.

There was a brilliant flash of blue light, and suddenly it was dead quiet. She was alone. The men were gone. Elena sat up and shakily wrapped her arms around her body tightly, checking for injuries while examining the room. The smell of overcooked meat filled her nose. Where had they gone?

As she stumbled down from the barrels, wiping sweat from her brow and fixing her skirt, she noticed four smoking piles of ash surrounding the barrels.

Quinn rushed in with Agon and Lyra on his heels.

"Are you ok?! What the hells just happened?" He held her at arm's length, trying to inspect her as best he could. Elena was in shock. She couldn't speak and she wasn't sure she'd know what to say even if she could. Quinn pulled her into him and hugged her tight. Elena was inexplicably exhausted and let him carry the majority of her weight.

"It's ok. You're ok. I've got you," he whispered over and over into her ear. "I've got you."

Agon clambered up the back of her shirt and perched himself on her shoulder, opposite Quinn.

"I heard a loud noise, then the door slammed shut, and I couldn't get it open. Agon said you were panicked and something was wrong. What happened? What was that blue light? Are you ok? Why does it smell like something's burning?"

Elena stood, stupefied. She didn't have any answers.

Quinn led Elena out of the storage room, and over to the far corner of the bar, then positioned himself between her and the rest of the dining hall.

"I'm ok. I'm not hurt," she squeaked as she felt her legs give out and she collapsed onto the barstool. "I'm not hurt."

16

BEATRICE

MADAME LABELLE HAD BREAKFAST with the faculty and students in the Great Hall, just like she did every morning, then came back to her chambers to deal with literal mountains of paperwork: letters from parents of prospective students, making cases for why their daughters were special and should be accepted into the school, the usual documentation that came with running a staff of some three hundred, and then the daily correspondence from the King. He wrote to her every day. She found him exhausting and needy. My Goddess, he was the ruler of the known world. He should have better things to do than constantly pen love letters to her.

"Beatrice, my beloved,
I miss you dearly. Words cannot express the impa-
tience I feel towards our next rendezvous. I desire
you. I need to feel the softness of your kiss and your
skin against mine."

The blithering fool. The words varied, but the sentiment was the same. He was completely under her spell, and she was completely bored with him. She continued the farce, though, because, through him, she ruled the country. She had all the power. He was a mere puppet. If that meant she had to waste precious time and energy feigning affection for the buffoon, so be it. It would be worth it all when she became Queen.

That was the end game, of course. Convince him to relieve himself of his current Queen, or do it for him if he was too squeamish or lazy. Marry the dullard. Orchestrate a "hunting accident." Rule the kingdom herself. It was well past time to remove the male authority in the world and replace it with a level-headed, maternal figure. Women were better at reigning. It was just fact. Men were too prideful and often went to war over petty vendettas. Women were cool, calm, and collected. Women were the stronger of the sexes. Men play a part, obviously, but only in the act of procreation. If women could procreate without men, the world would be a much happier, healthier, safer place. Men caused more problems than they solved. History had proven that time and again.

"Your lunch is ready, Headmistress." Madame LaBelle nodded to the servant who quietly bowed herself out of the room. Beatrice couldn't remember this one's name, but she had given up trying to remember their names decades ago. Her mental energy was better spent elsewhere.

Beatrice didn't consider herself a challenging matron, but she did expect things to be done a certain way, and the servants always seemed to struggle with that concept. Few seemed to last long in her employ.

She sat at the small wooden table under a north-facing, stained-glass window, casually calculating the number of servants she'd had since becoming headmistress. When the number reached triple digits, she chuckled to herself about the complete ineptitude of the non-magical community and turned her focus to the meal before her and the stack of applications beside her goblet of wine.

Madame LaBelle was reading through a petition for entry to Harbor Ridge when she felt it. A sudden surge of energy, power like she'd never felt before. It disappeared as quickly as it had emerged, but it was unmistakable. It was something new. It had pulsed through the air, passing through the room like a wave might crash along the shore; disappearing as quickly as it had arrived. The magic left an aftershock in the room that was faintly familiar, although Beatrice couldn't quite place it. The source of the surge felt close, but not inside the school. To the south? In the Dark Woods, maybe. Or perhaps farther, in the town at the bottom of the mountain?

Beatrice jumped from her seat, nearly knocking the chair to the ground in her rush to the south-facing windows.

Stop this. She thought to herself. *Don't be so careless and overeager. You don't know what it is, so you certainly shouldn't rush blindly toward it.*

Zied lifted his regal head and locked eyes with her. He'd felt it too and, like Madame LaBelle, he didn't like it.

"I've never known a power like that," he said, as he stood and stretched his lithe body from his position lounging beside her desk. His snowy mane seemed ruffled from the unexpected shock. "It feels like something new, but very, very old. And close."

Beatrice said nothing, but her agreement didn't require words.

"We need to investigate. Is this a threat or a potential new charge?" Zied hated change, and he despised the unknown as much as she did.

"We'll send some investigators to uncover the source of that power and assess the situation," Beatrice replied. Investigators. Enchantresses whose sole purpose was to seek out new powers and encourage them to attend Harbor Ridge. Beatrice called out to the guard outside her door. At all times, the head-mistress was accompanied by two highly trained combat en-chantresses, women were trained in battle magic, defensive and offensive spells, as well as camouflage, explosive, and healing magic. They could take out a single target in a crowded bazaar or implode a building with the flick of a wrist. They were the best in the business, and she took extra care to ensure that they were happy at Harbor Ridge and completely devoted to her.

Previous headmistresses attempted to keep the guard loyal by threats and coercion. That proved very fatal for those arrogant and foolish enchantresses. Madame LaBelle's method was far more effective. She encouraged the women to do whatever made them happy, showering them with gifts and freedoms denied the rest of the women in Harbor Ridge: a private and luxurious wing of the castle, overnight guests—on the condition that the guests only stayed one night and had their memories erased by one of the Cleaners before departure—whatever food they desired, and one night off a week to spend however they pleased.

The guards rushed in, spells poised in their hands, ready to attack. They must have felt the power surge as well and were on edge as a result.

"Stand down, ladies."

The guards immediately dissolved their magic and stood at attention. Seph's falcon, Archer, did a quick flyover of the room before landing gracefully on her shoulder. Baste, a small but ferocious ocelot, sat poised, statuesque, at Lillith's feet.

"Yes, Headmistress," they said in unison.

"I need you to escort two investigators into the town at the bottom of our mountain. Someone—or possibly some-*thing*—very powerful is nearby, and we need to know if they pose a threat. If they do, take care of it. If it's an enchantress, bring her here. She will need help learning to control the power inside of her." What she didn't say was that this power source could be an excellent weapon. It didn't need to be said. These women understood that a war with the magepts was inevitable. Men coveted power, and bloodshed was their favorite way to acquire it.

"Yes, Headmistress."

"Go now. Make haste. We need to know what's happening down there."

With that, the guards bowed and were out the door. Two more guards would take their place within minutes; they hated to leave their beloved Headmistress unprotected.

"We'll find the source of that power soon, Zied." Madame LaBelle gazed out her window while she stroked Zied's mane. She could almost make out the roofs of the pathetic buildings in the farming hamlet beyond the Dark Woods. The idea of anyone having magic in such a pitiful little place was almost laughable, and yet here they were. To find something new, after all these decades, scared her. Beatrice would never admit it, but this new power was unnerving.

17
QUINN

"**E**LENA? ELENA, PLEASE SAY something."

Her eyes. He'd seen something in them when they'd first broken into the storeroom. He thought they were glowing. *But that's impossible,* he kept telling himself.

Possible or not, he couldn't shake the memory. Her eyes had been blue, and for a split second, he was sure he'd seen lightning bolts flash across them. He'd seen blue lightning like that before, in the Dark Woods when they first met. It looked like the same lightning that Agon had used to incapacitate them.

Her eyes were back to their normal color, that warm brown that reminded him of fresh honey. They were still unfocused and distracted, rather than their typical quick, sharpness, but she was coming back to him.

"Elena. What happened? How did you get stuck back there? What was the light?"

Lyra jumped onto the stool next to Elena and gently nuzzled her hands in her lap. Lyra didn't say much, and he was certain she'd deny it later, but he could sense how anxious she was. Something strange was going on here, and Elena was at the center of it.

When the gentle nudging didn't work, Lyra looked to Agon wrapped around Elena's neck, "You could try a little zap. Maybe a light shock will snap her out of this."

As appalling as the suggestion was, Agon seemed to be considering it.

"Don't you dare." Q's voice carried more threat and rage than he'd intended. "I just mean, I've been on the receiving end of those shocks, and I don't think that will help Elena. We can all agree that something happened back there. Something traumatic to make her close up like this. Why don't we move her to her room? Agon can stay with her, and Lyra and I will take a second look in the storeroom. Maybe there's something in there that can explain what's going on."

He wasn't confident that they'd find anything, but it was a much better plan than mild electrocution.

As he walked her back to her room, Q was reminded of some marionettes he saw putting on a show at the last harvest festival. She was oblivious. He'd seen her like this once before, immediately after she was attacked by those drunken bastards.

Mux.

Quinn carefully closed the door to Elena's room. She was laying in her bed, curled around Agon, but still seemingly unaware of her surroundings. Agon assured him that he would alert them the second she came back around, so Q and Lyra crept out of the room and headed back to the storeroom to investigate.

The storeroom smelled a bit like burnt meat, but not any meat he'd ever tasted before. The scent was familiar though. Faint, like a memory long since buried in the back of his mind. Something about it was painfully familiar, but he just couldn't place it.

The room seemed dark. It wasn't poorly lit, but the room felt as though it had just witnessed something horrific. A barrel of salt lay on its side in the middle of the room, white grains spread across the ground. Q tapped into his hunting skills and examined the salt.

"So she came back here for supplies, right? Probably salt for the tables before the lunch rush. There are five different footprints in this salt. Elena's are smaller and softer than the rest, but it looks like there was a fight of some kind. She backed into the barrels and the other footprints encircled the barrels.

Where did these ashes come from? The footprints lead to the ashes... oh Mother Goddess. That can't be... no... how?"

Quinn knelt next to a pile of ashes and gently touched it, bringing some of the ashes to his nose, and took a deep breath. *Mux.*

Lyra crept gently around the spilled salt and over to a second ash pile before taking a few investigative sniffs.

"That's human." Lyra was never one for sugarcoating things. "These are human ashes. Drunk humans, by the smell of it. I can also smell dirt and a hint of wheat."

"They came back." Quinn was numb. "They came back to finish what they started. They waited until she was all alone, trapped her, and attacked."

How had he let this happen again?

"Clearly they didn't get what they wanted. Or, if they did, they didn't get to enjoy it for very long. Someone roasted them rather effectively. I'm not gonna lie, I'm a little jealous. I would have loved to have that honor."

"Lyra, you don't mean that. And even if you do, you sure as hells can't say shyt like that." Quinn was still kneeling next to the ashes. "How did this happen?"

Lyra hopped up onto a barrel, sat down, and wrapped her tail around her feet, flicking the tip casually back and forth. She didn't know any more than he did. They needed Elena to snap out of her stupor and tell them what happened.

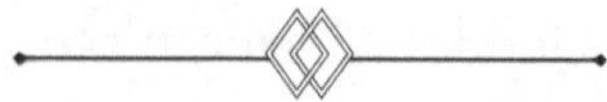

Q had told Amelia that Elena wasn't feeling well and needed to rest, then he'd helped cover the lunch rush.

After lunch, Amelia had brought a tray of food to Elena. She seemed to be more alert but didn't want to talk to anyone yet. Amelia told Q that she was upright, but still in bed. She'd backed herself into the corner and was huddled in a ball. Agon was in her lap, and Elena didn't seem willing to let him go. Amelia had left the tray and an extra blanket before leaving the room.

Q tried to distract himself with chores around the inn, but it didn't really help. By the end of dinner, he thought he might climb right out of his skin.

Lyra crept into Elena's room while Quinn cleared the last table and locked the dining hall door.

"She says she'd like to talk to you now." Q jumped at Lyra's words and practically raced down the hall to Elena's room. When he got to the door, he slowed and gently knocked. He waited for a response before entering the room.

18
ELENA

"**C**OME IN." ELENA'S VOICE sounded strange. Charged and raw.

Q and Lyra walked into the room, carefully closing the door behind them. Q took a seat in the chair by the window. He didn't say anything. She didn't know what she expected him to do but she had thought he'd have questions. Instead, he just sat there in silence. Even Lyra was uncharacteristically passive. She'd taken up residence under Q's chair and looked content to take a long nap.

After what felt like an age, Elena finally spoke aloud the words she'd been thinking since the attack. Elena felt the tears fill her eyes, but she didn't care. She needed to tell him what happened because she truly couldn't comprehend it, and she needed him to help her make sense of it all. "I don't understand what happened."

Q didn't move. He didn't react. He didn't say a word. He just waited. He was giving her the time and space she needed to find the right words.

"They came back... Those men that attacked me before. They cornered me in the storeroom and they attacked me again." The words poured out of her faster than she could think of them. Once she started, she couldn't stop, and she didn't want to. "They held me down on the barrels, and he was going to hurt me. They were all going to hurt me. I was certain I was going to die. Then something happened. I don't understand it, but I felt a shock, like Agon's, pass through me. It was stronger than anything I've ever felt before and suddenly they were gone."

She looked at Q and saw the calm clarity on his face. The realization of what had happened and what she'd done hit her.

"Q, I... I think I killed them."

Nothing. He said nothing. His face betrayed no emotion, but he held her stare. He already knew. How? Why didn't he say anything? She'd killed four people today. FOUR! And he had nothing to say?

"Say *something.* Call me a murderer. A killer. An evil enchantress who used selfish magic to take the lives of FOUR men! I'm evil. I don't deserve to be here. Mother Goddess, banish me to the depths of hells now. I deserve the fires of the pit. I'm a killer." Her voice was barely above a whisper. She was unraveling. The tears streamed down her face, but she didn't care. She'd taken the lives of four people today. She was a demon.

Q moved from his chair by the window to sit on the edge of her bed. He gently took her face in his hands and wiped the tears from her cheeks. He lifted her head until she looked into his eyes. He looked so sad and broken. His dark green eyes locked her in and calmed her mind. He didn't say anything, but he held her face and took slow, deep breaths with her until her body eased. When he spoke, he never took his eyes from hers.

"Those men were going to hurt you. They would have raped, beaten, and ultimately killed you. You are not a murderer. You defended yourself. You did exactly what you needed to do to stay alive. You are *not* evil. You are an amazingly strong woman who fought off four murderous bastards. You are a good person. A good enchantress. A *survivor*."

He emphasized the last word with a light squeeze of his hands on her cheeks before he pulled her into him and wrapped his arms around her whole body. Elena couldn't hold herself together anymore. She felt her body fall into his as she released the last of the strength that had been holding her upright.

Elena felt the tears begin to fall again but with fewer hysterics this time. It was her body's way of releasing the tension and pressure. Quinn kissed the top of her head and slowly rubbed her back.

Elena came to a strange realization as she drifted off to sleep in his arms: He wasn't scared of her. He had every reason to be, knowing everything she'd done, but he wasn't afraid.

19
QUINN

T HEY DIDN'T TELL ANYONE else what happened. Hells, they didn't even tell Amelia the whole truth. They just told her that Elena was confronted by the same men as before, but that she fought them off, and they weren't coming back. She didn't need to know all the details of the fight, Q decided. The fewer people who knew, the better. He didn't think Amelia would be scared of Elena if she knew, but he didn't want Elena to have to worry about it.

In the days that followed, Elena seemed distracted and distant. She carried on with her routine, but he could tell that her mind was elsewhere. If he was being honest with himself, his mind was elsewhere as well. He kept picturing her glowing, blue, electric eyes. Q had yet to bring up witnessing Elena's eyes glow when she was in the storeroom, for obvious reasons, but he still hadn't figured out a way to ask her about it. Was that normal? Had they done that before? He was more curious than concerned because she seemed fine, physically, but it did open a lot of questions. He'd been waiting for the right time to bring it up with her, but there never really seemed to be a good time to discuss her recent trauma.

After dinner a few nights after the attack, she and Q sat at the table near the large dining hall hearth, having a late meal, and he decided to just ask.

"So... I know you don't want to talk about what happened, but I have one question."

She flinched slightly but nodded for him to continue while she took a bite of her turkey breast.

Quinn paused for a second, trying to find the right words. "When Lyra, Agon, and I burst in the room, after the electric blast, you looked... well it looked like... ok, I'm just gonna say it." He took a deep breath and looked her in the eyes, "Your eyes were glowing. Blue. And it looked like there were lightning bolts *in* your eyes. Has that ever happened before?"

Elena looked stupefied. Either she thought he'd lost his mind, or she had.

"I'm sorry, what?"

"Your eyes. They were glowing bright blue, like Agon's lightning, and it looked like there were bolts of electricity flashing across them. Like you were literally filled with bolts of lightning that were trying to get out through your eyes."

"No. No, that's never happened before. I've never been able to wield that much power before. Ever. That 'blast,' as you put it, was the first bit of real, strong magic I've ever done. I don't understand it. I don't know how it happened, and I can't seem to recreate it. I've been trying, at night after everyone goes to sleep. I sit up in our room and try everything I can think of to create even the slightest hint of that power, but I can't."

"Maybe we should find that witch," Agon spoke, lifting his head from its sleepy position resting on his paws. He and Lyra were curled quite comfortably together on the stone hearth.

At the mention of the witch, Lyra flicked her tail to cover Agon's face, "There is no such thing as witches, you twit."

Agon responded by sending a small spark up Lyra's tail. It wasn't enough to hurt her, but it felt like a strong static shock to Q's hind end.

"Hey! I didn't do anything! Keep your shocks to yourself." Q glared at Agon and massaged his ass for a moment. "Lyra's right, there are no witches. They were all killed off ages ago." He paused and looked at Elena, a single eyebrow raised incredulously. "Weren't they?"

"Not according to Nikki." Agon stretched his long, slinky back before sitting up next to Lyra and looking at Elena.

"She did say she met a witch recently." Elena sat up a little straighter as she remembered the conversation. "The woman told Nikki that the baby she carried would be a girl and that she'd need me to save her life and the life of the baby. Nikki seemed pretty confident that the woman was truly a witch. Maybe we should go and talk to her. It wouldn't hurt. Either we find out she's a fraud, or we get some advice on what's going on with me."

"A witch? In Andover? You've got to be kidding me. Why? Why would a witch set up shop in this tiny place?" Quinn was truly baffled. It just seemed so outrageous.

"Probably because no one would believe it, and she could live in peace. Witches weren't all bad, you know. Most of them were honestly good people. They just wanted to live as one with nature, worship the moon and sun, celebrate the seasons, grow plants, drink tea, and dance naked in the woods. But people don't like things that are different. Witches were persecuted for ages before they were finally extinguished. Witches weren't that different from enchantresses, so we had to study their history at Harbor Ridge. To learn from their mistakes and avoid the persecution they faced."

It was Q's turn to be stupefied. Witches might still exist. Well, mux, that added a whole new layer of shyt for him to process. His brain was going to explode.

"We should talk to Nikki in the morning." Elena was already in action mode while Q was still hung up on this new shift in his reality. "Q, you don't have to come with us. You are clearly thrown by all of this. Agon and I can go talk to the witch by ourselves and catch you up when we get back."

"No," he shook his head, "no, we'll come with you. I'm not thrown, I just need a minute to wrap my head around all this.

Lyra and I will go with you. I don't want you to go see this witch alone. Yeah, you've got fancy new powers, but you can't control them, and I don't want anything to happen to you if I can avoid it."

They agreed to go see Nikki first thing in the morning and head to the witch as soon as possible. Elena seemed anxious to understand and gain control of her newfound powers, and Q completely understood that sentiment. It was a feeling he almost related to, but he couldn't quite remember why. There was a memory, drifting just out of reach, that he couldn't place, but it made him empathetic to El's concern nonetheless.

The next morning, Q was in the kitchen, loading some lunch for himself and Elena into his pack. He wasn't paying too much attention to what his hands were doing as his mind wandered to thoughts of witches and electrified blue eyes. The steady hum of the diners having breakfast in the next room offered comfort and allowed his brain to wander freely.

Q was shaken out of his thoughts when he noticed the normal buzzing of the breakfast crowd had gone silent. Not just quiet, like they were all waking up slowly this morning, but utter stillness, as if they'd all been frozen.

He stepped out from the kitchen, into the dining hall and followed the gaze of all the silent and stunned—but thankfully not literally frozen—patrons. Four women, dressed head to toe in black robes, had entered the room. Two of the women had their faces fully covered by the hoods of their cloaks, but the other two removed their hoods as they walked further into the room. The looks on their faces were akin to that of hunters stalking their prey. These women were more intimidating than any man Quinn had ever seen.

He knew, instinctively, that they were here for Elena. He didn't know why or how, but he knew he needed to get Elena out of here, quickly and quietly.

Without a word, he nodded to Lyra, who understood him implicitly, and carefully disappeared back into the kitchens. She would slink around the outside of the building to get to Elena's window. Elena and Agon needed to disappear. Now.

Q put on his "gracious host" face and walked right up to the aggressive blonde.

"Mornin', ladies! Welcome to the best and only inn in Andover. You look like you've been traveling for quite some time. I bet you're hungry. What would you like for breakfast? The eggs are fresh, just collected them this morning, and the bacon is absolutely delicious. Have a seat! What can I get for you lovely ladies on this fine morning?"

Q had perfected this happy personality many years ago before he came to live here with Amelia. He might have been a homeless wreck, but he could fake it with the best of them, and it helped him swindle people out of their cash. They thought he was so friendly and adorable, they never noticed that he was picking their pockets clean as he was pulling out their chairs.

"We aren't here for food. We are looking for someone." The blonde spoke with a curt tone. No bullshyt, no mincing words.

"Well, I know just about everyone in this little hamlet. Who are you looking for? Maybe I can help." The breakfast crowd slowly turned back to their meals; they all had work to get to and now that Q had taken the brunt of the attention from the women, the townsfolk were losing interest.

The blonde looked Quinn up and down, inspecting him with a look that settled somewhere between disgust and boredom. There was something almost familiar about them. The vibe coming off these four robed figures was unlike anything he'd encountered in town before, and yet he knew they were powerful.

These women were enchantresses. Probably from that school. Why were they here? How did they know Elena was even here? What could they possibly want with her now, after kicking her out only a few moons ago?

The other woman, a fiery ginger with alarming red hair, surveyed the room but didn't say a word. She raised her arm, and a falcon flew into the room through an open window. Several women shrieked and covered their heads. One of the men, the town leatherworker, grabbed his bow and notched an arrow from the quiver he'd slung across the back of his chair.

Before he could fully draw the bow, the blonde raised her hands and shoved the air in front of her. The archer flew into the air and across the room, smashing into the wall with a sickening crunch. The redhead drew her own bow from under her cloak and stood poised, arrow at the ready, casually inspecting the guests as if inviting one of them to move.

Amelia rushed out from the kitchens when she heard all the commotion.

"What in the name of the Mother..." She stopped when her eyes landed on the four women. A flash of recognition, followed by outrage and a fury Quinn had never seen in her, raced across her face.

"Everyone, the kitchens are closed for the remainder of the morning. I apologize for the inconvenience. I'll see you all back here for lunch." Her voice was strained and tight. She was trying her damnedest to control her temper long enough to get the townsfolk out of the dining hall.

Within moments, the hall was empty. Amelia calmly closed and locked the doors and windows before turning on the robed women.

"What in the bloody hells are you demons doing here? Lillith, you *threw* a man! A customer and a dear friend. What on earth were you thinking? That is not the way to endear yourself to a community. Seph, put that damn thing away before I throw it in the fire. Maddy, is that you under there? You and your sister might as well remove the hoods now. I'm not talking to a cloak."

What the... Amelia knew these women? And she was ordering them around like she had known them for a while. Like she was their mom. Like she does with me... Q had no idea what was going on, but he definitely wasn't going anywhere. He knew Amelia had a life before he'd met her, she'd even hinted at having some magic over the years. But this...? This was unreal.

The last two women removed their hoods to reveal two identical faces and long, wavy brown hair. One had an owl perched on her shoulder. The other held a brindle rabbit in her arms.

"Maddy, Noelle, it's lovely to see you girls. It's been so long. So long, it seems, that Madame LaBelle has changed her tactics and would rather terrorize the communities than build a relationship of trust. I can't imagine this new stratagem has helped to boost enrollment."

"He drew his weapon first," the red-head—Seph, wasn't it?—replied calmly and coolly. She adjusted her robes and her falcon repositioned himself on the string notch of the bow she'd replaced on her shoulder.

"If you hadn't scared the whole dining hall with that damned bird, he wouldn't have drawn a weapon at all!" Quinn's voice had a much higher volume and rage than he'd intended. Every woman turned toward him as if they'd forgotten he was even there. Seph glowered at him, and Q swore he could feel a warmth spread across his face and neck, almost like a sunburn.

"Seph, stop that right this second," Amelia snapped at the woman and Q felt the heat leave his face. "I know you, and I know Q," she continued. "He's right. You wanted shock and awe. Lillith wanted to show off her powers and send a 'message of strength' to the crowd. Congratulations. If there is a magical child in this town, no one is going to let her go with you now." Amelia motioned to Quinn, "Come sit down, sweetheart. We need to talk." Then she turned to the women with a much firmer tone, "We all need to talk."

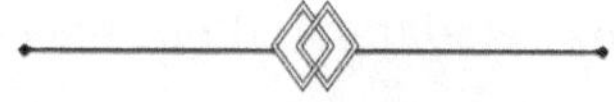

"A long time ago, ages really, I was a student at Harbor Ridge. I loved my time there, but I disagreed with some of the basic tenants of the school. Harbor Ridge dislikes men. If it were up to the headmistress, women would rule the world, and men would be used exclusively for breeding purposes. Madame LaBelle distrusts all men and refuses to hear anything to the contrary. When I finished my tenure as a student, I left. I had no interest in working with or for that narcissistic, arrogant, close-minded woman. Instead, I came here. I met my beloved Herb, and we opened this beautiful inn.

"After a while, Madame LaBelle sent an emissary to speak with me. She had a proposal: I would refer any magical children to her investigators, and she would pay me a small bounty for each child they accepted. I didn't take her up on the offer until after Herb passed. I couldn't handle this place all alone, and I didn't have the funds to hire someone right away. We don't have a lot of magical children born here in Andover, but as an innkeeper and bartender, I hear a lot of rumors, and I would send anything that sounded promising to the investigators.

"I'm much older than I look, Q. Enchantresses have a considerably longer lifespan. You never met Herb, because he's been gone for nearly seventy years. He knew who I was, and he loved me anyway. Ours was a love for the ages. Madame LaBelle hated it. That's why she didn't reach out to me until after he was gone. She didn't approve of emotional entanglements.

"It's been a few decades now, and I've referred maybe a dozen potential students to Harbor Ridge. That's how I know these ladies. Lillith and Seph are part of the Guard, and they are quite fantastic at their jobs, if not a little overzealous. Maddy and Noelle are the best of the best, which has me wondering," she turned to address the twins, "why are you ladies here? If there were a magical child around, I would have requested an intervention, but I haven't seen or heard anything."

"We were tasked with investigating the power surge from a few days ago. Madame LaBelle sent us to assess the situation and bring the source of the power back to the school for proper training, if possible. If not, we are here to neutralize the situation." Lillith spoke with the same matter-of-fact tone one would use when discussing the weather or the wheat harvests.

"Neutralize?" Quinn asked. "You mean kill? You're here to kidnap or kill someone because they have power?"

"I didn't say kidnap. She will be invited to come. It will be her choice."

"But the choices are to go with you or go unto the fade, am I right?" He could feel the heat rising in his face and tone, but he didn't care.

"I wouldn't have put it so crassly, but yes, that is the gist of the offer." Her words dripped with disdain.

"That's crazy! This is all complete insanity! You can't kill someone just because they don't want to disappear into your black hole of a school." This was lunacy. Q slammed his hands on the table and shot to his feet, glaring at the women.

"Q, please sit back down and take a deep breath. They aren't going to kill a child, are you, girls?" Amelia's tone left no room for discussion or disagreement.

Noelle piped in. "Of course not! We would never hurt a child. We have never felt a power like this, so we are here to assess the threat it may or may not pose. It's very likely that this girl doesn't know or understand her powers or her full strength. We want to help her and train her so she can reach her full potential and control her abilities."

"And if she decides not to go?" Q pressed.

"Well, it would be in everyone's best interest that she accompany us to Harbor Ridge. If only for basic training so she can control her powers and not cause another episode," Maddy said with a kind, but firm tone. They weren't going to accept no for an answer.

"Do either of you know what caused that massive pulse?" Lillith asked, taking the seat across from Q, next to Amelia. Her familiar, an ocelot, jumped gracefully into her lap and sat at attention, glaring at Quinn.

"No," Q said flatly.

"No, dear, I'm sorry. I'm not sure where it originated from, but it felt distant. Like maybe someone was in the Dark Woods. I haven't heard anything from the regulars either. And no new folks visiting in the last few weeks." Amelia glanced toward the window. "It will be time for lunch soon, and I need to get back to the kitchens to start cooking. You girls are welcome to stay; we always have a few rooms to spare."

"No, we should keep moving. We need to find the source of this power and take care of it." Lillith stood from her chair and motioned to the others. "It was nice seeing you again, Amelia. We'll try to stop back by on our way out of town."

They each gave Amelia a quick hug before departing.

As soon as they were sure the enchantresses were gone, Amelia turned and grabbed Quinn by both shoulders. "I know you have a lot of questions, and I'm sorry I didn't tell you all of this sooner, but it's too late to change things now. You have to get Elena out of here. It's not safe for her here anymore."

"I already sent Lyra to take Elena out of the inn. She should be waiting in the stables for me now."

"Fetch her things and yours, then meet me in the kitchen." Amelia let go of his arms and rushed from the room.

Q grabbed his pack and hurried down the hall to Elena's room. She hadn't collected too many things since arriving in town, so he was able to pack all of her clothes and a spare pair of shoes into the bag Nikki had gifted her. His mind was reeling, but he didn't have time to process these new revelations. Q had always suspected there was something more to Amelia. Her orange tabby, Marty, had been around since before Q had arrived at the inn, and he never seemed to age. He had long believed that Amelia was more than what she appeared, trusting his gut that there was something magical about that woman, but to have it confirmed so abruptly was jarring.

He rushed from Elena's room to his own, collected the remainder of his belongings and shoved them far less carefully into his pack, then headed back to the kitchens. Amelia was waiting with two large cloaks.

"This was Herb's. His favorite traveling cloak. It kept him safe and warm on many long journeys. Wear it, and take good care of it. Give this one to Elena. It was my own, and the pockets have been enchanted to hold far more than she'll ever need. Be safe. Take care of each other. I'll miss you both so much." There were tears in her eyes as she gave him the tightest hug he'd ever experienced. "I love you, my son."

"I love you too, Mom." He'd never actually said those words to her before, but he had no idea when he would see her again. That feeling pushed him to be direct. "I never would have made it this far without you. You saved me, and I will never forget that."

He returned her hug and kissed her forehead, then ducked out through the backdoor for quite possibly the last time.

20
ELENA

WHEN LYRA JUMPED INTO her room through the open window, Elena had been startled. When she announced with firmness and a hint of anxiety that Elena and Agon needed to pack their things and follow her out the window immediately, Elena had been nervous. Hiding in the stables behind a massive pile of horse manure, Elena was nauseated. Partly because of the smell, but primarily because she could sense that something was wrong. She could feel strong magic nearby. Magic she'd felt before. She didn't know exactly who was in town, but she recognized powerful investigators when she felt their presence. They were the most powerful enchantresses Elena had ever felt, aside from her own mother. And from the tingling sensations Elena felt on the base of her neck, she could tell that they were pissed and not looking to invite anyone back to the school. They were on a mission to neutralize a threat.

What in the name of the Goddess are they doing here? No one here is a threat to Harbor Ridge. No one even has magic.

"Except you," Agon whispered, ever perceptive to her thoughts and emotions. He climbed down from his perch on her shoulder to look her in the eyes. "You know that's why they're here. They felt your magic all the way on the top of that damned mountain of theirs. They are here for you."

"But I'm not a threat to them!" Elena argued as if that would change the facts.

"That may be true, but you annihilated those four *men*," he spat the word *men* out as if it were poison, "reducing them to ash, and you have no idea how you did it. You might not see yourself as a threat, but that kind of uncontrolled magic will definitely threaten your mother."

Lyra wasn't saying anything, she paced back and forth in front of the closed stall door. Every few moments, she'd freeze and tilt her head as though she were listening for something.

"What do you hear?" Elena finally asked.

"Nothing. But I can feel Q. He's feeling anxious and something else... shock? It's hard to tell at this distance exactly what he's thinking. Something about Amelia and those strange women. There was some commotion a few minutes ago. Breaking glass. Some screaming. But that all seems to have died down. I can't hear anything anymore."

"Is he hurt?! Is Amelia ok? Who was screaming? We need to go help them!" Elena jumped up and was at the door, but Lyra grabbed ahold of Elena's skirt with her sharp teeth.

"What are you doing? Let go of me! I have to help them!" Elena struggled, but Lyra managed to twist her skirt around Elena's leg, tripping her and causing her to land on her ass in the shyt.

"We aren't going anywhere. You aren't going anywhere. Agon is right. They are here for you. If you go in there and they try to take you, you will only make things worse. People will die if you run in there right now. Look at you, your hands are glowing. Do you even know how you're doing that?"

Elena looked at her hands. They felt warm, and there was a blue glow emanating from her fingertips.

"What the...?" Elena lifted her hands and studied her fingers. An arc of electricity passed between her fingers, then the light began to fade. As quickly as it appeared, the glow and warmth were gone.

"You are in no position to defend anyone right now, Elena. We will wait here just like Quinn said, and he will come out as soon as it's safe for us." Lyra sat at attention in front of the door. She was not willing to argue or debate the issue. It annoyed Elena to no end, but Lyra was faithful and obedient to Q's commands. He had told to Lyra to get Elena to safety and stay until he gave them the "all clear" so that was what they were going to do. End of discussion.

It felt like hours had passed, but in reality, based on the sun's lack of movement from the window in their shyt stall, it had been less than one. Lyra hadn't moved from her sentry location in front of the door, but when they heard someone rustling at the entrance to the barn, she stood.

"Elena?" Quinn's voice was barely above a whisper. The threat wasn't gone, but it must have faded for the moment.

"We're back here," Elena whispered and pushed the stall door open ever so slightly.

Q came in and quietly shut the door firmly behind him. He gave Elena a quick once over and ruffled Lyra's ears. "Thank you for keeping them safe," he said as he lowered the items he'd been carrying.

"We need to get out of here. Andover isn't safe anymore. Here, put this on." He tossed Elena a large fur-lined cloak. "Amelia loaded it up with everything she thought we'd need, and she said it's enchanted so the pockets will hold a lot more without weighing you down."

"What? I didn't know that was even possible anymore. Spacial magic hasn't been practiced in decades. None of the scholars at Harbor Ridge even understand how to do it." Elena thrust her hand into the first pocket she saw, and it seemed there were dozens of pockets hidden in the fur. She tried to reach the bottom of the pocket, but the further she shoved her hand in, the deeper the pocket went. When her arm was buried in the pocket up to her shoulder, she gave up.

"Q, where did she find this?"

"She said it was hers. She didn't go into a lot of details. We were in a bit of a hurry." Q sounded annoyed, but Elena reminded herself that he was just scared. He'd met investigators and their guards. They weren't known for their friendliness, especially towards men.

He busied himself, loading all the things they'd grabbed from her room into various pockets in his bag and her cloak. Elena stopped fiddling with the cloak's pockets and took a good look at Q. He was pale, his hands were shaking, and he was breathing as rapidly as a scared rabbit. She grabbed him by the shoulders and turned him to face her. He looked like he'd seen a ghost.

"Quinn." She spoke calmly to try and reach him through his panic, just as he had done for her before. "It's going to be ok. You're ok. I'm ok. Amelia is ok. We will go to the witch and find out what's going on and what I am. Then we will find somewhere safe. We are all ok."

Q searched her face, looking for signs of doubt and fear, but she showed none. He needed her to be calm and focused right now. She could process her emotions later when they were a safe distance away. If she shared her panic with him right now, it would only make things worse.

At Harbor Ridge, the girls were all taught to clear their minds of all emotions and mask their feelings in order to control their magic and the situation they might find themselves in. Elena put her enchantress mask on and held it, and her emotions, in place. Now was simply not the time.

"Take a deep breath." Elena held his eyes with her own and breathed with him. "Again. That's it, one more. Ok, good. Let's just get out of here, and we can talk once we're safe."

Quinn held her stare for a moment longer, then he nodded, quickly finished loading their belongings, and shouldered his pack.

"Let's go ask Nikki about this witch, but we'll need to stay off the main roads. Those women are sure there's a threat in town, and they'll be searching everywhere." He nodded once to Lyra, and she crept to the stall door, sniffing the air before poking her head out of the stall.

"It's clear," she said.

Elena donned her new cloak, closed the clasp at her neck, and placed Agon on her shoulder. The cloak seemed to shimmer a moment, then the color shifted to match Agon's fur perfectly.

"Where did she find this? This isn't a normal enchanted cloak," Elena pondered.

"I think the fact that you just referred to any enchanted cloak as potentially 'normal' should be indicative of how abnormal your entire life is," Lyra responded pointedly. She wasn't being cruel, just incredulous. Elena got the feeling that Lyra was having a hard time wrapping her mind around the idea of magic and all that it entailed.

"Oh, hush you. Your tail starts fires. You have no idea what 'normal' is either," Elena poked back at her with a smile.

Lyra flicked her tail, sending some harmless sparks toward Elena, then crept out of the stall and toward the backdoor of the barn. It was the closest route to the woods that encircled the town. They would trek through the woods, along the edge of town, until they reached Nikki's. Hopefully, she'd be willing and able to tell them where she saw the witch and, if they were very lucky, where they could find her as well.

21
QUINN

N IKKI WAS NO HELP. *Surprise*, he thought bitterly. She had a vague memory of the witch's home being in the woods, near a small waterfall, and it smelled like honeysuckle. What the hells were they supposed to do with that? Q and Lyra ran through the woods day in and day out for cycles. They had never seen a waterfall. Big or small.

"That was a waste of time," Q said as they disappeared into the trees again, wondering where they should go now. Their whole plan hinged on Nikki knowing where to find this damn witch. Q was starting to believe she'd made the whole thing up. Either that or she was crazy.

"No, actually, it was very helpful. It's not Nikki's fault that the witch has magic protecting her home. I would too if I only knew how." Elena stepped carefully around the entrance to a rabbit's burrow at the base of a large oak.

How is she still positive after all this?

"All right, take a minute and think. Is there a spot in the Dark Woods that you avoid? Somewhere that feels ominous or imposing and the idea of going there makes you nervous? So anxious that you've never even attempted to venture there?"

An image popped into his mind almost instantly. There was a spot. It was always shrouded in mist, no matter what time of day or year. Always gloomy and foreboding. He froze mid-step. Lyra stopped walking as well and began to twitch her tail anxiously. Agon eyed her cautiously like he was waiting for a forest fire to erupt at any second.

"There is, isn't there? Where is it? I'll bet everything in this fancy cloak's pockets that *that* is where we'll find the witch." Elena's enthusiasm was unexpected, and as far as Quinn was concerned, insane.

"It's about a day's hike upstream from our hut." Q felt like there was ice in his veins. He'd attempted to hike to the source of the stream one day when he and Lyra had first set up their little home. He had thought there might be more fish farther upstream. They never found the source. They'd only made it a few steps into the mist before he'd started hearing things, horrible things that he knew were impossible and that he never wanted to hear again. The sound of a house burning and warping under the heat of a tremendous fire. Shrieks and screams from his abusive foster parents as they burned alive in that awful place.

"Then that's where we need to go." Elena's cautious tone brought him back to reality. She was studying him, speaking calmly and quietly, "You don't have to go with us. You can wait for us at your house. It shouldn't take too long to talk with her. A day, two at the most. You don't have to go in there."

"No. I'm not letting you go in there alone. That's not happening. Let's head to the house. We'll eat and rest there tonight. It will take a full day to get to the mist from the hut, and we're not venturing into it at night."

Q hated this plan, but it was the only one they had.

It took the rest of the day to make it back to their forest home. If they'd been able to take the main roads, they could have made it in half the time, but he didn't want to risk running into those women again. They took their time and did a little hunting on their way. Amelia had packed enough food to feed an army, but Q thought it would be better to save the hard cheeses and dried meat for an emergency. They could easily hunt and cook a rabbit or two tonight and save the food from Amelia for their hike through the mist. He had no idea how long that would take, if they'd be able to hunt, or if there would even be anything to hunt in that hells. Better to hunt while they had the opportunity.

It was nearly dark by the time they made it to his home. Lyra set them up with a fire while Elena took the cooking pot to collect water from the stream, and Q skinned and prepped the rabbit for the cooking spit. Agon ran out to Q's little garden and came back with a few carrots. He dumped them, unceremoniously, on the ground next to Quinn before heading back out and returning with some radishes. He made one more trip for a single potato, which he had to roll across the floor with his nose because it was too big for him to carry.

Elena used a small knife from Quinn's bag and sliced the veggies before adding them to the fresh pot of water she'd hung over the fire. It was weird to have someone else cooking in his hut, but he liked having her there to help.

"I found these out near the garden too," she said, holding up a few stems of something green.

"What is it?"

"Parsley," Elena answered. Q's face must have betrayed his confusion, so she continued. "It's an herb. It grows wild around here. I'm adding it to the stew for some extra flavor."

She started tearing the tiny leaves off the stems and dropping them into the boiling water, smiling to herself.

"How do you know they're parsley and not poison?" Q asked. He wasn't much of a plant person. If he didn't grow it, he didn't eat it. He'd made the mistake of eating some berries by the river once when he was younger. He would *never* make that mistake again.

"We all had to take Basic Plant Identification when we were young. Herbs and other plants are great for natural remedies and potions. When we turned eight, the botany scholars poisoned our familiars, and we were sent to the gardens to create a remedy. If you failed, you'd be sick for a *very* long time, and more often than not, your familiar would change to a sickening green color for weeks."

"What the hells? That's insane and cruel." Q was astounded. How could anyone purposely poison a child or their familiar? Especially for some sort of test.

"It was a rite of passage. The enchantress who cured her familiar the fastest got to sit at the head of her class' table for a moon and determine the dining order." Elena's mind seemed to be drifting back in time. Her face bore an expression of sadness and loneliness.

"I take it you didn't cure Agon first," Quinn said, encouraging her to continue.

"No. I wasn't last, and neither of us got sick, but I also wasn't very popular. I didn't get much to eat that moon, and I was forced to sit at the very end of the table." Elena quickly brushed the tears from her eyes and went back to her parsley. Q's protective instincts surged and he suddenly wanted nothing more than to meet the enchantress who'd been at the head of the table and punch her in the nose.

They cooked the rest of their meal in silence, both stewing in their memories and worrying about what tomorrow would bring.

"This stew is delicious, El. That parsley of yours really makes a difference." Q tried to lighten the mood and bring them both back to the present.

"Thank you. This rabbit is perfect too. You're a very skilled hunter." Elena beamed at him.

"Years of practice will do that," he replied casually. Q never knew how to accept compliments. He'd spent too many years never hearing a kind word that when he did receive compliments of any kind, he had no idea what to say.

"I'm sorry I screwed everything up. My magic brought those investigators here. I've put the whole town at risk. I should never have come here." Elena stared into her bowl and poked a carrot with her spoon, clearly lost in her thoughts.

"Stop that," Q said firmly. "Look at me. Elena, please, look at me."

He waited for her to look up before he continued.

"You are not at fault. You were defending yourself. *Never* apologize for that. You are amazingly strong. Sure, we might not understand it, yet," he put a hard emphasis on *yet* and paused until she looked into his eyes, "but we will figure it out. Together. You are not alone in this. You will never be alone. Whether you like it or not, we're here for you and we," he pointed to Lyra and himself, "will be with you every step of the way. You are family now. We are a family now."

"You don't want me in your family. I'm a curse. My own family didn't want me." The tears welled in her eyes again. She was so scared and raw. Too many things had pulled and torn at her over the last few moons, and it was all coming to a head. She truly believed she was cursed.

"El," Quinn said as he put his bowl down on the packed earth floor beside him, and grabbed her hands, "you are not cursed. No more so than I am. Bad shyt has happened to us, but that isn't our fault. We didn't ask to be put in these situations. We are strong because of the things we've had to endure, and we will only get stronger."

He squeezed her hands in his, then carefully wiped the tears from her cheeks and pulled her into him. He hugged her and held her as if his life depended on it. It took a few moments, but Elena relaxed into him, letting him take her weight and unleashed all the pent-up emotions she'd been holding since the attack.

Quinn held strong. He could feel her body shaking with all the stress and anxiety she'd been trying to hide from him. He'd seen it in her eyes back in the barn, but he didn't push. He knew she'd let go when she was ready. Just as he had when he'd come to Amelia. All of the fear, all the confusion, all the anger at being taken advantage of and used, it all flowed from her body in waves.

That sat like that for several moments, as he held her and allowed her to release all the feelings she'd been bottling up. Q rubbed his hand up and down her spine and noticed an unexpected warmth. It wasn't coming from the fire, but from between them. The heat radiated from her chest. A warm sensation like a ray of sunshine, directly from her chest to his. The more she cried and let go of it all, the hotter the feeling grew. When the heat became disconcerting, Q pushed her back and held her at arm's length, to examine the source. Her clothes looked the same. No sign of fire or electric charge emanating from her chest.

"Q," Elena gasped, "What happened to your shirt?"

Quinn looked down at his own chest and saw several small holes had burned through the fabric of his shirt, singeing the linen.

"What the... did you do that?" He looked from his shirt to her face, utterly confused.

"No. I think I would have noticed if I burned your shirt."

"Did you feel the heat?" Q asked.

"What heat?" Elena looked nervous now, carefully reaching out and gingerly touching the damaged fabric.

"I swear, I thought it was coming from you. I felt this warmth growing in my chest. I assumed it was just your powers again. I don't understand. Didn't you feel it? It got so hot…"

"I didn't feel anything," Elena responded, staring at the holes in his shirt. "I don't understand this either. First, you have a fire-starting familiar. No man is supposed to have a familiar. And now you're radiating heat so warm that it's burning your clothes from the inside… who are you? What are you…?" The last question was muttered more to herself than to him, as she continued to examine the fabric of his shirt.

"I'm just a guy," Q said defensively.

"You, Quinn, are far from 'just a guy.' You are something else. Something magical and unlike anything this world has seen in a *very* long time." She took his face in her hands and locked eyes with him. "We are ok. We will be ok. The witch will be able to help us both."

"Mother Goddess, I hope so," Quinn said, placing his hands over hers. Even his hands felt like they were on fire compared to hers. "If not, we are so muxed."

22

ELENA

A S THE MORNING SUN crested over the distant mountain peak to the east, Elena and Quinn had already finished packing their things for the journey ahead. Q hadn't said much all morning, but Elena had heard him tossing and turning throughout the night. She knew his mind had been plagued with terrible dreams or memories, but she didn't push. Rather than talk, they worked in silent harmony to make breakfast, break down their campsite, and prepare for a journey into the unknown. Hopefully, they would be back in a couple of days, but there was really no way to know.

"I always disguise the hut with fallen branches and bushes to keep prying eyes away while we're gone," Quinn said as he tossed his pack onto his shoulder.

"Good thinking." Elena wrapped her new enchanted cloak around her shoulders and picked Agon up off the hut floor. He climbed up her arm and settled onto her shoulder, blending in perfectly with the fur-lined hood of her cloak.

"How far did you say this fog was?"

"It will take about a day to hike upstream. We'll stick to the riverside and make camp just outside the fog boundary tonight. I'm not attempting to make it through that mess in the dark. We can breach the fog at first light tomorrow." It was clear he didn't want to breach the fog at all, but no amount of persuasion was going to sway him from this course. She had spent hours on their trek back to his hut the night before trying to convince him to let her go find the witch alone, but he steadfastly refused.

Elena drifted off that night to dreams of being chased by demons, and disappearing into the menacing mists, filled with disembodied cries of agony.

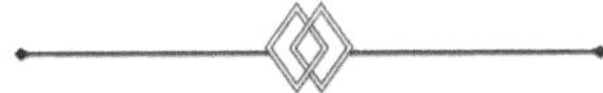

They spent the morning with minimal conversation, both still wrapped up in their thoughts of their respective fears of what was to come. Elena tried to distract herself from her anxieties about their future and the growing cold that nipped at her nose by trying to understand what Quinn was and how he had such intense and unusual magic when no man was supposed to be capable of having magic at all. She wanted to ask him about his parents, but she was fairly certain he didn't know anything about them. She knew he'd grown up in the terrible orphanage, on the streets, and with Amelia. In the few moons that they'd known each other, he'd never once mentioned his parents. Elena thought it was likely because he didn't know anything about them himself.

They stuck close to the riverbank and snacked on the bread and hard cheeses that Amelia had packed for them. It was going to be a long day, but they wanted to make it to the fog edge before nightfall so they could find a safe, relatively secluded location to make camp for the night.

"This place is really beautiful. Why does it have such a foreboding name? The Dark Woods. I haven't seen anything dark or menacing." Elena was making small talk, trying to get out of her head. She needed a distraction and she assumed Q did too. Plus, he always seemed happiest when he shared his knowledge of the woods and the creatures within them.

"Huh? Oh, I'm not sure. There are some nasty beasts that live here, but they mostly stay deeper in the woods, more toward the mountain. I think the name is probably just meant to keep people away. You know, since your school is in the middle of these woods. I'm pretty sure an enchantress at that school named the woods just to deter random... what did you call normal people?"

Elena flinched a little at his words. *Normal.* As if there was something abnormal about her.

"Magept," she replied simply.

"Yes, magept. I think the enchantresses named the woods something scary and intimidating so that the magept would keep away from their precious school."

"Oh." Elena didn't know what to say. She was hurt that he'd implied that she was weird or abnormal simply because she could do magic. She had always felt like there was something wrong with her because she wasn't as quick to grasp spells or as powerful as her classmates at Harbor Ridge, and now Q had literally told her that she wasn't normal.

Her mother had reminded her daily about how abnormal she was, how disappointingly unusual she and Agon were. The other girls as Harbor Ridge mocked her mercilessly for being so different. In Andover, she'd been forced to hide her true self, or risk being considered strange and threatening. Q was the one person Elena thought she could finally be herself with.

They walked quietly for a bit longer before Elena snapped, grabbing his sleeve and turning him around abruptly to face her.

"There's nothing *abnormal* about me, Quinn. There's nothing *abnormal* about having magic." Elena could feel her frustrations building. "Yes, I can do things that some people can't, but that doesn't make me weird or wrong or unusual. It just makes me different."

"Wait, El, that's not what I—" Quinn said, confusion painted his face, as he tried to explain, but Elena wasn't interested in his reasoning.

"And another thing," Elena ranted on, pacing back and forth along the side of the creek, "you aren't exactly 'normal' yourself. You have a familiar, which is weird enough in itself, but she has magic of her own! That's *definitely* abnormal. You burned a hole through your shirt, *from the inside*. I've never seen that, and I've seen a lot of strange things. There's no such thing as 'normal', Q. Just things that are more common."

Q caught her arm mid-pace and turned her to face him.

"I'm sorry. I didn't mean to upset you. It was a bad choice of words. I know you're not abnormal or weird. You are one of the most amazing people I've ever met," Quinn said quietly, locking eyes with her to make sure she really heard him.

Elena studied his face for a moment. It was so familiar to her now. She'd spent the majority of the last few moons with him. Learning from him, connecting with him, teaching him a few new things as well. He was her best friend—after Agon, of course—and the only human on the planet that she truly trusted.

"I'm sorry too. I overreacted."

"So... we're good? Because I don't want to set off another Elena-rant. Especially when you might blow me up or something," he joked, squeezing her arm gently before letting go and turning back to continue their journey upstream.

"Hey, don't get too comfortable. I might change my mind!" Elena taunted.

With the tension broken, they spent the rest of the day in casual comfort. Elena pointed out more edible plants and tried to teach Q how to identify them for himself. She collected more parsley as they walked as well as some lavender, rosemary, and even some blackberries.

Elena savored the peace she felt in knowing that Quinn truly accepted her and all of her "abnormalities." It was a first for her, and she desperately hoped nothing would ever change that.

They reached the boundary as the sun was starting to disappear behind the mountain. The fog didn't slowly rise like a morning mist over the lake near the gardens at Harbor Ridge. "Fog" wasn't even the right word. The so-called fog was more like a thick curtain made of clouds. It came into view suddenly and without warning, appearing like a barricade that surrounded a castle or fortress of some kind. The look of it alone would deter visitors, but the feeling Elena got as she crept closer to investigate was enough to drive away even the most heroic of adventurers. A sense of dread, misfortune, and distress made her want to turn and run as far away as possible. Even though she knew it was only the work of the witch's magic, Elena had a hard time convincing her feet to step forward or her heart to slow its beat.

"This is definitely the place," Elena said to no one in particular. It was fairly apparent that this was the fog Q had talked about, so stating the obvious seemed unnecessary. But nervous talking was better than uneasy silence, as far as Elena was concerned.

"Let's make camp back this way," Q turned to point behind him, the way they'd come. "We'll set up at the bend in the river and get a fresh start in the morning."

"Are you sure we'll be ok this close to that... fog?" Agon asked, a slight tremor of doubt and concern in his voice as he eyed the wall of clouds suspiciously.

Both he and Lyra had been rather quiet all day, most likely as a result of their connection to their humans. While Q and Elena opted to largely ignore their anxieties for the day, their familiars carried that weight for them. Now that they seemed to be settled in for the night, Agon voiced the concerns that everyone was feeling.

"We don't have a lot of options," Elena replied. "We need to see the witch, and we have to get through her fog to do that. If you have another idea, I'm all ears."

When Agon said nothing, they made the quick hike to the river's bend in search of some form of shelter to help keep them warm and shielded from the elements for the night. The upside of being this far into the forest was that the trees here were huge, at least a couple hundred years old. They would provide shelter from strong winds, rain, or snow if any could permeate this deep into the Dark Woods. There was a chill in the air, and an untold number of mysterious and magical creatures living in the woods, however, so they found a few large pine branches that looked to have fallen during a storm.

"These will be perfect. We can use them to make a small shelter. No one will see us through these needles, and the scent from the pine sap will help hide us from any curious creatures." Quinn dragged an exceptionally large branch over to the base of a pine near the riverside, propping it up, needles on the ground. It wasn't a huge space, but it would do for the night. "I'll grab a few more of these larger branches to reinforce the walls and make us less visible. Why don't you and Agon see if you can find some dry branches, and we'll make a small fire to cook tonight."

With Agon still nestled around her neck, Elena turned to face the unknown depths of the forest. Being back in these woods unsettled her, sending her mind back to the last time she'd been in the Dark Woods. She'd been terrified, homeless, and completely lost. Both literally and metaphorically.

"We're ok. We're all ok, and everything is going to be fine." Quinn's voice was quiet and calm. She turned to see him standing beside her. He moved so quietly, she was startled to see him so close. He looked confident, so sure of himself.

He's in his element, Elena thought. She felt the tears welling in her eyes, but she wiped them away. They didn't have time for her to have some kind of emotional breakdown. This wasn't the time or place. Any good enchantress knew how to reign in her emotions and maintain control. Emotions could get you killed.

She nodded to Quinn and stalked off in search of firewood.

23
QUINN

D RY WOOD WAS FEW and far between during the frost season. Too bad those *investigators* couldn't have waited until the planting season. The woods were really beautiful and welcoming then. Now? Now they were just wet, cold, and miserable. Not the ideal time for running from crazy, magic-wielding bitches on a mission. Q knew Elena wouldn't like him calling them that, but he couldn't have cared less. They were being hunted, and he wasn't overly concerned about hurting the feelings of their predators.

Elena had only managed to find a single armful of firewood, so they didn't attempt cooking, opting instead for more of the food Amelia had sent with them. Q built a small fire at the opening of their pine shelter. It wasn't much, but it was enough to keep them warm. If he added wood sparingly, he felt confident that their meager supply would last through the night. He'd taken the first watch because El had looked completely drained. With Agon curled at the entrance of their shelter—resting but alert—Quinn and Lyra took up watch with their backs to the river facing the woods. Q was fairly certain that no person in their right mind would venture this far into the Dark Woods, but the animals who lived this deep in the woods would be curious and not altogether friendly.

"What if this doesn't work?" Lyra inquired as she paced between two large fir trees, flicking her tail back and forth leaving light scorch marks on the damp forest floor.

"Can you stop with the sparks? I don't want to wake Elena because you started a forest fire. Again."

"What? I didn't start that fire! I've told you a hundred times. You must have left the fire going and fallen asleep."

Q chuckled. It hadn't been a full-blown forest fire, but it had burned down their first shelter when they had initially run away to start a new life in the woods all those cycles ago.

"I heard you. You don't have to yell." Q made a soft bed of green pine needles on the riverside next to the boulder he'd been sitting on, then patted for Lyra to come and sit with him. "I honestly don't know," Q added, getting back to her initial question. "Something big is happening or has happened here, and we need to figure out what the hells it is. If the witch can't help us, then maybe she'll know someone who can."

"And if this witch *won't* help? What then?"

Q stared off into the darkness, in the direction of the fog. "I don't know."

When the time came to wake Elena for her night watch, Q couldn't bring himself to do it. Instead, he added the last of the wood to their fire, settled onto the ground beside their shelter, leaned against the tree, and closed his eyes. Agon and Lyra were both awake and would alert them if there was any trouble.

He woke to the sound of footsteps in the woods to his left. Slowly, without opening his eyes, Q slipped his hand to the knife at his waist and gripped it tightly. He jumped suddenly and grabbed for the source of the sound. As soon as his fingers made contact, he felt a force of air so strong it pushed against his chest and threw him into the shallow edge of the river. He struggled to find his footing, grateful to find his dagger still clenched in his fist. He felt Lyra ahead of him, to the right of their shelter. Q sensed that she was awake, on alert, and poised to strike the thing that had just attacked him. He wasn't sure if Elena was awake yet, but he knew Lyra would protect her.

Q tried to see the thing that had attacked, but it was called the Dark Woods for a reason. Their fire had gone out, and the only light was the faint glow of the sun rising behind him. It didn't offer much assistance, and whatever he'd heard stalking toward them seemed to have frozen in place.

Probably debating its breakfast choices, Q thought to himself.

Q decided his best option to protect Elena was to draw the beast's attention and try to lead it away from their camp.

"Hey, ugly! You wanna fight? Let's go!" Quinn yelled, jumping and splashing in the water to ensure he had the thing's attention.

He heard footsteps shuffling ahead of him and a little to his right, moving closer to their shelter.

Panic rose like bile in his throat. He had to protect Elena. He wouldn't let this thing hurt her. She was only here because of him. He had to keep her safe.

"Hey! Over here!" He splashed even more, yelling and whistling at the creature. "Come on, you big, dumb, ugly beast! You want breakfast? You're gonna have to work for it today!"

Q picked up a river rock the size of his fist and hurled it toward where he'd last heard the beast move. He was careful to avoid hitting their shelter, knowing that Elena was in there somewhere, and he didn't want to hit her or Lyra. His rock missed their shelter, but it also missed the beast.

He threw another and another. Q heard something large moving toward him. He had the beast's attention now, and he wasn't going to back off. He needed to draw it away from their camp. It was still too dark to see what it was, but he hoped that he'd be able to get it closer to the river and into the faint light of sunrise, out of the shadows of the woods.

"Come on, beasty! Come face me, and let's see if you're really as scary as you want us to think!"

"Must you be so rude?" The voice was female. Deep. Smooth. Calm. Slightly irritated, but with a hint of amusement.

What the...

The creature seemed to glow as she stepped closer to the river. She was gorgeous. Long, flowing green hair that blended in perfectly with the evergreen trees surrounding them. Her skin was the same color as the river silt he'd been standing in just moments before. Q studied her with bewildered fascination. She had eyes that seemed to change color as she walked toward him, from soft gray to crystal clear blue. She came closer, and he caught a hint of jasmine in the air.

"What are you?" Quinn whispered the question so quietly, it might have been mistaken for a simple exhale, but her eyes flared at his words.

"What am I?" Her tone was slightly accusatory. "*What* am I? Well, my dear ignorant magept, I am the thing they warn you about in these woods. I am the guardian and protector of this place, and you are trespassing in my home."

Q was so focused on her voice that he barely registered her words at first. He caught a glimpse of movement behind the female and was jarred out of his trace.

Elena.

The female creature followed his line of sight and turned, swatted her hand through the air, and knocked their shelter down, as if she controlled the wind by sheer desire. Elena stood, Agon around her neck and Lyra poised to attack at her feet.

Q wanted to run and place himself between this female and Elena, but he couldn't move. He looked down to find that the tree roots had wrapped up his legs, holding him fast and not allowing him to move.

"Leave them alone!" he shouted. Using his dagger, Q started cutting at the roots around his legs.

"That's enough of that," the female said, and with a twist of her fingers, more roots grabbed hold of him, removing the dagger from his grip and pulling him down to a seated position on the riverbank.

Before he could hurl any more threats or insults, the female flicked her hand one last time, and the roots wrapped around his mouth, stifling his voice.

Elena looked horrified, but she didn't move as the female slowly, calmly, crept closer to her, inspecting her and examining the familiars around her.

The silence seemed to drag on forever, as Quinn struggled to break free from the roots, he heard Elena speak calmly and quietly to the female.

"I apologize, but we didn't know this place belonged to anyone. We're just trying to speak with the witch who lives beyond the fog, in the hopes that she can give us some answers."

"Answers about what?" the female inquired.

"My friend Quinn and I," Elena gestured toward him, "have recently discovered some unusual magic within ourselves, and we are hoping the witch could help us make sense of all this." El held up her hands as evidence, blue sparks flashing between her fingertips.

"How intriguing," the female said, carefully reaching out and grasping Elena's wrist in her hand. Quinn tried to yell, struggling against the binds, but the roots tightened themselves around him, sending a clear message: you're not going anywhere.

Elena locked eyes with Q and gave him a small smile. She was trying to tell him to be calm, but that wasn't going to happen. This creature had strong magic, and he wasn't about to sit back and do nothing.

Lyra was torn between Q's feelings and her desire to keep the peace. He could feel her body tense, like a coil about to be sprung. Agon must have noticed because he clambered down Elena's cloak and onto Lyra's back. Lyra *hated* the feeling, Q could sense it, but Agon whispered something in her ears and some of the tension left her body. She was still prepared to attack, but she'd switched to a more defensive stance. Q could only watch as events unfolded before him.

"You say your friend," the female glanced over her shoulder at him, "has magic too? That's impossible. Men are incapable of having magic. Their bodies are too weak."

Quinn jerked at this comment. *Muxing bitch*, he thought to himself.

"That's what I thought too, but he has a familiar," Elena pointed to Lyra, electricity still sparking between her fingers, "and he seems to have some kind of connection with fire that I've never seen or heard of before."

"A familiar..." the female muttered, seemingly to herself, and knelt to Lyra's level. Lyra didn't move, but Q could feel the tension building in her again.

The female held up her hands, cautiously, and asked, "May I?"

Lyra weighed her options, Q could sense her internal debate, but she finally consented with a simple nod.

The female placed one hand on Lyra's head, gently, just between her eyes, then closed her own eyes. Q didn't feel anything change within Lyra, but a moment later, the female thanked Lyra, removed her hand, and stood.

"This is highly irregular, but I've been expecting you. Your arrival was foretold."

With a casual wave of her hand, the roots containing Quinn fell away and retreated back into the ground around him. Unfortunately for Q, he wasn't expecting to be released so suddenly, and he ended up face-first in the wet leaves and mud that lay along the riverbank.

The female smirked and turned back to Elena, "Come with me, and we'll see what answers we can find for you."

Finally able to speak again, Q voiced his objections instantly.

"Hold on a second, lady. We don't know who, or what, you are or what you want with us. Why would we go anywhere with you?"

The creature turned to face him, a single eyebrow raised in apparent disdain. In the span of a heartbeat, she'd crossed the distance between them and was standing toe to toe with Q at the riverside, eyes locked on his. Elena gasped but didn't move.

"I am the one you came to see. I am the one you hurled insults and stones at, then turned around and asked for help. I am the wicked witch of the wood, and you can either come with me now or take your chances with my fog."

She didn't move. She didn't even blink. She simply awaited his response. Q lowered his eyes in concession, and she stepped back.

"I fear we might have gotten off on the wrong foot here," she stated simply. "My name is Belladonna. These are my woods. I am the nature witch who protects this place from the ever-encroaching menace that is magept-kind."

With that, she turned and headed north, toward the ominous fog and, apparently, her home.

24
BEATRICE

"WE HAVE AN UPDATE from the investigators searching for the source of that power surge south of the Woods." The guard handed Madame LaBelle a wax-sealed envelope. She cringed internally. All this magic and power and they still had to communicate with investigators in the field through muxing coded reports and messenger birds.

The guard returned to her post outside the office door, as Madame LaBelle broke the wax on the missive and mentally translated the coded update.

> *Source still unknown. Amelia offered no insights.*
> *Caught the faint trail of magic leading into the*
> *Dark Woods. Will pursue and send updates with*
> *any new information.*

Amelia. Madame LaBelle had nearly managed to forget the damned-stubborn woman was living in the town at the bottom of the mountain. And apparently, she wasn't being helpful. That wasn't surprising. Annoying and infuriating, but not surprising.

"I find it hard to believe that she's in the town where the magic incident occurs, but doesn't know anything about it," Madame LaBelle muttered mostly to herself.

"We could always go pay her a visit ourselves. Might be fun." Beatrice could feel that Zied wasn't entirely serious, but there was a hint of sincerity in his words.

"That wouldn't be productive, and you know that," she responded with a sigh of frustration. Unknown magic irked her. She liked knowing exactly what sort of powers were out and about in the world, and she demanded to be in control of such powers. Either by teaching and earning the loyalty of any and all enchantresses or by eliminating the untamed threat.

Whoever or whatever the source of this new power was, she needed to get her hands on them as soon as possible. The magic had felt unlike anything she'd ever met, and yet oddly familiar. Beatrice wracked her brain, trying to recall specific feelings from the creatures she'd met before becoming headmistress. Unfortunately, the magic had felt nothing like that of the Fae she'd encountered in Rolam, or the sprites she'd parlayed with when brokering a deal for a kidnapped child enchantress.

For the source of this new magic to be running and hiding in the Dark Woods meant it was likely that the source wasn't a young child. The reputation of the Woods alone tended to keep children and all magept at bay. However, if they knew they were being pursued, they would flee into the Woods, hoping to hide. Hoping to escape.

"The Woods won't protect them. The investigators will find this source and bring it back to us, or remove it from the world." Zied was trying to bring her comfort, sensing her stress.

"I'm less concerned about this source getting away as I am what they are running toward. That muxing witch is still living in the Woods. We can't control or sway her, and she doesn't seem interested in relocating, despite our best efforts."

"Maybe the investigators will get lucky and catch the source *and* free us of the witch as well. That would be lovely," Zied said through a yawn. For being such a massive and imposing creature, he was admittedly quite lazy. He spent most of the day and night sleeping or lounging in the sun. He might have looked like a snowy lion, but he behaved like a common house cat.

"Judge not," he stated, standing to stretch before repositioning himself to lay in a patch of sunlight on the stone floor of her office. "We both know you're jealous of my lifestyle. *Common house cat*? Please, if anything, I'm far too majestic to ever be labeled a common anything."

Madame LaBelle didn't respond to his description of himself. She knew he was trying to get a rise out of her, to break some of the tension that had been weighing on her for days. He did make a good point though; if the investigators could take care of this new source of magic and remove the witch from their realm, it would simplify things for her immensely.

Madame LaBelle moved from where she'd been standing by the window, looking out over the treetops as though she might be able to spot the witch's hideout or locate the power source, and returned to her desk. She penned a quick missive of her own, reminding the investigators of the presence of the witch in the Woods and instructing them, in no uncertain terms, that they were to do whatever was necessary to bring the source back to Harbor Ridge.

She was determined to contain this magic and end the threat. One way or another.

25

ELENA

She was expecting them. She'd said as much, hadn't she? She knew they were coming. What did that mean? Did this nature witch, Belladonna, have the power of foresight? If so, why did she attack them? Why did she threaten Q like that? What was her issue with him? What had she seen in her connection with Lyra? So many questions.

They followed the witch in silence, Q right by her side, refusing to take his eyes off Belladonna. Elena had to admit that the woman was stunning. She had flowers in her hair that appeared to be literally growing in the green expanse of her locks, rather than being braided in as Elena had done for festivals and solstices as a child. And she smelled of wildflowers: jasmine, magnolia, and lavender.

Aside from her hair and skin, Belladonna wasn't at all what Elena had pictured when they'd studied nature witches at Harbor Ridge. She wasn't tall and willowy as the books described. She was built more sturdy, like a centuries-old sequoia. Strong legs and lean arms. Clearly, this was a woman who spent a great deal of time hiking and climbing the woods she protected. She was barefoot, which Elena found off-putting, simply because there were so many broken branches and dried evergreen needles on the forest floor that it had to be at least mildly painful to walk without some form of protective covering on her feet.

"It's actually quite nice," Belladonna stated, as though she'd been reading Elena's mind. "The forest floor is soft and the trees offer their branches, needles, and leaves to make a soft cushion on the ground. Almost like a rug, but far more natural."

She didn't look behind her as she spoke, but it was clear she had been speaking to Elena, answering her unasked questions.

"Can you... did you read my mind?" Elena asked incredulously.

"Not exactly," Belladonna replied. "I can't read minds, but I can sense your feelings and emotions as well as you can feel that of your familiar's. I'm an empath. If I let my guard down, I feel all of your emotions. Including all the rage, disgust, and distrust of your friend here. Which is how I know he hates everything about me without actually knowing me at all."

Q looked stunned. He opened his mouth to respond, but no words came out. He just stared at the back of the witch's head in shock.

"It's ok, boy. I don't hold it against you. You were raised in an ignorant and close-minded town. Not to mention you had a rather intense run-in with my fog not too long ago, and you've had a fairly traumatic life thus far. I'm sorry to tell you that it isn't going to get any less traumatic for quite some time."

She said all of this with the same casual air of someone discussing the weather.

"I don't mean to be so blunt," Belladonna stopped and turned to face them. "I'm not used to this much interaction with humans. I love the animals and plants here, but they aren't much for social cues or niceties. It seems I've lost some of my polite conversational skills. I apologize. Please, forgive my rudeness." She was looking directly into Q's eyes as she apologized. She looked as though she wanted to touch him, but was holding back.

Good choice, Elena thought.

Q searched her face for a moment, possibly looking for a hint of sarcasm or deception, or maybe he was just admiring the almond shape of her now emerald-green eyes. Regardless, Elena felt a twinge of discomfort at seeing their closeness. She pushed the feeling away and grasped Q's hand to give it a squeeze of reassurance. Q took his eyes off the witch, muttered a simple, "Ok", and squeezed Elena's hand in return. As the witch turned back around and continued leading them to her home, Q didn't let go of her hand.

It wasn't until they stepped into a clearing that Elena realized they'd passed through the fog without her even noticing.

"How did we make it through the fog? I didn't see it and I didn't feel any of its effects." Elena looked around her to see that the clearing they were now in was encircled by Belladonna's fog.

"That's because I brought you here," Belladonna stated, matter-of-factly. "I'm immune to my fog, and I extended my protection to you. I created a small, fog-free bubble if you will, encompassing the both of you to bring you in without incident."

Q surveyed the clearing they were in, a look of discomfort with a dash of nausea spreading over his face.

"Does that mean we're trapped in here? Surrounded by the fog until you escort us out of here?" There was a touch of panic in his voice.

"No, boy. The fog only affects those coming *toward* the clearing. Toward my home. When you are walking away, the fog doesn't bother you. Picture the barb of an arrow. The barb only causes serious damage when you try to pull it out. If you just push it through, the damage is far less."

"You realize that your analogy still involves me getting shot with an arrow, don't you?" Q asked.

"Hm, yes, I suppose it does," Belladonna smirked again and directed them to the fern-covered cottage in the center of the clearing. "This is my home. You are both welcome to stay here while we figure out what's going on with your magic. Unfortunately, you won't be able to stay very long or get all the answers you seek before things get messy and you have to run again. I promise, I'm not the looming threat, but be sure that a threat is, without a doubt, looming and moving ever closer."

Elena felt an icy chill fill her chest.

Agon nudged her chin with his nose, silently encouraging her to breathe and focus on the matter at hand. Elena took a deep breath, tightening her grip on Q's hand before releasing him and stepping toward the witch's cottage. It was surprisingly lovely and, under different circumstances, Elena would have taken more time to admire the beauty of the thatched roof covered in flowering ivy, the mossy stones that built the outer walls, the sound of the river lazily flowing just beyond the fog, the massive garden that appeared to be consuming the back half of the clearing, and a small but deep-looking pond. It would have been a very peaceful and relaxing place to rest after the stress of the last two days. However, the witch made it clear that rest wasn't in their future.

"How long do we have?" Elena asked flatly. There was no need to pretend like they were surprised by her warning. Elena and Quinn were well aware that they were being hunted. She just needed to know how much time they had.

"By my count, I'd say a day, maybe two. Things are coming for you, young enchantress. The likes of which this world hasn't seen for nearly an age. You worry about your hunters, but you should be more concerned about the Brotherhood and the *turmio*."

Belladonna opened the door of her home and gestured for them to go in before walking over to the well by her garden gate to draw the bucket of water from its depths.

Elena and Quinn walked into the witch's cottage and were instantly greeted by a pair of bright red eyes and a threatening caw from a shadow in the far corner of the room.

"Hush, Castor. They're guests, not invaders, you twit," Belladonna scolded as she carried the bucket of fresh water over to the hearth. She turned to Lyra and casually asked, "Would you mind, dear?"

Much to Elena's surprise, Lyra didn't hesitate. She didn't look to Quinn for advice or permission. Instead, she sauntered over to the hearth, flicked her tail into the neatly arranged pile of firewood, and stepped back to admire her handiwork as the blaze burned brightly.

"My, that is quite handy," Belladonna muttered, "Thank you, ma'am," she said, turning to Lyra and offering a gentle scratch under her chin.

"What in the name of the Goddess is going on here?" Quinn demanded. He glared at Lyra as if she'd betrayed him. Elena was equally confused, although not nearly as enraged as Q suddenly appeared to be.

If she'd been capable, Elena was sure Lyra would have shrugged or rolled her eyes at Quinn's outrage. "What? She already knew. Besides, I do it for us all the time, and building a fire the regular way is a time-consuming waste of energy. Especially if we really are as pressed for time as she says."

Not for the first time since they'd been roughly awakened that morning, Quinn looked stunned into silence. Elena decided to follow Lyra's lead and get right to the point.

"Here's the thing, Belladonna, we don't understand how or why, but I have powers no one has ever seen or talked about at Harbor Ridge. I unintentionally reduced four men to ash a few days ago, and I have no idea how I did it or how I can stop myself from doing it again."

Belladonna gave her a knowing look. "I felt that power surge. Are you sure you wouldn't like to do that again? I imagine those swine deserved what happened to them."

Quinn grunted in agreement. It was the first time those two had agreed on anything, and it seemed to melt some of the icy tension between them.

"I don't want to accidentally kill people. I don't want to kill people at all!" Elena tried not to yell, but the stress of the week's events was starting to take its toll.

"I understand, dear. I'm not sure I can fix things the way you would like me to, but I can promise that with time and practice, you will be able to control your powers and only kill people when you intend to. I'm sorry to say that there will come a time, sooner rather than later, that you will be forced to defend those you love and take a life. I don't envy you that, but I can reassure you now, it will be the only way to save your loved ones, and it will be the right choice. Killing is always a difficult thing to do when you have a soul as pure as yours, my darling, but it will be the best option."

It was Elena's turn to be stunned into silence. She never wanted to use her powers again, especially not to bring harm or death to another living thing. Yes, the men who attacked her were horrible, violent monsters who'd intended to do a great deal of harm to her, but she still hated that she'd murdered them. That's what it was, despite Q's reassurances that it was self-defense. She had taken their lives from them. It was murder.

Elena's fingers began to warm and emanate a faint blue glow as she thought about the events of that day. She felt the sparks skipping between her fingertips, but she couldn't make it stop. She tried to rub her fingers and massage the magic away, but it didn't help. Agon, who was still curled around her neck, unfurled and climbed down the sleeve of her cloak to her hands.

He forced himself into her grasp and attempted to absorb her electricity.

Quinn came into her field of vision. He didn't touch her, but he locked eyes with her, then without saying a word, started taking dramatic deep breaths, silently encouraging her to breathe with him. Lyra came to sit between her feet, pressing her little furry body into Elena's inner calves. Elena tried to breathe with Quinn, but she could feel the power building, rather than subsiding.

Belladonna didn't move. She watched the four of them closely for several moments, waiting to see what would happen next. When it was clear that Elena was only getting worse, Belladonna focused her attention on Quinn.

"Lyra, will you please take Quinn to the garden and collect some vegetables for the stew?" Her voice was calm and casual, as she took a boiling bucket of water from the hook over the hearth and poured it carefully into a porcelain teapot. It seemed like she either didn't notice that Elena was about to combust, or she didn't care. Quinn tried to argue, but Lyra grabbed his pants in her sharp teeth and pulled him out the door and towards the garden.

Agon was still attempting to absorb the magic in Elena's fingers, to no avail, when Belladonna quietly said, "Elena, tell me about the room you grew up in. Did you share it with anyone? Did you have a window? What color were your sheets? What sort of feathers filled your pillows and mattress?"

Elena was confused by her questions, but she decided to humor the witch because honestly, she didn't know what else to do.

"I shared my room with three other girls. My bed was on the north wall of our tower room, with a window above each bed. From my bed, I could look out and see the gardens below." Elena continued to describe her room with as much detail as she could recall. The more she talked, the more her breathing regulated and the warmth and tingling diminished from her fingertips.

Once Elena was able to regain control of herself, she asked the obvious question, even though she was fairly certain she already knew the answer.

"Why does that happen?" Elena asked, after taking a sip of the lavender and honey tea Belladonna placed in her now spark-free hands.

"Our powers are tied to our emotions. When you bottle things up, like you have clearly been doing all of your life, your powers will behave erratically. If you want to control your magic, you will first need to gain control of your emotions."

Elena let out an exasperated sigh.

"I've been trying to contain my emotions my whole life. That's one of the basic lessons at Harbor Ridge. Emotions aren't meant to be shared or shown. I've never been good at it. How am I supposed to just shut down my feelings to control my powers? Please, tell me how to disconnect from my feelings!" Tears streamed down her face as Elena verbalized her frustrations. The tingling was already coming back in her fingers.

Looking at her hands, watching the glow grow and the sparks return, she started crying even harder. "How am I ever going to control this? What if I hurt someone? Gods, what if I kill someone else?! I'm not safe to be around. I should just let my mother's investigators lock me up somewhere so I can't hurt anyone ever again."

The tears flowed freely as Belladonna took Elena's face in her hands.

"Dear girl, no one needs to lock you up. You need to set yourself free. You've spent your whole life locking away emotions and feelings. That is not how you control your emotions. Let it out. Let all of the rage, fear, frustration, and anxiety out. Give it the freedom to run its course, then release it. You can't keep avoiding negative feelings. Acknowledge their existence, then thank them and send them on their way."

Elena wasn't sure exactly what Belladonna meant, but the floodgates were open and she had no way of stopping the out-pour of emotional baggage as it raced down her face. The more she cried, the more her fingers glowed. Soon, the glow spread from her fingers, through her hands, up her arms, and into her chest. It was only a few moments before the warmth and electricity spread through her whole body. She could feel the power burning through all of the mental blocks she'd built in her mind over the years. Walls meant to lock away all the feelings of hurt and neglect every time her mother ignored her or worse, berated her in front of her classmates. Her power burned through her feelings of rejection when she was kicked out of Harbor Ridge. Her fear of being alone and helpless. Her pain and terror at being attacked not once, but twice by those awful men. Her power grew until her entire body was giving off heat and a blinding electric blue light.

Agon stood watching, from his perch on Belladonna's dining table. He seemed unsure of what to do, but he could sense that she wasn't in pain. In reality, as her electricity burned through her emotional blocks, he could feel the weight that had been growing within her for as long as he could remember, lighten. She was burning off all of the negativity that she'd been holding onto for so long. She was freeing herself from her baggage, and Agon was content to sit and watch her heal herself.

26
QUINN

"**H**OLY MOTHER OF LIGHT!" Q looked up from pulling carrots in the garden to see the entire house glowing radiant blue from the inside and bursting through the windows. He dropped everything he and Lyra had collected and ran toward the house.

He stopped short at the threshold of the open front door. Elena was glowing. The small bolts of her lightning that bounced between her fingertips weren't an unusual sight, but the currents of electricity that raced through her hair and flashed in her eyes were new and deeply unsettling. The most alarming part of the whole scene was how calm, peaceful and serene Elena looked. Sure, she was a bright, glowing mess of deadly blue electricity, but she seemed content. Q had never seen that look of tranquility on her face. It completely contradicted the pulsating lights that radiated off her skin.

"She's ok." Agon's quiet voice brought Q out of his trance. Elena was mesmerizing and he had a hard time taking his eyes off her.

She's ok. "Are you sure? She doesn't look ok."

Elena hadn't seemed to even notice his arrival or acknowledge his presence.

Agon climbed along the edge of the furniture, bounced from the table to the back of a chair, to the floor, darted across the room, and jumped onto Q's shoulder. Quinn nearly threw him off. He didn't know a lot about familiars. Hells, he didn't even know what a familiar was until Elena explained to him that that was what Lyra was and why they were connected. However, Quinn was fairly certain that touching another person's familiar was wrong, a violation, or at least frowned upon. Lyra instantly tensed at the contact between Q and Agon. Evidently, she wasn't any more comfortable with it than Q was.

"She's ok, I promise," Agon told him. "Elena is working through some... emotions that have been weighing her down for a very long time. She's not hurt. If she could talk, she'd tell you herself that this is the best she's felt in years. Elena has spent her whole life repressing emotions because enchantresses aren't supposed to let their feelings be known. She's finally unleashing all the things she's spent all this time trying to bury, and it's liberating."

Q gave Agon a suspicious glance out of the corner of his eye but didn't turn away from Elena. If Agon said she was ok, Quinn would trust that. After all, they were connected. If Elena was in pain, or scared, Agon would know, and he wouldn't just stand by and watch. Still, it was a pretty unnerving sight to behold.

"Where are the vegetables?" The witch's tone was dull, almost bored.

This woman... doesn't she care that Elena is muxing glowing in her home? Or does this sort of thing happen all the time?

"It's not a normal occurrence, but as Agon said, Elena is fine and she'll need sustenance when she's finished. So I'll ask again, where are the vegetables for the stew?" Belladonna was sitting at her table, sipping what looked like herbal tea, and casually stroking the head of a large, black, hawk-looking bird.

"Castor is not a hawk, ignorant boy," she commented. "He's a moonbird. All witches have a moonbird. They are similar to the standard familiar, in that they are connected to their witch on a psychological level, but far more useful. Moonbirds, for instance, can travel miles and miles from their witch, unlike traditional familiars who are incapable of venturing more than a half-mile, at best. They can carry nearly a hundred times their own weight, meaning Castor here can carry me and enable me to travel far distances in a matter of moments. The most wondrous thing about moonbirds, though, is their shape-shifting abilities. I've read tales of moonbirds transforming into dragons to protect and aid their witches. Castor has never tried anything that dramatic, but I know he could if he wanted." She ruffled the feathers on the back of her moonbird's head as she said those last words, like a grandmother might affectionately muss the hair of a child. Like Amelia had often mussed Q's hair when he was younger.

Q knew she was trying to distract him from the state Elena was in, since sending him to fetch food hadn't worked, now she was attempting to sidetrack his mind by telling him impossible things about her bird.

"He's not merely a bird. He's got more magic in one feather than you've seen in your whole life, boy. Well, your life prior to today." She took a sip from her tea and waved a casual hand in Elena's direction.

"Would you stop that? Stop reading my mind. It's *my* mind, dammit."

"Then stop thinking so loudly."

"What?" Q snapped. "What the hells does that even mean? How am I thinking too loudly? They're my thoughts, in my head. You shouldn't be able to hear them at all."

"And you shouldn't have a firefox or burn holes through the front of your shirt that you can't explain. We all have our crosses to bear, boy."

The patronizing tone in her voice grated on him. Q could feel the heat rising in his body. How dare this witch talk down to him like he was some ignorant child. Q hadn't done anything to deserve this level of condescension and contempt.

Q saw Agon jump down from his shoulder, but he barely registered the shift in his mind. He was already spiraling down a dark tunnel. Everyone had always talked down to Q, pushing him around, insulting him, spitting on him—literally and figuratively—kicking him when he was down—again, literally and figuratively—and generally treating him as something less than.

"Lyra, take the boy outside before he burns another house down, dear. I rather like this place."

"That's it! I have a name, witch! My name is Quinn, and I don't deserve this shyt. I'm only here to help my friend, and you've been nothing but rude and insulting to me the entire time. What is your pro—" His question was cut off by Lyra pouncing into his chest and knocking him out the door and onto his back in the soft grass.

Q was stunned when he looked down at her on his chest and saw that she was on fire. She immediately hopped off his chest and sat at attention beside him, flame-free. Q could still feel the heat and smelled something burning. He turned his attention back to himself only to see that he was on fire and his shirt was nearly gone.

He cried out in shock before he started rolling in the grass, trying to smother the flames. When it was clear smothering wasn't going to work, Q ran and jumped in the witch's small fishing pond. The water sizzled and boiled around him, but the flames refused to be extinguished. No matter what he tried, the blaze only seemed to burn hotter and brighter.

Lyra stood at the edge of the pond, joined by the witch and her moonbird.

"Get out of my pond, you fool," Belladonna yelled. "You're going to boil my fish. Water won't put out those flames anyway. Or did you not learn that the first time?"

Q waded back out of the water as her words sank in. *The first time.* Oh, gods. The first time. When he set the orphanage on fire. He'd worked so hard to block that memory out, but it all came rushing back as he fell unconscious at the water's edge.

Q was a young boy, maybe eight or nine, although he had no way to be sure as he'd never known his actual birthday. A fact that the orphanage "mother" and "father" liked to taunt him about regularly. They were cruel people. The house was always filled with at least a dozen kids. Mother and Father, as they made the children call them, should never have been allowed to raise children. They hated kids almost as much as they hated each other. They were constantly yelling and throwing things, and those were the good days. The day the house had burned down had not been a good day.

Father had spent the day, and all of the money, at the tavern and came home stumbling drunk and looking for a fight. Mother quickly directed his rage at one of the youngest children, a little boy just four solar cycles old, who had broken a plate earlier that day while trying to wash the dishes. He was too small to properly reach the washbasin and should never have been tasked with this chore in the first place, but Mother certainly wasn't going to wash dishes when she had so many servants at her disposal.

Quinn saw the murderous look in Father's eyes as he removed his belt and approached the small boy who cowered in the corner. The boy had already been beaten by Mother with her favorite wooden spoon and bore the welts and bruises on his backside and legs. He wouldn't have survived a beating from Father. Quinn positioned himself between the drunken man and the little boy, then told the other children to take the boy out and run to Ms. Amelia's inn. They were all so terrified that they ran out the door and never looked back. Q was the oldest child in the home, so they all looked up to him and trusted him.

"You'll regret that, boy." The drunk spat and swung his belt toward Q. He missed, as drunk as he was, and nearly knocked himself to the ground. Mother stepped forward to grab Quinn and punish him herself, but Lyra lunged from her protected position under the kitchen table and attacked. It was the first time she'd ever attacked anyone before, and it was a bit clumsy, but it did the trick. Mother shrieked in pain and rage as she

clutched her leg where Lyra had just taken a chunk out. Lyra didn't move quickly enough though, as Mother lashed out with her uninjured leg and kicked Lyra across the room.

Quinn felt the impact of the wall into Lyra's spine on his own and cried out.

Father struggled to his feet when Quinn felt the heat rise in his body for the first time. All the terror and rage he'd felt since being placed in that house, the only "home" he'd ever known, swelled within him until he erupted.

Quinn never fully understood how it happened, but suddenly Father's belt was aflame, as was Mother's spoon. They screamed as the flames quickly spread to their flesh. The flames spread so rapidly that the entire house was on fire in a matter of moments. Quinn didn't move. As he stood there and watched it all burn, he felt an immense sense of peace and freedom. He was aware that the screams had stopped, and the house was falling down all around him as he walked over to the wall and picked up Lyra, still unconscious.

Quinn calmly walked out of the house and into the night, seemingly unfazed by the scene that unfolded behind him as the townsfolk tried without success to quell the flames. He knew—although he had no idea how—that the flames wouldn't spread to any other homes, no one else would be harmed, and the fire would put itself out when the house had been reduced to nothing but rubble and ash.

27
BELLADONNA

"**C**OME ALONG, CASTOR, LYRA. Agon!" She called back into the house. "Come help us collect food for dinner. The children will be hungry when they awake."

With Castor's assistance, she had moved Quinn farther from the pond, fully into the field, just in case he rolled over, so that he couldn't drown himself. That just wouldn't do.

"Has Elena settled yet? Relaxed her muscles so that we might move her to the bed?" Belladonna asked Agon.

"No, ma'am," he replied, hopping along next to her toward the garden. "I will let you know when she releases the tension holding her upright so we can move her before she falls. She seems a bit frozen right now."

"Aye, that can happen." Belladonna talked like she knew what they were going through, but in fact, this was all very new to her as well. Sure, she'd read about the arrival of these two and studied the prophecies extensively, but research and books can only prepare you for so much. She was just grateful that they hadn't seemed to notice how surprised and nervous she'd been at their arrival.

Agon and Lyra helped her fill a basket with fresh vegetables for the stew—carrots, radishes, a head of cabbage, and some potatoes— then she sent them to carry the basket back to the house while she and Castor went to the well to fetch more water.

Once they were out of sight, Castor transformed into his second favorite shape, a man. Tall and lithe, with a slightly more pointed nose than a typical man, jet black hair, dark eyes, and skin tone so dark it rivaled her kitchen cauldron.

"You can't tell them about the prophecy, you know. It would disrupt the natural order of things. They can't know he's coming for them or you might throw off the entire plan and cost them the war."

"Castor, don't talk to me about what I can and cannot say to these children," Belladonna rebuked. "I'm well versed in all things prophecy, and I remember clearly what happened the last time a witch tried to alter the Mother's Plan. Witches paid dearly for Esmerelda's arrogance, and I will not repeat her mistakes. That doesn't mean I have to send them in blind. I will simply prepare them as best I can, set them on the right path, and pray to the Mother that she takes pity on their ignorance."

"Do you honestly think they'll survive? Doesn't the prophecy say that one must die for the world to survive?"

Despite his human legs, he still walked with a bounce in his step, much like a bird hopping through tall grass.

"The exact words were *'one must fall.'* That could mean a lot of things. That's the thing about prophecies. They always work out the way they were designed and rarely in the way you'd expect."

They filled the bucket with cool water from the well and walked back to the house in companionable silence, Castor returning to his moonbird form as they reached the pond. Belladonna paused to check on Quinn before she ventured into the house to begin the stew.

28
ELENA

ELENA WOKE UP IN a bed covered with her cloak, to the sounds of a crackling fire and hushed conversation. There was a small bowl of stew on the bedside table along with a steaming cup of what smelled like lavender and chamomile tea.

"Oh, good, you're awake! The stew is still quite warm, but the tea should be at the perfect temperature now. Take a sip, and let me know if you'd like to add any honey or peppermint to the mix. I wasn't sure exactly what you'd be in the mood for. Calming, invigorating, or a bit of both. I decided it was safest to start with calming. We can always add the mint to perk you up if need be, but you can't exactly un-perk someone, can you?"

Belladonna was doubtless an expert on perkiness. She was practically vibrating with enthusiasm.

Elena took a sip of the tea and a groan escaped her throat. "Oh my goddess, this is amazing." On the second sip, Elena felt a wave of tension leave her body, replaced by a sense of calm.

Agon slunk over from his spot on a pillow by the hearth and crawled into her lap. No words were exchanged because they already knew what the other was feeling. Just being able to touch him and physically connect was enough to quiet her anxious mind.

Elena absentmindedly sipped her tea and stroked Agon's fur, nose to tail, trying to process everything that had happened. She felt different. Lighter. She'd burned off a lifetime of baggage, but now what? Sure, she felt more at ease than ever before, but she still didn't know how to control her powers. She couldn't very well keep bottling everything up and exploding in bright blue, electric energy every decade or so.

"You're right, but you've proven to yourself that you have the power and the control. You just need to work more on directing that energy and master your emotions rather than letting them continue to reign supreme. You can do it, Elena. It will just take time and practice."

Elena nodded and took another sip as Quinn stumbled into the house. He looked rough. His shirt was in tattered ashes, hanging off his shoulders. His belt appeared to be gone and he was holding his singed pants up with one hand while steadying himself in the doorframe with the other.

Elena jumped out of bed, accidentally knocking Agon to the ground as she rushed to Q's aid. Agon gracefully rolled to his feet, grumbling and returning to his pillow by the fire, unbothered by Quinn's haggard appearance.

"What happened? Are you ok?" Elena's eyes searched his skin, noting the smooth and strong shape of his chest and stomach, as well as his muscular arms. She'd never seen him without a shirt before. It made her blush.

She gave herself a mental shake, then moved to catch him under the arm that he was using to support himself as she shifted his weight from the doorframe to her own frame and guided him to the bed. Neither Belladonna nor Lyra offered to help, but Lyra came to sit beside him at the foot of the bed and rested her head on his knee

Quinn's eyes were unfocused like he wasn't fully with them, mentally, but he refused to lie down. Instead, he sat on the edge of the bed and gazed into the fire. Elena quickly wrapped him in his cloak and searched his pack for a new shirt and a second belt, or, more likely, some rope to use as a belt.

"I started the fire." His voice was gravel, rough, and barely above a whisper.

Elena didn't need him to repeat it though; she'd heard him loud and clear. That wasn't news though. She had already known he started the fire. She wasn't sure why he brought it up now, but she decided to just wait and see if he said anything else.

For the next several minutes, no one spoke. Belladonna minded the stew and stoked the fire. Night was falling, and it would be getting colder soon. The faint scent of snow was in the air, indicating that in the coming days, the clearing would be covered in a smooth blanket of white. Elena ate her stew and studied Q's face, looking for any sign that he might tell her what happened to his clothes. She offered him some of her tea. Initially, he declined, but he smelled it and seemed to realize it would bring comfort. Ultimately, he consented and took a large swig. As if by magic, the tension in his shoulders and eyes eased. He took a second, smaller sip and turned to face her.

"I started the fire," he said again.

"I know, Q. You told me before." Elena eyed him cautiously.

"No, I mean *I* started the fire. Me. My body. I burned that place to the ground. First them, then the house. *My fire.* I controlled it. I directed it. I burned that place to ash and walked away, unharmed. How did I do that?" He looked at her, begging her to have all the answers, but she simply didn't. She had never heard of this sort of power before. She didn't understand how he had a familiar, much less how either of them, Lyra or Quinn, had any magic. It wasn't supposed to be possible.

"You, boy, are FlameBorn. Elena is StormBorn. Neither has existed in an age, maybe two, I'd have to check my records. Either is rare, but to have two born in the same generation is... prophetic."

29
QUINN

*P*ROPHETIC. *WELL, MUX EVERYTHING. Of course there would be a gods damned prophecy. Isn't that always the case?* Q could hear Elena and Belladonna talking around him, but he wasn't listening. He didn't give a damn about any prophecy. He was still reeling from the realization that he controlled the fire within him, and he used that power to murder two people.

Yeah, they were two of the world's worst humans, but still. Murder? Deliberate and intentional murder by burning them alive. What in the world was he supposed to do with that knowledge now? How was he supposed to cope with all this shyt? Clearly, he'd blocked it all out for a reason.

I wonder if I can block it out again? No, that wouldn't really be a solution. Q needed to find a way to move on, and quickly. If he was meant to be part of some ridiculous prophecy, then he desperately needed to get his head on straight. Elena would need him.

"But what does it mean?" Elena's raised voice brought Q out of his internal debate.

"No one knows for sure, dear. Prophecies are tricky. No two people will interpret a prophecy the same way, and no one ever seems to decipher them correctly." Belladonna ladled more stew into their bowls, setting them around the table along with a large pot of tea. "Come eat. You will need your strength. You've got a long journey ahead of you, and you will be leaving at first light."

"What? Why?" Q didn't really *want* to stay in the witch's cottage, but they also didn't have any plan or any real answers to their questions.

He roughly pulled on the shirt Elena had placed beside him on the bed and fed the length of rope she handed him through the loops of his slightly toasted pants. Once he was decent again, he moved over to the table and the steaming bowl of stew.

"Because, boy, the investigators will be here by midday and you don't want to be here when they arrive."

"I thought you said we had a few days! We still need answers. How can I control my powers? I don't want to kill anyone else. I just want to go home." Tears silently slipped down Elena's face. Q rose from his chair and went to her side, pulling her into a protective one-arm hug.

"Darling, do you even have a home?" Belladonna's quiet tone wasn't cruel, but her words were needlessly harsh.

"Of course she does," Q said, jutting his chin and glaring at the witch. "Her home is with me and Lyra."

"So then she's already home. There's nowhere to 'go.'" She sipped her tea and waited patiently for Elena to stop crying.

Q stroked her back, comforting her as best he could. He'd never been much of a hugger, but Elena was different. Holding her felt as natural as breathing. They belonged together. He wasn't exaggerating or simply being kind when he said she was home with him. He meant it. He knew it in his bones. It felt as though this was how it was always meant to be.

"You should really eat," Belladonna said, as she motioned to the steaming bowls of stew on the table. "Both of you. Then sleep. Castor and I will keep watch over you tonight, so you can both get some much-needed rest, then we'll send you off as the sun rises. I can guide you north, through the Mist, but that's as far as I'll take you. I should be here when the investigators arrive. If not, I fear they will make a mess looking for the two of you."

Elena wiped her cheeks, took a seat at the table, and took a sip of the relaxing tea. Quinn kept his eyes on her trying to gauge her emotional state as he sat back down in the chair beside her.

"Do they know they are looking for me?" Elena quietly asked.

"Not yet, dear. The four of you give off very distinct magical energies, and I imagine that's confusing the investigators. They've never tracked anything like any of you before. They probably believe they are searching for four different enchantresses at the moment. Although, once they see you, they'll realize their mistake. Your best option is to stay hidden for as long as possible."

"Then where do you suggest we go?" Q tried to keep the annoyance out of his voice, although he wasn't entirely successful.

"North, boy. I already said that. Pay attention."

Q could feel the heat rising in his body again. His jaw clenched, his hands were balled into fists again.

"Boy, if you start another fire, you will be sleeping outside." Belladonna eyed him with clear disdain.

"What is it about me that you hate so much? You don't even know me!" Q slammed his fist on the table, leaving a distinct burned print of a clenched hand on the surface of the table, ready to rise and face off with Belladonna and all her condescending glory.

Elena quickly grabbed his arm, careful not to touch his scorching hand. It was her turn to calm him down. Q tried to jerk his arm away, knowing he was seconds from bursting into flame, and he didn't want to hurt her. Elena wouldn't let go, however, so Q was forced to calm himself down or risk causing her injury.

Elena spoke again, while Q was working to reign in his rage.

"Perhaps you could explain why we are going north? What are we looking for? Maybe someone who can explain why we even have these powers? What it means to be StormBorn and FlameBorn?"

Elena always knew the right questions to ask. After burning through her "emotional baggage" as Agon had called it, Elena seemed more level-headed and focused than ever. Probably best if Q backed off and let her handle this mess for a few minutes. He decided to put all of his rage energy into shoveling the stew into his mouth before he said anything else and started another fire. It was clear he wasn't in control of himself right now. Best not to risk burning everything to the ground. Again.

"In a matter of days, three maybe four, you'll be forced to make some tough choices, and you'll uncover some life-altering information. No, don't ask, I can't tell you. You have to find out on your own. You wouldn't believe me if I told you anyway. Trust me. I've seen it before." Belladonna took a sip of her tea, then nodded towards Q's bag and Elena's cloak. "I have restocked your supplies as well as added in more herbs and bandages. You will need it."

"Are we heading into a fight?" Q asked, between mouthfuls.

It turned out, the witch was a decent cook; the stew was delicious, and it seemed to have a calming effect on his fried nerves.

"Yes, boy, you are. There is a war coming, and you two are at the center of it. The prophecy states that two magical beings such as yourselves will come as the war for magic is beginning. It will be up to you to preserve magic, or we will all lose it forever."

Elena nearly choked on her spoonful. "WHAT?! What in the name of the Mother are you talking about?"

"Breathe, dear. Eat your dinner, and I'll tell you a story."

Belladonna offered them both a fresh slice of bread, took a sip of her tea, and began her story.

"Ages ago, a group was formed with the singular intent of ridding the world of 'the scourge of magic' as they called it. The Brotherhood of the Healing Light was founded by a man by the name of Lucien who'd been scorned by an enchantress. She used him for his seed, as enchantresses do, and abandoned him. Lucien was a foolish man, arrogant. He did not take kindly to being used. He spent decades trying to find this enchantress, but he was unable because, as you know, Elena, enchantresses never use their true faces when they are with a man. He had no idea who she truly was or what she looked like. When it was clear that he would die without ever finding her again, he created the Brotherhood.

"The first members were chosen by Lucien himself. All men scorned or slighted by enchantresses or witches. They led the very first witch hunt back in the Age of Fire. They killed hundreds of women. Some were witches, but most were merely women whose only crime was denying a man his desires. It was a blanket excuse for men to murder women who didn't submit to them. It was a very dangerous time to be a female.

"When Lucien died, the mantle of leader was passed on to his son and second in command, a man by the name of Damen. Damen was as cruel as he was creative. He invented dozens of new ways to torture 'confessions' out of women. The witch hunts lasted a full solar cycle before the enchantresses finally stepped in and assassinated him. Hundreds, probably thousands, of women were killed at the hands of the Brotherhood. All because one man's ego was hurt and he decided violence was the best solution. Men always think violence will solve their problems." At this comment, Belladonna cut her eyes to Q.

"Not all men are like that." Elena piped in, coming to his defense, but she seemed to freeze as soon as the words left her mouth.

Quinn got the feeling that her mind had been transported back to that storage room at Amelia's. To the men who had attacked her. She didn't say another word and turned her attention back to the bowl of stew sitting before her on the table. "Not all men" was true enough, but you never really knew which men were actually wolves hiding among the faithful hounds.

"We shall see. Since the fall of Damen, the Brotherhood has had a steady stream of equally cruel and clever leaders. They went underground for an age and slowly started resurfacing during the Age of Blood. If you studied history in at Harbor Ridge, you might recall that was the last time we suffered through witch hunts. They were quite thorough, and their methods had evolved to become far more effective. The Brotherhood managed to drive witches to near extinction. Now, only a handful of us remain in the world. Despite the group being founded to avenge Lucien's wounded ego by an enchantress, the Brotherhood shifted its focus over the ages to mainly hunting witches. We are typically solitary creatures, which should keep us safer, but somehow the Brotherhood found a way to use it against us. We don't have allies and sisters-in-arms like the enchantresses, so we are easier targets.

"The prophecy that I mentioned before refers to the Brotherhood as the harbingers of the end of magic. It would seem, with the arrival of you two, that the end is in fact nigh, and it's up to you to save all of magic."

They sat in a stunned silence that seemed to drag on forever. Neither Q nor Elena said a single word. What could they possibly say? It seemed pretty clear to them both that this woman was out of her mind.

"I am not, and that's rude," Belladonna said, locking eyes with Q.

"Look, lady, I'm sorry, but this is all crazy. Some secret society has been hunting witches for ages, and now they're going to kill all the magic in the whole world, and it's up to us to stop it? That's just... well it's muxing lunacy."

"You don't have to believe me, boy, but you are meant to stop this, and if you don't, all the magical creatures in the world—witches, enchantresses, familiars, questing beasts, dragons, even the fae—will die. Like it or not, boy, you are at the center of this, and you must fight to preserve and protect us all."

Q looked to Elena, hoping she would back him up and tell this witch she'd lost her mind, but Elena seemed frozen in thought. Agon, still perched on a pillow by the fire, appeared to be locked in a staring contest with her, leading Q to believe they were communicating without words. Lyra paced back and forth along the hearthstones, flicking her tail, creating sparks in her agitated state.

Several moments passed and, just as Q was about to suggest they pack up their things and leave, Elena spoke in a quiet, raspy voice.

"Are you sure it's happening now?" Her question was directed at Belladonna, although her eyes hadn't broken their unfocused stare into Agon's.

"Yes, dear, I'm sorry, but I am quite sure," Belladonna replied in an equally quiet and surprisingly apologetic tone.

"What do we do?"

"Go north. Find what's destroying all the magic in our world. Stop it."

"Oh, just like that, huh? If it's really that simple, why can't you do it?" Q demanded.

"It's not that simple, and I can't do it because it has to be you. The first FlameBorn and StormBorn to exist in ages. The prophecy requires the combination of you both to combat the *turmio*." Quinn was startled to see the look of helplessness on her face. "I would do it for you if I could. This isn't my quest, it isn't my prophecy, and I can't change the outcome. Only you can, FlameBorn."

It was the first time she'd called him something other than "boy" and she said it without even a hint of disgust.

"Finish your stew and your tea, then rest. Castor and I will be outside if you need anything, but you both should get some sleep. Things are going to get much worse before they get better."

With that, Belladonna and her moonbird departed, closing the door behind them, leaving Q and Elena in the silence of the cottage.

Neither of them said a word, too lost in their respective thoughts and fears. Elena quietly drank the rest of her tea but left her bowl untouched before climbing into the bed and curling into the fetal position. Quinn finished his bowl and downed the last of his tea. He removed his travel cloak from the hook on the wall where Belladonna had placed it and laid down on the floor between the door and the bed.

Q didn't really know what to say, but he felt responsible for Elena and desperately wanted to comfort her. He wanted to tell her that everything would be ok, they'd figure out what to do, no one would get hurt, but he had no idea if any of that was true.

Instead, he said nothing. Agon moved from the pillow on the hearth to the bed with Elena, curling up within her human ball shape. Lyra stretched out alongside Quinn, placing herself between him and the door, as always. Within minutes, despite all their anxieties, they were all fast asleep.

30

ELENA

THEY LEFT AS THE sun was beginning to rise from behind the low mountains. Not many words were exchanged as Elena and Quinn followed Belladonna through the Mist. Castor the moonbird circled lazily overhead. Lyra trotted alongside Q to Elena's left and Agon claimed his regular perched around her neck, blending in seamlessly with her magic traveling cloak.

Time and distance seemed irrelevant in the Mist. Elena wasn't sure if they'd been walking for hours or moments but when they reached the edge of the Mist, the sun was nearly directly above them.

"This is where I leave you. Head to Nexton, and seek out a man named Fàidh. He's a bit of a nutter, but he's also a prophet of sorts and will hopefully be able to advise you on how to stop the *turmio*. Follow the path," she waved her hand to reveal a thin, winding path heading decidedly east through the trees, "and you should reach Nexton by nightfall. Don't stop. Don't delay. The *turmio* is coming quickly, and you only have a matter of days to stop it or we'll all be doomed."

"No pressure then," Q muttered under his breath.

Elena spoke up quickly before Belladonna had a chance to respond to Quinn. "Thank you for all of your help. We truly appreciate everything you've been able to do for us." Elena couldn't figure out what was going on there, but something about Q seemed to truly irk Belladonna.

"You're welcome, child. Just remember you can't bottle everything up. Feel your feelings, and let them go, or they will overwhelm you, and you may end up exploding again. Emotions aren't your enemy. Controlling them will not help you. Coexist with them. That's the only way to truly master your powers." Belladonna turned back to Q. "That goes for you too, boy. Figure your shyt out before you burn everything you love to ash."

With that, Belladonna bid Elena farewell, scratched Lyra on the head just behind her right ear, and disappeared into the Mist.

"I will never understand why that witch has to be so damn hostile towards me, but she's so nice to the two of you. Hells, she's nice to Agon even though he's a male, so it's not just a guy thing. She hates me, and I haven't even done anything to deserve it. Yet."

Quinn adjusted the pack on his shoulders and headed down the path Belladonna had unveiled for them. Elena decided to let it go. There was no point in trying to understand a woman they barely knew, or guess as to her motives and logic. For all they knew, she simply disliked all men. With all the witch hunts over the ages being led by magept men against any woman who offended them, it would be easy enough for Belladonna to write off the entire gender. Regardless, it didn't seem to matter now. They had a quest: Get to Nexton, find Fàidh, stop the *turmio*. Whatever that was...

31
BELLADONNA

THE MAGIC IN HER fog allowed her to sense when someone had crossed the barrier and was attempting to venture through. She felt the enchantresses enter her fog the instant they stepped foot over the border. Castor circled overhead, flying higher and wider with each cycle, waiting to catch a glimpse of them.

Despite how strongly the fog had affected Quinn during his first encounter with it, trained enchantresses like these investigators wouldn't be overly impaired by the magic, unfortunately. These women were well trained in defensive magic and would pass through her fog without succumbing to any of the dark thoughts, fears, or anxieties that her fog usually drew out of people. Which meant that Belladonna needed to be back at her cottage and waiting for them. She didn't want them to reach her home and find it empty. Too many ways that would end badly. Belladonna could sense the irritation radiating off these women in waves. The investigators were anxious. The guards with them were aggressive.

Well, this should be fun, she thought to herself, crossing from the far edge of the fog, through the grassy field toward her garden and cottage.

Castor let out a loud caw from the opposite side of the clearing; he'd spotted them.

They should be entering the clearing in a matter of minutes. Belladonna wasn't looking forward to this encounter. She wasn't worried about the enchantresses being a threat to her; she'd been alive for nearly a century, and these girls didn't have enough magic, even combined, to be a real threat to her. She was worried that she wouldn't be able to deter or delay them. She collected some herbs from her garden, then brought the bucket up from the depths of the well.

Belladonna chuckled to herself as she walked into her cottage. She lived in the middle of the Dark Woods surrounded by a fog of her own making, specifically designed to keep people out, and yet here she was hosting guests for the third day in a row.

The enchantresses knocked on her door just as she was taking the boiling water off the hook on the cooking spit over the fire. She added the water to her waiting tea kettle, preparing a special tea for her "guests" before opening the door with the flick of her wrist.

"Good afternoon, ladies. Would you like some tea? I just started a pot, herbs fresh from the garden." Belladonna hadn't bothered to turn to face the women. She knew they were there, and they were going to come in whether she invited them or not.

The investigators took seats at her table, but the guards stayed standing, blocking the exit.

They think they're going to trap me in my own home? Ridiculous, arrogant children.

"To what do I owe this delightful visit from Beatrice's finest?"

She never called their headmistress by her title. It irked the guards, and that always made Belladonna chuckle. She hadn't had a great deal of interactions with them, but she knew they didn't like her and it amused her to push their buttons and watch them scowl.

"We're looking for the source, or sources, of some immensely powerful magic. Most recently, we felt surges of power coming from within your fog in the last day or so. We've been tracking these surges over the last few weeks. Have you seen or heard anything that might indicate what is causing these surges?"

The enchantress who spoke held her stare, which was an impressive accomplishment in itself. Most didn't dare maintain eye contact with a witch. Too many superstitions about the curses and hexes a witch can cast through mere eye contact. It was all foolishness, of course. No self-respecting witch needed eye contact to curse or hex someone. Any witch worth her salt could simply use a piece of their intended victim's hair and the proper herbs.

Belladonna almost respected this young enchantress's boldness. Almost.

"I'm sorry to disappoint you, but I can't say that I've seen any unexplained surges." She poured the tea and handed a cup to each of the women before pouring one for herself and taking a seat in the chair closest to the fire. Belladonna made a point of pausing and sipping from her teacup, subconsciously encouraging the women to do the same.

"You are all welcome to stay the night here, before continuing your journey in the morning. Get a decent night's sleep, secure in the boundaries of my fog. I'm sure you've had quite a long and tiresome trip. I have fresh bread and a hearty stew over the fire." Her voice was casual, but she let a little of her magic seep into her words, gently swaying their decision.

"We don't have time for that." The gruff voice belonged to one of the women standing guard at the door. Her tea remained untouched, and she glared distrustfully at Belladonna.

"Well, we can't keep going like this, Seph. We need a proper meal and some real, *restful* sleep." These words, said with frustration and conviction, came from one of the younger, softer-looking enchantresses seated at the table. Belladonna noted that her teacup was nearly drained.

Splendid, she mused. The sleeping draught that she'd slip into their cups would be working soon. With any luck, these women would sleep for a full day, giving Elena and Quinn plenty of time to reach their destination.

"Maddy's right, Seph. You and Lilith might be trained to survive in such rough conditions, but we aren't, and we can't keep surviving on half rations of dried meat and cheese. We could all benefit from a solid night of sleep." The second brunette, whose teacup was equally empty, spoke with an air of authority. The guards were serving as security for the investigators, but they were not the ones in charge. The investigator twins were running this party, and the guards were forced to submit.

"As I said, I have plenty of food for you all. Unfortunately, I don't have a spare bed. I don't usually have guests, but you are welcome to make camp in my clearing. The grass is quite soft, and you'll have a lovely view of the stars. Feel free to make a large fire to keep yourselves warm. I have plenty of wood that has been gifted to me by the forest and I'm happy to share with you all. Then you can refill your water skins and start fresh in the morning." Belladonna thought she was being a fairly gracious hostess, despite her lifestyle as a self-imposed hermit and never actually inviting these women into her clearing to begin with.

"Thank you," Maddy said, placing her empty teacup back on the table. "We truly appreciate your hospitality. We don't want to impose, and we will be gone at first light."

"It's no trouble, dear," Belladonna cooed, filtering more magic into her words. "You are no imposition. It's been a while since I've hosted such powerful guests. You are welcome to stay as long as you need."

Laying it on a bit thick, eh? Castor's voice resonated in her head.

Hush, you. I need to make sure they stay. Those damned guards didn't drink my tea, so slipping verbal magic into their arrogant minds is the best I can do. We need to ensure that Elena and Quinn have enough time.

I'm sure your knock-out stew will keep them pliable for the next day or so. Castor knew all her tricks.

That's assuming the guards are willing to eat it.

She served them all heaping bowls of her "knock-out stew" and prayed to the Goddess that the magic would hold these hunters in a sleeping stasis long enough for Elena and Quinn to speak with Fàidh and find the answers they needed.

Belladonna knew it was very likely that Elena and Quinn wouldn't be able to stop the *turmio* from starting, but she was hopeful that they'd be able to end it before the damage it wrought became irreversible. She needed to give them as much time and space as she could to ensure their success.

32
ELENA

THEY SPENT THE REST of the afternoon walking in tense but surprisingly calm quiet, snacking whenever they got hungry, pausing only once to watch a family of deer playing in a creek for a few moments. Elena could almost convince herself that they were just two friends, enjoying a peaceful nature walk rather than the products of an ages-old prophecy sent to save the world from some unknown magical apocalypse: the dreaded—and rather vague—*turmio*.

The reality of their situation was just too much to think about. If she let herself dwell on the severity of the threat and all the unknowns, she would end up in a ball on the forest floor crying. That wouldn't help anyone.

However, bottling up her fears and anxiety wouldn't be helpful either.

So what should I do? How do I process my feelings and coexist with them without being overrun by them? Elena wondered.

"What do you think *turmio* means?" Q asked, interrupting her mental spiral.

He'd been leading them through the woods, following the path Belladonna had shown them, but as he spoke, he turned around to face her. He was so confident in the woods that he didn't miss a step as he walked backward along the path. Elena felt a twinge of jealousy at his comfort level amongst these trees, in a part of the forest he'd never been to. He was always so self-assured, especially in woodland environments. Elena never felt that level of confidence in her life.

It took her a moment to realize he had asked her a question and was still waiting for her response.

"I'm not really sure," she finally said, secretly hoping he'd trip over the tree root that rose up a few paces ahead of them on the path. "It kind of sounds like 'terminal' or 'turmoil.' Either way, pretty ominous. I'm curious, is it a person? An illness that only affects the magical? She made it sound like the magept wouldn't be harmed, since that is the goal of the Brotherhood, right? A world without magic? You'd still have magept people and animals in a magic-less world."

Without looking, he smoothly stepped over the root and continued his backward trek. "Maybe it's like a wildfire, but instead of burning trees and brush to ash, it only incinerates magical beings."

"It's always got to be fire with you, doesn't it?" Lyra chimed in.

"Hey, you use what you know." He shrugged and ducked under a tree limb that he couldn't possibly have seen. "Besides, it could happen. We have literally no idea."

"I hope it's not fire. That sounds painful," Elena said.

"Can't be more painful than being electrocuted," Quinn said with a wink.

"Well, we wouldn't have shocked you if you hadn't been sneaking up to steal from me!" She quickened her pace and reached up to push his chest, adding just the tiniest shock to her fingertips as she made contact, hoping to catch him off guard just a bit. Maybe this time he'd trip and wipe that smug look off his face.

No such luck.

"That's not fair," Q whined while dramatically rubbing his chest where she'd shocked him. "I can't lightly burn you."

"All right, you big baby, no more powers. I promise." Elena held up her hands to show she'd put the sparks away. "But you have to stop being so damned cocky!" He ducked under another branch without looking and she exclaimed, "How the hells are you doing that? I know you don't have eyes on the back of your head, and there's no way you can see these branches and roots, so how? How are you managing to miss them every time?"

"I'm warning him so he doesn't fall on his ass and look like an idiot," Lyra stated.

Elena froze mid-step. "You... you cheat! I thought you were really that clever! But you're not! You've just got a very canny partner warning you of all the hazards."

"There's no such thing as cheating. That's just a lie they taught you at that fancy school. Cheating doesn't exist." His smirk was infuriating and charming all at once. "Plus, how can I be cheating if we aren't competing? We're just a couple of kids, off to save the world from the *turmio*." He waved his arms in front of him as though the word turned him into some sort of spooky poltergeist that haunted the attics of Harbor Ridge.

Elena smiled to herself as they walked on, thinking how nice it was to have someone to talk, tease, and play with like this. She'd never really had a close friend before, besides Agon, and it was really quite lovely to have someone to be so comfortable with.

He winked at her again and tripped over a root. Lyra barked a laugh and Elena had to cover her face to hide her own snickers of amusement.

Q quickly bounced back up, dusted off his pants, and glared at Lyra, "What the hells? I thought you were helping me."

"I was, but then I thought this would be funnier," Lyra replied between fits of laughter. "I was right!"

33
QUINN

IT WAS JUST PAST dusk when they wandered into Nexton. The shops were closing up, shopkeepers heading home for the day. This was not the ideal time to start searching for some random "nutter," so Q suggested they find the town inn and get some sleep, then start fresh in the morning. Elena agreed, though she was visibly disappointed. Quinn was grateful that she saw the value in his logic. No one in this town would want to give aid to a couple of scruffy outsiders who'd literally just stumbled in from the depths of the Dark Woods. Better to get a decent night's sleep and wash up before asking around for Fàidh.

Q led the way down the main road through town until he found a small pub and inn, much like the one he'd called home for so long. As soon as they walked into the pub, he was hit with an undeniable wave of nostalgia. The sounds of the rambunctious crowd coupled with the smells from the kitchen and bar made him homesick. He wondered how Amelia was doing, running the whole inn and kitchen without him.

"Wha canna get ye, love?" a woman shouted at them from behind the bar. It took Quinn a moment to realize she was talking to them.

"A room, please. And some dinner would be wonderful," Elena piped up, gently pushing Q closer to the woman and taking an empty seat at the bar.

"We got rabbit soup tonight. A bowl for the both of ye, then? Would ye be wantin' one room or two?" The last question was said with the hint of a smirk and a wink toward Q.

Elena's face instantly turned bright red and Q felt himself heating up at the implications.

"Two rooms," he answered quickly and the woman barked in laughter.

"Whate'er ye like, dearie. I'm no judgin'." With that, she walked back to the kitchens, presumably to fetch their bowls of soup.

"I can't believe she... I mean to think or imply that you and I..." Elena was clearly frazzled, but Q understood her sentiment and nodded.

"I'm sure she's used to clandestine meetings in a place like this. And with how filthy we look, it's pretty obvious we've been sleeping together in the woods."

"We most certainly have not!" Thoroughly shocked by his words, Elena practically fell off her stool. Quinn caught her elbow before she landed on her ass in the middle of the bar.

"Oh shut it. That's not what I meant. I mean we have been *literally* sleeping together. In the woods. In Belladonna's cabin. Hells, we were practically cuddling back in my hut the first night we met." That felt like ages ago. When he took a moment to think about it, that truly had been only a few moons ago, at the beginning of the harvest season. They were barely into the frost season now. He felt like he'd only just met Elena, but also as if he'd known her his entire life.

The barmaid returned with their soup, two thick slices of bread, a mug of ale each, and a mischievous glint in her eyes.

"It seems we've a small hiccup with yer sleepin' arrangements. Only one room left in the house. Looks like ye'll be sleepin' together after all." There was that hideous attempt at a wink again as she set the single key on the bar between them. Mux.

"You take the bed. Lyra and I will be fine here on the floor. We've slept in much worse places before." Q immediately took his cloak off and started rolling it into a ball to serve as his pillow as he walked into their room. The fire was already burning, so he wasn't too worried about getting cold in the night.

"Don't be an idiot. The bed is big enough for both of us, and you made a good point. We have been sleeping together for a while now." He could tell Elena wasn't entirely confident in her proclamation.

"Really, El, we'll be fine on the floor. Besides, you need your beauty sleep."

"My what? Are you seriously implying that you think you are prettier than me and therefore do *not* need beauty rest? Because I will tell you right now, Quinn Whatever-your-last-name-is, you aren't looking as fresh and fanciful as you might think."

Banter. He liked when they bantered. It cut through any potential awkwardness of being forced to sleep in this small room together and put them back on level footing.

"Listen here, princess, you've never had to rough it, and I can promise you would wake up grouchy and miserable, and we would all," he gestured to Lyra and Agon then, "suffer for your arrogance."

"Oh-ho, *my* arrogance is the problem, is it? Look who's talking!" At this, she took a roll of bandages from one of her many hidden cloak pockets and hurled it at his face. Quinn caught it with ease, leaving her with a look of frustrated disbelief.

"Enough of this nonsense. You're both ridiculous and arrogant. Happy? It has been a long day and I'm tired. Agon, would you like to join me on the bed? These two idiots can bicker all night." Lyra hopped onto the bed and curled into a ball right in the middle. Without a word, Agon leapt from

Elena's shoulders, landed gently on the bed, padded over to Lyra, and curled up beside her. Both familiars glared at their human counterparts before lowering their heads to rest on their respective tails.

"Well, there's something I thought I'd never see. I didn't know Lyra knew how to cuddle," Q scoffed. Lyra had so often only expressed annoyance and disdain for Elena and Agon. She'd grown attached to them, just as he had, and it was clear that those two would never willingly part from each other for long. Which was just fine with Q, because he felt the same way about Elena.

"This has been a truly weird day. But if they can get along and sleep in the bed together, there's no reason we can't do the same," Elena said as she removed her cloak and hung it on a hook beside the hearth. "We have no idea what tomorrow will bring. We should both get the best sleep we possibly can."

Quinn knew she made a good point, but he wasn't sure just how restful a night in bed with her would actually be. Elena didn't wait for his answer, however, before kicking off her travel boots, and crawling into the far side of the bed, directly under a small square window. The sun had truly set now, and the window offered a peaceful view of the night sky and the moon in all her glory. Well, not "all her glory" as she was currently just a tiny sliver of a crescent in a sea of black. She'd be completely invisible in a couple of days. Amelia always told him that the Black Moon was a time for rebirth and new beginnings.

He'd met Elena on the night of a Black Moon. She had definitely been the start of a new beginning for him.

Stop being such an ass and get in the bed. Idiot. Lyra's voice in Q's head was a bit of a shock, knocking him back into the present.

Mux it, he thought, as he removed his boots and took the remaining side of the bed, closest to the door, making sure to keep the familiars as a buffer between himself and Elena.

It was the most restful sleep Quinn had ever experienced.

34

ELENA

ELENA WOKE WITH THE warmth of the sun on her face and the warmth of Lyra and Agon pressed against her spine. Q was there too, she could feel the bed weighed down on his side, although she couldn't feel his body touching her own. She had slept the most peaceful and dreamless sleep she'd ever experienced. It was bizarre. Like coming home, except her home had never given her this sense of calm. Elena decided not to look into this thought too much; no need to ruin a good thing by overthinking it.

Slowly, and as quietly as she possibly could, Elena slipped out of the bed. Agon awoke within seconds of her and was upright, gently stretching his lithe body on the bed next to Lyra before hopping down.

Where do you think you're going? Agon was in her head. He opted for silent communication either in consideration for their still-sleeping roommates or because he thought she was trying to sneak out, and he didn't want to disrupt her plans until he knew what she was up to.

I'm going to head back down to the kitchen for some breakfast and see if anyone can help us to find Fàidh. You can come if you'd like. Or stay here with your new best friend. Elena smirked at Agon. Regardless of his previous words and actions, she could see that he was thoroughly attached to Lyra and even Q. They were becoming more like family than mere travel companions.

Agon scoffed at her but said nothing. He simply waited for her to put on her shoes, then climbed onto his perch, as per usual.

They silently crept out of the room and made their way down the stairs to the now empty dining hall. Apparently, this inn didn't have the same popular breakfast crowd that frequented Amelia's.

There was a different woman behind the bar this morning, older with her stark white hair braided down her back and a stained white apron wrapped around her comfortable waist.

"Good mornin', lass. We got porridge an' goat cheese ifin yer hungry. Ma boy went to fetch eggs from the market a moment ago, ifin yer willin' te wait." She spoke with the easy cadence of a woman in charge. This was her domain. Either she owned the inn, or she was married to the person who did.

"Porridge would be lovely." Elena took a seat at the bar, directly in front of the woman, despite there being plenty of empty tables. "I was actually hoping you could help me find someone. My friend and I arrived late last night and we are looking for a man called Fàidh. Do you know him? Perhaps you could point us in the direction of his home or place of business?"

The woman gave Elena an odd look.

"Lass, I kin e'eryone in this gods forsaken town, and I ne'er haird of a Fed. Ye sure yer in the right place?"

Elena's heart sank. How could he not be here? Why would Belladonna send them here if the prophet wasn't?

Before Elena could respond, a young boy ran through the dining hall carrying a very full, and heavy, basket of eggs.

"Careful with those, lad. Ye break them an' ye'll be workin' it off in the mule stalls fer a moon." Though her words carried a threat, it was clear by her tone and her smirk that it was an empty one. "Oy, Iain, ye haird of a feller named Fed down at the market?"

Iain, a freckled-face boy who looked to be around ten, gingerly set the basket of eggs down on the counter behind the bar and turned, eyeing Agon curiously. "Fed?"

"Fàidh, actually," Elena interjected. "He's meant to be an older man. Bit isolated and a little... odd."

"Ye mean tha ol' daft fool who lives in a hut near the creek?"

The woman swatted Iain in the back of the head with a bar towel. "Iain! Ye dinna speak like tha. Hermit or no, ye dinna speak o' people in sucha way. Ye hear me, *balach*?"

"Yes, Ma. I jus meant he's strange, is'all. Always talkin' in riddles. No one kins wha he's rattlin' on about." Iain's cheeks had turned bright pink.

The woman turned back to Elena, "Yer lookin' fer the hermit? Why would ye wanna do a daft thin' like tha?"

"I've been told he might be able to help me and my friend on our journey," Elena replied before turning to Iain. "Would you be able to point me in the direction of his hut? I desperately need to find him."

Iain glanced from Elena to his mother, who nodded subtly before Iain agreed to take Elena and Quinn to find the hermit's hut.

"Ye point 'em to the path down to the creek, then ye come straight back. I dinna want ye anywhere near tha man, *balach*. His mind's not all there."

Elena thanked them both, inhaled the last of her porridge, grabbed a couple of fresh biscuits, and raced back up the stairs to wake Quinn so they could be on their way. Between their hike through the woods and their awkward, albeit quite restful, night in the inn, they'd lost a full day and night, which meant they only had a couple of days left until the *turmio* occurred. Happened? Began? She didn't really know, but she was cautiously optimistic that their meeting with Fàidh would offer some clarity on the subject.

It had taken more time than she liked to wake Q and explain everything she'd learned from her conversation with the barkeep and her son. It was during this retelling that Elena realized she'd never gotten the woman's name. She felt rude now, for having not asked, but also felt like it would be far more insulting to ask the woman after having had such a lengthy conversation with her that morning.

Regardless, Iain was waiting for them outside the inn to escort them to the creek before leaving them to their fates with Fàidh. The path that Iain spoke of, the one that would lead them to the man's hut, wasn't exactly a path at all. Elena would have described it as more of a deer trail, based on what little experience she had with nature trails since leaving Harbor Ridge.

Iain had led Elena and Quinn along the main road through town, and down a trail that passed through a grassy meadow on the outskirts of town. He pointed out the path for them to follow and told them to travel north along the creek. Iain explained that the hermit's hut was upstream a bit, bid them good luck, and quickly turned back and ran home to the inn.

"Well, that's comforting. He wouldn't even take us to the creek. Are you sure this crazy hermit is the guy we're supposed to talk to? This seems like a great set-up to kill us and steal all of our shyt." Q, ever the optimist, watched the boy disappear down the dusty road.

"Oh shut it. At least I found some useful information. While you were sleeping in like a baby, I might add." Elena turned back to the path and headed into the tall grass of the meadow. "Come on, then! We don't have all day."

"Hey, remember when you were all meek and shy and polite? I miss those days..." Quinn was always more comfortable wandering through nature than he was in cities. He jumped off the path, disappeared in the grass, and reappeared a few paces ahead of her, back on the path with Lyra at his side.

"Show off," Agon mumbled from his perch.

The path to the creek was quick. The trip upstream, in search of a supposed lunatic in a grass hut, took considerably longer than Elena would have liked. The sun was shining brightly overhead when they finally spotted a clearing with a hut at the water's edge.

Looking at the place, Elena wasn't sure "hut" was the right word. The grass of the meadow was nearly shoulder height. It seemed to Elena that Fàidh had taken a sickle to a small section of grass, cropped it, then built a circular structure by curving the tall grass in on itself and lashing the top together with a braided rope of cut grass. Elena had read about the use of similar housing in nomadic tribes during one of her history lessons. Decent temporary housing, but not meant to be a permanent homestead.

Elena noticed a man sitting on the grass outside the hut, feet dangling in the slow-moving water, staring directly at the sun.

Fàidh was, in fact, absolutely insane. Iain's mother had been right. He muttered a constant stream of nonsensical words under his breath.

And he was completely naked.

Gods, she needed to stop being so damned hopeful.

35
QUINN

NAKED. OF COURSE, HE was muxing naked. Because when you go searching for a batshyt crazy prophet in the middle of muxing nowhere, why on The Goddess' green planet would that man be wearing a single stitch of clothing?

"Oh, my... um, excuse me, sir? Are you Fàidh, by chance?" Elena asked, looking straight up, almost as though she were addressing the sky, rather than the filthy, exposed man before them.

"Giggle sputtle luck sack."

"Oh, gods. What the hells are we supposed to do with that shyt? I thought Belladonna said he could help us." Quinn looked around, hoping that perhaps they had found the wrong crazy man in a hut by the side of a creek near a town no one had ever heard of.

"Bell don caw," the man started quietly chanting. "Bell don caw bell don caw bell don caw"

"Wait, what is he saying?" Elena turned back to the man and knelt beside him.

"Bell don caw," he said again, only this time the final word sounded more like a cry from a crow than an actual word.

"He's a lunatic. That's been well established. You honestly expect to decipher anything useful from his nonsense?" Quinn was annoyed. He thought this man they'd been sent to find would be able to offer some help. Some insight. Some clue as to what they were dealing with, why they had to be the ones to handle it, and maybe how they were meant to fix it all.

"No, listen to him. What is he saying? 'Bell don caw.' I think he means Belladonna." The instant the word left her mouth, Fàidh turned to face her, nodding violently. "Belladonna? Do you know Belladonna?"

He continued his vicious head bouncing, matted hair flopping wildly around his face, to the point that Q worried he might be having some kind of fit or trying to shake his head off his neck.

"You do! Thank the gods! Are you Fàidh? Can you help us?" Elena seemed so excited that the man was communicating with her that she didn't even appear to be bothered by his state of undress anymore. Quinn, however, was not over it.

He stepped forward, positioning himself between Elena and the naked crazy man, then dug into his bag and threw a rough blanket over the man's lap.

Fàidh looked down, staring at the blanket with complete confusion. It was obvious that he either didn't realize or didn't care that he was naked in front of strangers. Q imagined that this was his natural state. Exposed and unashamed. *Likely because he's completely out of his mind*, he thought to himself. Lyra caught his eye and nodded before maneuvering herself to block any potential physical contact Fàidh might have with Elena.

Quinn had no interest in trying to bond with the old fool. They didn't have all day. After all, they were being chased by Elena's mother's overly-aggressive, magic-hunting mercenaries.

"What can you tell us about the *turmio*?" Q tried demanding answers from the old man, but he wasn't listening. He wasn't chanting anymore or nodding his head like a broken doll. No, the crazy, homeless, naked man was shrieking like a banshee from one of those fairy tales Amelia used to read to Q when he was a child.

Fàidh jumped up and ran into his little grass hut, still making that otherworldly noise. Q could feel the heat rising in his chest again, felt the warmth of the fire licking the tips of his fingers. Lyra was tense and alert at his feet. Glancing at Elena, he could see the spark of her blue power as it flickered between her fingertips. Agon remained on Elena's shoulders, but he was fully alert as well, hair standing on end with blue sparks pulsating down his spine.

Q had a vague thought that maybe all of their flame and scorching powers were not ideal for a large, dry, grassy field, but he wasn't putting his fire away until they were sure Fàidh wasn't going to try and kill them all.

As quickly as his screams began, they stopped. The sudden silence was deafening, leaving Elena and Quinn frozen in place.

"What do you think he's doing in there?" Elena whispered.

"Getting dressed, I hope," Lyra quipped.

"I just hope he doesn't come out armed. I'd feel guilty if I murdered a crazy man. Even if it is self-defense." Quinn leaned forward, trying to hear anything that might indicate the man had weapons in his hut.

Without a word, Agon jumped down from Elena's shoulders and slunk through the grass, mostly invisible, toward the hut.

"Agon!" Elena hissed, "Get back here! It isn't safe!"

Agon, however, did not heed her command and continued his silent trek across the short distance to the hut. Low to the ground and glowing ever so slightly, Agon slipped inside and disappeared into the darkness.

No one moved, but Quinn could tell that Elena was communicating with Agon. Time stood still as they waited to see what Fàidh was going to do next. Without a word, Elena visibly relaxed, quelling her lightning and motioning for Q to do the same.

"Hells no! Not until I know what exactly is going on here."

"It's ok, Q. He explained everything to Agon. Well, he didn't, as he can't actually speak in coherent sentences. An unfortunate side effect of his gift. But he has someone with him who can explain everything to us. Just put away your flames, and they will come back outside."

"What are you talking about? Why the hells would I put out the best defense system we have right now? Because that naked lunatic has a friend? Not muxing likely."

Elena paused for a moment, before asking, "Would you be more comfortable if he were dressed?"

"Not by much, but it wouldn't hurt."

After clearly relaying that message to Agon and getting some sort of affirmation in response, Elena locked Quinn with a hard stare until he released his hold on the fire inside and allowed it to fizzle out.

Inwardly, Q was quite proud of himself and his ability to control his fire with such ease. He had no idea how he'd managed that but hoped it wasn't a one-time thing.

He nodded to Elena and followed her over to the front of the hut, taking a seat beside her in the grass while they waited for Fàidh to get some damn clothes on.

36
ELENA

D ESPITE HER OUTWARD APPEARANCE, Elena was quite nervous about actually speaking with this man. He was supposed to have all the answers. What if she didn't like his answers? Or worse, what if he didn't know anything at all? Or he did know things, but his brain was too scattered to tell them anything useful? There was so much riding on their encounter with him, she felt like her entire world hinged on his answers.

Agon had assured her that Fàidh's "companion" would be able to translate his gibberish and help them interpret his responses. Whatever that might be.

Gods, please, help us. We have no idea what we're doing or what we're even up against. Please, please, we need your guidance. Elena wasn't much for prayer; the last few moons had taught her that the gods were likely not listening, and if they were, they didn't give a damn, but desperate times being what they were, she didn't see the harm in trying one last time.

Agon came bounding out of the hut followed closely by a now-dressed Fàidh, with a small yellow songbird on his shoulder. Fàidh shuffled over to them, wearing a torn and tattered shirt that draped down to his knees, trailing casually behind Agon like he didn't have a care in the world. Looking at him now, it was as though his outburst only moments ago had never even happened.

"Fàidh, are you ready to speak with us now?" Elena posed the question in the softest, most non-confrontational voice she could muster. Inside she might be wound tight, but she knew that wasn't Fàidh's fault, and aggressively coming at him would only make things harder for them.

"Bell don caw. Trible hunger mellow mark. Stick thick hick bick. Weldon hale. Fla wa boom nocker skittle mugher flot."

"What in the name of the Goddess are we supposed to do with that shyt?" Q exclaimed through gritted teeth.

His barely contained irritation, bordering on rage, was evident in the flames warming his skin, just beneath the surface. Elena was impressed. She didn't know how he managed it, but the self-control he was displayed in containing his powers when he was clearly on a knife's edge was truly something to behold.

"Pukmle figs agus jart flurry wham. Zealty kilty magno. Bugget whail yeti manster billdy drawn muffer."

Just as Elena opened her mouth to ask Fàidh to explain, the songbird hopped down from his shoulder to his knee and began to sing.

"Dragon's hoard treasure, a truth we all know,
Adventurers creep into the mouth of the beast,
Questing for fame, fortune, or stories to crow,
Within their teeth lays a yawning mouth,
A chasm of secrets and score below,
Stories told and histories revealed,
Beware of the words that seem hollow,
When venturing into the belly of the beast
Allies wear the mask of foe
Three storms will collide, but one must fall
For only two can withstand the impending turmio. *"*

"Well that was lovely, but what does it mean?" Lyra didn't bother trying to hide her annoyance.

"I think the beginning is clear enough," Agon replied. "First, we need to head east, to the mountains. Some of the villagers in Andover would call them the Dragon's Teeth. That must be what the first line of the song is talking about."

The songbird flew off, back into the hut, leaving Fàidh mumbling incoherently under his breath. He wasn't going to be any more help. Elena just hoped his words, and the songbird's lyrical translation would make more sense soon. She considered that this song would be like following a treasure map made by pirates in storybooks. The map and its landmarks only made sense the farther you went.

"Agon is right," Q said confidently. "Those mountains aren't too far from here, a day's hike at most, and they definitely fit the description well enough. It's better than sitting around on our asses listening to the ramblings of that man for another minute." He was already standing up and dusting the grass from his pants as he spoke. "The sooner we get going, the better. We should head back to town and resupply. Fresh food. We can refill our waterskins in the river, upstream from this mess." He gestured vaguely around them. "And be on the road before midday. We can make camp safely in the meadow tonight and with any luck, we'll be in the 'mouth of the beast' by midday tomorrow."

After walking a few dozen paces upstream from Fàidh's camp, they refilled their waterskins and quickly set back on the path to town. Elena went back to their room at the inn with Agon to make sure they hadn't left anything behind while Quinn and Lyra haggled with merchants for the best prices on their supplies. When they met back up at the edge of town, the sun was nearly directly overhead. Quinn distributed the supplies as evenly as possible between the many pockets of Elena's cloak, before forcibly placing a heavy metal item into her hands. Elena glanced down to see a small sheathed dagger in her palms.

"What in the world are you expecting me to do with this?" Elena wasn't comfortable being armed; nor did she feel it was necessary. She had already proven she was capable of defending herself. "You know I can easily zap someone if I need to protect myself or anyone else."

"Yeah, you can, but what happens if you deplete that energy? Do you even know? Your powers aren't endless. This is just in case you need a little backup and for some unforeseeable reason, I'm not there." His tone was conversational, but Elena could feel the guilt and possibly regret in his words. It was almost like he felt responsible for what happened—or rather almost happened—to her back in Andover.

Elena tucked the knife into her belt, then turned and took Quinn's hands in her own.

"Thank you. I will be safe. What happened before was not your fault. You couldn't have known what they were going to do, and I don't blame you or hold you responsible for their behavior. Nor do I blame you for what became of them. While I feel terrible that I took their lives, they were willing to take what they wanted from me, and what happened was a direct result of their actions." Q avoided her eyes while she spoke, so she dropped his hands and put her hands on his cheeks, forcing his eyes to look into hers. "I do not blame you."

Elena couldn't be sure if tears were forming in his eyes, because she couldn't see past the tears in her own. Q pulled her into a tight, warm hug, nearly knocking Agon off her shoulders, before resting his chin on the top of her head.

"I've never felt this connected to another human. Amelia comes close, but I've never felt responsible *for* her. I feel like it's my job to keep you safe. I have ever since you attacked me in the woods that day."

Elena pushed back at these words, "Hey, you attacked me first!"

Quinn smiled down at her and pulled her back into his hug.

"Yes, fine. The point is, I feel it, down deep in my chest. The same spot that burns right before the fire comes through me. I'm supposed to keep you safe. I don't know why I feel that way or where it came from, but I can't shake it, and I can't help feeling like I failed you."

He spoke into her hair, arms wrapped securely, but gently, around her shoulders with her cheek pressed against his chest. She could hear his heartbeat, strong and unwavering. Elena couldn't help but compare the steady beat of his heart to the solid, steady sense of security and safety she felt when he was with her. With one final squeeze, he released her and turned to grab his pack off the ground.

"We should get moving. We've got a long trip ahead of us."

37

BEATRICE

"**H**AVE WE RECEIVED ANY updates from the investigators searching for the source of these power surges?"

Madame LaBelle was on edge. It had been two days since their last communication, in which Lilith had stated that they were entering the witch's boundary. She was certain that whatever was delaying her communications with the unit was entirely that damned witch's doing.

Madame LaBelle had had exactly one direct interaction with the witch since becoming Headmistress. In an attempt to make an alliance, she had ventured into the witch's clearing with a plan of peace and an allegiance that would be mutually beneficial. That damned woman rejected all of the headmistress' offers and suggestions, claiming she didn't need or want any ties to her or the magical community at large.

It was in that moment, many cycles ago, Madame LaBelle had decided she would have to find another way to secure her power and authority in Waverly. Shortly thereafter, she had begun to cultivate alliances and "friendships" with the King's court which ultimately led her to the King and all the influence he provided her through their relationship.

It was so long ago, it was hard for her to remember exactly how she'd first been introduced to the King himself, but cultivating that relationship and permitting that ruddy-faced buffoon access to her body had gained her many privileges. Not to mention all the power she wielded as a result of that connection. She had more power and authority in the entire country of Waverly than any headmistress, or any woman for that matter, that had come before her.

"No news, Headmistress."

"Damn," she muttered to herself before turning to the guard. "Notify me the instant we get any communication. I don't care if it's the middle of the night. Wake me up."

"Yes, Headmistress." With a quick bow, the guard turned and exited her office quickly, gently closing the door behind her.

"Damn that witch," she murmured mostly to herself while stroking Zied's mane.

"We should have had her removed cycles ago," he purred into her touch.

"We tried that before. She dug in, planted muxing roots, and it didn't seem worthwhile to start a war with her. She agreed to stay in her woods, and we agreed to not pick a fight with her."

"Well then, she didn't break her agreement, so what can we do?"

"Exactly," Madame LaBelle seethed.

This was the problem with being diplomatic. She had to step lightly or open herself up to the potential for war. If they were facing the *turmio*, as she suspected they were, she didn't have the resources to spare.

As irritated as she was to admit it, Madame LaBelle knew the best option she had right now was to wait and give the investigators more time to deal with that witch.

Who knew, maybe she would actually be helpful this time. That thought made her chuckle. *Belladonna? Helpful? Not bloody likely.*

38
QUINN

T HE SUN WAS SETTING behind them when Quinn decided it was time to stop for the night. He sent Lyra
ahead, off the trail, to find a decent spot for them to make
camp. Lyra knew the requirements for a good overnight place
to rest their heads: sheltered from the elements, far enough
off the road that other travelers wouldn't notice them, ideally
close to a source of fresh, clean water. With their waterskins
still mostly full from their morning by the stream, the last one
was more of a personal preference than an actual requirement.
Q always preferred to make camp near water because it would
mean they could refill again and wouldn't have to waste their
stores.

Q turned back to Elena, walking a few paces behind him.
She looked tired. No. Tired didn't cover it. She looked completely drained. Despite their amazingly restful night's sleep
last night. *Gods, was that really just last night?* Elena looked
dead on her feet. Quinn felt exhausted as well, but he was so

wired that he wasn't sure he'd be able to get any sleep. Especially in the shadow of such formidable-looking mountains.

"I'll take first watch. You look like you're about to pass out just standing there. And before you start arguing, don't. I'm wide awake, and I couldn't sleep now if I tried."

Elena grumbled something about him being a bossy know-it-all, but she didn't fight him on it.

Q led them off the well-worn path to the spot Lyra had found for them. A semi-circle of tall stones that looked to be the result of a rockslide off the mountain, with its mouth a handful of paces from the river that came down from the snowy peaks. The same river they had been by this morning, where they had learned almost nothing new and were visually assaulted by that nonsensical naked man and his singing bird.

Q shook his head in an attempt to knock the image from his memory.

I'm never gonna be able to forget that, he thought to himself with a shiver.

"Oh, this is perfect, Lyra. Thank you for finding this space for us tonight." Elena scratched Lyra between her ears then removed her cloak and laid it out inside their temporary home. "I'll fetch some water for dinner. Q, would you and Lyra get the fire started and pull out some vegetables from my cloak? Vegetable stew will keep us fortified for our journey ahead. I'll add a few extra herbs to boost our energy and give us added protection. I might not have been the best herbology student, but I know enough to make a tasty protection stew."

Quinn stared after her for a moment as she pulled a tin pail from a pocket in her cloak and then headed down to the water's edge with Agon hopping along behind her. He still couldn't fathom how that damn cloak worked. It just wasn't logical.

Neither is shooting fire from your fingertips, but here we are, he heard Lyra's snide voice in his head.

"Mux off. Go see if you can find any wood, and if not, start collecting as much dry grass as you can. I don't want to make a huge smoke signal, but we will need a fire to make her fancy magic stew."

Lyra didn't respond, but simply slipped off to find the wood he asked for, and Q got to work making a firebreak and clearing out a safe space for their cooking pit.

By the time the sun had fully set they had a small but warm and secure camp for the night. Lyra had been able to find just enough wood to make a decent cooking fire, but Q was confident it wouldn't last the night. Still, it served its purpose. Elena made her magic stew—vegetables for sustenance, wild rosemary and fennel for protection—then she and Q ate their fill. Agon and Lyra opted out of meals, since they didn't actually *need* food, and Elena promptly fell asleep, tightly wrapped in her cloak against the frosty chill of the night.

Agon didn't go with her, which surprised Q a little. Sure, technically familiars didn't need sleep either, but he couldn't think of a time when Agon wasn't right by Elena's side, awake or asleep. Quinn was about to question him about it when Lyra spoke up.

"You should get some sleep too. No, don't argue. We," she shared a pointed look with Agon, "have already discussed this, and we will be taking first watch, and second watch, and most likely any other watches from now on."

"That's comple—" Quinn started, but she cut him off with a glare and a sharp snap of her jaws. He knew she'd never actually bite him, or anyone for that matter. Why bite someone when you can flick your tail and set them on fire? That was just her way of saying the conversation was over, and he wasn't going to change her mind.

It was kind of sweet, honestly. Seeing the two of them work as a team. Annoying, but sweet.

"Fine. But wake me at the first sign of any trouble. Assuming there's no trouble, we need to get moving at first light."

Agon made a noise that sounded like a hiss and a bark rolled into one. Quinn took that as confirmation with a dash of condescension, possibly the magic weasel's version of a scoff. Regardless, Q went into their little shelter for the night. Unfortunately, sleep didn't come as easily for him as it had for

Elena. He tossed and turned for a while, but when he did finally drift off to sleep, it was a peaceful, dreamless sleep.

The morning was uneventful, and Quinn thanked the gods for that. They had a quick breakfast of bread and cheese, refilled their water skins once more, and headed back to the main trail and into the mountains. The Dragon's Teeth.

Quinn had always heard stories about these mountains: people going into the mountains and never being heard from again, strange noises being heard from travelers who dared to venture too close but never actually attempted to cross the mountains themselves, and stories of mythical monsters living in the caves within the Teeth. He wasn't sure he believed any of the tales, but seeing the mountains rising so forebodingly before him and beginning their ascent into them, he understood why people were so apprehensive.

The mountains themselves faded from a dark gray at the base of the mountains to a bright white at each peak. Quinn assumed they were all topped with snow but he had no intention of finding out. The road that led to the base of the Dragon's Teeth quickly devolved into a rocky, rough path through the mountain range. Q had no idea how traders made it through those mountains. Soon they were climbing rough, jagged terrain without any sense of direction other than to keep putting one foot in front of the other, making their way farther into the depths of the Teeth.

They tried talking at the start of the day, but by midday, they were both too focused on finding good footing and continuing onward without falling or getting lost, that conversation came to a halt.

When the sun had risen directly above them, Elena and Quinn took shelter in the shade of a cliff to rest and have a small lunch. Agon and Lyra, in their new capacity as best buddies, decided to scout ahead a bit while Q and Elena took a moment to catch their breath and refuel.

"We have to be getting close, right?" Elena asked, pink-faced and slightly out of breath, leaning her back against the cool stone of the mountain.

"Gods, I hope so. Although we don't really know where we're going, so your guess is as good as mine," Quinn moaned as he slid down to the ground beside where she stood.

"We're supposed to be looking for the *'mouth within the teeth'*," she replied, as if that would somehow clarify their situation. Elena sat down and handed him a small loaf of bread from one of her pockets.

"What the hells does that even mean? A mouth inside teeth? I mean, if it's literal, that is not something I want to find," Q quipped. He took a bite of his bread and mockingly growled at her.

"It's a prophecy, you child. Of course, it's not literal," she said as she rolled her eyes at him. Then she froze. "Oh, Gods! What if it is literal?! Are we being sent off to fight some freakishly horrifying, double-mouthed beast? I'm not trained for that! I never took any combat classes at Harbor Ridge. My mother wouldn't allow it. She said, 'No daughter of mine will learn to fight with the lower levels and weaklings.' Gods, we'll be killed!"

She was spiraling, and Quinn felt instantly guilty. He didn't mean to scare her; he was just being an ass.

"I'm sure it's not literal, but even if it is you've already proven you can handle yourself. When push comes to shove, I have no doubt that you'll take down anyone who tries to hurt you. You're a kick-ass enchantress! The first of your kind in over a century, StormBorn. No one with half a brain would mess with you." He bumped her with his shoulder, then offered her his waterskin. "Take a deep breath. Prophecies are never that straightforward, anyway, right? It's probably just a hole in the ground or something. We are already in a mouth of sorts, aren't we? Dragon's Teeth? Teeth are typically found inside mouths."

Elena accepted his water and took a small sip. "So... you think we should be looking for a hole? Or maybe a cave?"

"Maybe. Makes more sense than looking for a double-mouthed demon to slay." He nudged her again, smiling to ensure that she understood he was joking again.

"I think you're right," Lyra said, coming around the bend she and Agon had disappeared behind moments before.

"I never get tired of hearing you say that," Quinn said smugly.

"Damn, I owe you a biscuit." Agon slunk out from underneath Lyra and headed straight for Elena who was holding out a piece of cheese for him.

"I told you," Lyra replied with a smug tone of her own.

"What's that about?" Elena asked.

"Lyra bet me a biscuit that she could get Quinn to be an arrogant ass by only saying four words to him." A small blue bolt of lightning rippled down Agon's spine. Q couldn't decide if that was a sign of amusement or irritation. He scooted over a bit, giving Agon some space, just in case.

"Wait, what?" Q asked, after registering what Agon had just said. "Come on now! I'm not the only cocky one in this group. If anything, Lyra is more arrogant than me!"

Q was surprised that the laughter that followed his proclamation didn't cause an avalanche. Elena looked like she was going to choke on her last bite of bread, Agon was literally rolling on the ground laughing, and Lyra was sitting proudly beside him chuckling and thoroughly enjoying her victory.

"Fine. Whatever. Mux all of you." Quinn dug a biscuit out of his pack and chucked it at Lyra. Much to his annoyance, she jumped and caught it cleanly.

"So, wait," Elena started once she'd calmed down enough to speak coherently, "does that mean Q was actually right about something? Or were you just messing with him?"

"Oh, right, that," Lyra stood up and stretched, licking her muzzle clean of the last few crumbs from her victory biscuit. "He is actually right. Or he could be. Agon and I found a cave not too far ahead of us that might be exactly what the prophecy mentioned. Your 'mouth within the teeth' nonsense. It even has a nasty smell. Just like a dragon's breath, I imagine."

"It's worth looking into. We are in a bit of a time crunch, so we should move quickly. Hopefully whatever we're looking for to cure or stop this *turmio* will be right at the entrance and we can get back to living normal, relatively peaceful lives back in Andover." The optimism in Elena's tone was impressive.

Quinn had a sinking feeling that whatever was waiting for them in that cave wouldn't be so easy to find. He was also pretty confident that "normal" was over for them.

39

ELENA

T HE WORD "CAVE" WASN'T exactly an accurate description of the foreboding opening that greeted them as they rounded the bend in the path through the Dragon's Teeth. It looked more like an entrance to the Pit. The entrance to the cave was fringed in stalactites, eerily giving off the appearance of a yawning mouth. Beyond the faux-teeth was pure darkness. It was as if the light was incapable of breaching the threshold.

"This isn't a cave," Quinn hissed. "This is the muxing gateway to hells."

Elena couldn't help but agree with him, but what were they going to do? Ignore the prophecy? Leave the entire world to its fate because their quest had gotten too intense?

"We need to go in there. Whatever is going on, there's something in this cave that we're meant to see or use to stop the *turmio.* The sooner we go in, the sooner we get to go home, right?" Elena was trying to be optimistic, but she couldn't help feeling like this cave would be the end of them.

"I hope to the gods you're right. I'll go first and light the way. Keep some of that lightning ready to go, in case we meet some unsavory characters in there." Quinn stood up from the boulder they'd been huddled behind, Lyra quick on his heels.

"Unsavory characters? Really?" Agon prodded, the sarcastic tone in his voice almost hid his apprehension.

"Yes. That's what I said. And *you* can owe *me* a biscuit when it turns out I'm right. Again."

"Oh dear Mother, if you all keep gambling with our food, we'll be starving by dusk." Elena cut them off before their banter could evolve into bickering. Agon slipped down from her shoulders and joined Lyra at the head of their little troupe. Between his lightning spine and her fiery tail, the chasm they stepped into was no longer pitch black. Elena thought she might be able to see a few paces ahead of them, but that was it.

Upon entering the cave, it felt as though the world behind them vanished. They were plunged into near-total darkness and pure silence. The only sound Elena could hear was that of her heartbeat pounding in her ears. She glanced back over her shoulder to make sure they could leave the same way they'd come in, but the entrance was gone. The opening to the cave had been replaced by a solid stone wall. It was as if the entrance had never existed.

"No. No, no, no!" Elena whispered in a panicked rush as she ran her hands across the entirety of the wall, searching for a seam or a latch. Something, anything, to reopen the way out and provide an escape route she now desperately needed. "We're trapped. How did this happen? What are we going to do?"

"The only thing we can do," Q said, placing a steady hand on her shaking ones. "We keep going. If we can't go back, then we have to go forward. Something or someone sent us here, with a purpose. I guess this is their way of ensuring that we don't back out. Literally."

With that, he intertwined his fingers with hers and turned back toward the tunnel leading deeper into the cave.

Lyra and Agon led the way, stopping on rocks, and warning Q and Elena of any holes in their path, but otherwise no one spoke. Being trapped in a black hole with no idea what lay ahead made them all considerably less chatty than usual.

Elena kept her lightning in check, just below the surface, at the ready in case something tried to attack them. Based on the heat she could feel in his palm, Elena knew Q was doing the same with his flames.

They continued deeper into the cave, following the tunnel as it gradually descended farther below the mountains when Elena heard a noise. She froze in her tracks.

"Hey, what are yo—"

"Sh!" she whispered. "Can you hear that?"

The group halted and listened.

In the distance, there was a faint repetitive sound of a single voice.

"Is that... chanting?" Agon wondered.

"I think so," Lyra said, twitching her ears to find the source of the sound. "It's coming from up ahead. Maybe fifty paces. Inside a large, open space."

"Let's keep moving. Stay low and silent. We don't know what we're walking in to."

Elena rolled her eyes at her own words. *Stating the obvious. That's helpful, El.* Of course, they'd stay low and quiet. They weren't a pack of idiots. Unfortunately, Elena couldn't control her tongue when she got nervous. Stating the obvious was her way of trying to control a scary situation. She knew it was a waste of time and energy, but saying nothing didn't make things any easier.

Slowly and carefully, they crept closer to the source of the sound. Elena listened hard, trying to decipher what they were chanting, but the words were too hushed, and the cave walls provided too much of an echo for her to comprehend what was being said.

Agon led the way, slinking between stalagmites along the edges of the tunnel, until he found a small opening. It ap-peared to serve as a doorway into a vast cavern. He flattened his body to the ground, making himself as small as possible, and inched into the large space. He relayed everything he saw to Elena, who then repeated it to Q and Lyra, where they hid in the tunnel just outside the cavern.

"It's one person. A guy," Elena's voice was barely above a whisper, "doing some sort of ritual. Agon and I don't recognize the language he's speaking, so I don't know if he's here to help or hurt. Based on what Agon is seeing though, it sounds like a very intense ritual. Maybe he's trying to stop the *turmio* or cast a massive protection spell against it."

"Maybe. Or maybe he is the *turmio*. We have no way of knowing," Quinn retorted.

"What do you want to do? Go in there and ask him? If he is trying to end the world or magic or whatever, it's not like he's just going to come right out and say it," Elena replied snidely. Agon reappeared at her side, looking on edge with his lightning pulsating up and down the length of his spine.

"Well then, what do *you* want to do?" Quinn snipped.

"I'd like to at least *try* to come up with a reasonable plan instead of just bursting in and hoping for the best, Q."

"Um, guys," Agon tried to interrupt.

"I'm not just hoping for the best, El, but sitting in this tunnel isn't getting us anywhere, and we are running out of time," Q continued as though he hadn't heard Agon.

"I know we're running out of time, but that's all the more reason to proceed cautiously. We have no idea what we're walking in to," Elena bit out.

"Hey, you two," Lyra hissed a little more forcefully.

"The only way to know what's really happening in that cave is to go in and see for ourselves," Quinn hissed through gritted teeth.

"We could be walking into a—"

"A trap," Lyra said.

The chanting had stopped. The silence was back. Elena and Quinn had been so busy arguing that they hadn't noticed the guy performing his ritual had finished. The entire cave started to shake.

Inside the cavern, Elena saw a huge crack split the middle of the floor, separating them from the guy and his ritual altar. The crack continued to expand until it became a chasm, then Elena watched in horrified awe as a massive, black swarm-like cloud flew out from the depths of the chasm and straight out of a hole in the ceiling of the cavern. The silence that followed was deafening, broken only by the words of the guy.

"Thank you so kindly for letting me finish my ritual. I wouldn't have been able to complete the initiation if I'd been interrupted." His voice was harsh, gravelly, and he spoke with an accent unlike anything Elena had ever heard.

They crept into the cavern, carefully sidestepping the edge of the newly created chasm, and she took a few moments to study the guy.

He was younger than he'd first appeared. He couldn't have been much older than she was, with dark, matted hair that covered much of his face. He seemed to have a hunched back, although that could have just been the result of bad posture. His clothes were simple, rough spun linen with unadorned leather boots.

His altar, however, was filled with some of the finest, most lavish tools she'd ever seen. A bejeweled chalice, an offering bowl that appeared to be made of solid gold, and an athame whose hilt was encrusted in gemstones. At least a dozen candles in silver holders. Bottles and jars filled with spices, herbs, and mysterious liquids. It was the sort of altar the young enchantresses at Harbor Ridge would dream about. So why in the name of the Mother was it all here in the middle of a cavern in the depths of a mountain with this guy?

"What sort of ritual?" Quinn asked, his tone bordering on interrogative.

"The most important ritual known to mankind," the guy responded. "The ritual to purge this world of this blight known as magic. The *Turmio.*"

40
BEATRICE

"IT HAS BEGUN." HER cold voice didn't betray the tension and sheer terror she felt. Having spent decades leading a school and guiding a country, Madame LaBelle was very practiced at keeping her emotions in check, never letting them show.

"What has begun, Headmistress?" Marsali looked up from the quill and parchment she'd been using while updating their classroom inventory. Her familiar, a dusty brown hare named Calum, twitched an ear as he perked up ever so slightly from where he slept comfortably in her lap.

"The *turmio*. Can't you feel it?" Madame LaBelle moved from her throne-like chair at her desk to gaze out her eastward-facing window, with Zied at her side, as always.

"The dark prophecy? Headmistress, are you certain? What should we do? I can call up some of our best investigators to find the source or trigger of this whole event and have them put a stop to it." The sudden drive to take action startled

Calum, and he jumped from her lap just as she rose to join the headmistress at the window.

Marsali was a sweet and proactive girl. She was always quick to find solutions and take things off the headmistress's plate. That was why Beatrice had chosen her to handle the day-to-day issues within the school. Beatrice was Headmistress, which meant she needed to be firm and authoritarian with the students. However, many of the students came to the school when they were girls, some as young as eight. Marsali was like a second mother or big sister that many of these girls needed, especially upon their arrival at Harbor Ridge.

Beatrice told herself that she kept her distance from the young girls so as to not intimidate them and maintained her strict persona as a way to ensure her imperious control over the school and all of its inhabitants never wavered.

The truth she would never admit to herself, much less anyone else, was that she refused to let herself get close to any of the girls because she knew she was a better leader than a mother. Her own daughter would attest to that. Beatrice was not a mother. Madame LaBelle was a leader and an exceptional, historically unprecedented enchantress, but she never had that maternal, loving side that one needed to be a mother.

"That will not be necessary, Marsali. The prophecy was triggered many years ago. There's nothing we can do to stop it now. If the *turmio* has been set free, and I assure you it has, then all of the players are already in the field of battle, and all we can do is wait to see who will prevail."

Beatrice anxiously stroked the fur behind Zied's ear. It was a habit she had developed as a child. A self-soothing method she used to keep herself calm. Their current predicament could not be soothed by the gentle warmth of her familiar's coat, but the habit always arose in times of great stress. Knowing her progeny was out in the world, meant to avert the end of all magic, naturally put Beatrice on edge. "For now, we will do nothing. Our best investigators are still in the field, searching for the source of that power surge we all felt the last moon. We can't afford to send any more out on blind quests. We will stay here and prepare for the coming war."

"War, Headmistress?" Marsali was not as practiced at hiding the fear in her voice.

"Yes, Marsali. According to prophecy, the *turmio*, if left unchecked, will absorb all magic from the world and leave us vulnerable to attack from the magept. We need to prepare our defenses. Once those fools realize we are without our magic, they will assume we are weak and powerless. We must be able to prove them wrong."

"Yes, Headmistress." There was a small quiver in her voice.

Madame LaBelle turned to face the girl. Marsali stood beside her, clutching Calum to her chest, the looming threat of tears in her eyes. Beatrice took pity on her.

"That will be all for tonight, Marsali. Thank you for your work today. Go down to the kitchens and have a cup of lavender and chamomile tea. Settle your nerves. We are safe here in Harbor Ridge."

"Yes, Headmistress. Thank you." Marsali offered a small bow of her head, then collected her quill and parchment before departing from the office.

"You know that's not true," Zied stated as soon as Marsali had closed the door.

"I do, but there's no reason to make the girl more anxious than is absolutely necessary." Beatrice turned back to her desk and started rifling through her drawers.

"We knew this was coming, and yet you still seem shocked by its arrival. What are you searching for?" Zied was always blunt, it was one of the things Beatrice loved most about him. Except in this moment.

"When we were young, I was cursed with being the mother of prophecy. I arrogantly believed that meant I would become a prophet. It did not occur to me that it meant I would literally give birth to a specific prophecy until I became pregnant. Now I know that all of this and the death that will follow could have been avoided had I simply terminated that pregnancy. I was vain. I thought I could control and guide the prophecy to suit my needs. Now, the world as we know it is ending."

"This prophecy would have come to fruition regardless of what you might have done differently. I would be willing to bet this entire school that you wouldn't have been able to terminate the pregnancy, even if you tried. This was destined to happen. Nothing anyone could have done would have averted this."

He was trying to comfort her, which she appreciated, but she wasn't convinced that he was right. Unfortunately, she reminded herself, they had no way of knowing if this disaster could have been avoided and, in truth, it didn't matter. The *turmio* had been initiated. It could not be undone, so they needed to focus on the problem at hand and stop playing childish games of "what if?"

"I'm looking for the prophecy. I need to know what will happen next so that we might prepare for it."

"I believe what happens next is magic drains, slowly at first and then exponentially until there's nothing left. Familiars fade away. Enchantresses become normal, magept women. Wards fail. Magical items lose all of their power and the world, as we know it, ends."

"Guard!" Beatrice shouted. She never shouted, so naturally, the guards burst into the room, spells and weapons at the ready, fully prepared to defend their headmistress against some vicious enemy.

"Stand down. I need to speak with the head of the guard as well as the commander of the investigators."

"Yes, Headmistress," the two guards said in unison and left the room as quickly as they entered.

"It's time to prepare for war and pray to the Goddess for protection. We're going to need it."

41

QUINN

"WHO THE MUX ARE you and what the hells did you just do?" Quinn strode across the cavern, Lyra quickly on his heels. Whoever this guy was, he had just admitted to triggering the *turmio* and labeled himself as the root of their problems as far as Q was concerned.

"*Ohhoh*, that is some colorful language. Didn't your mother teach you better than that? Oh, that's right. You didn't have a mother, did you, Quinn?" He looked up from his collection of shiny shyt on the large, flat boulder he had clearly used as an altar. His bright blue eyes glanced at Q with a hint of amusement.

Who is this guy? Q could feel the temperature rising in his body, the flames tickling his fingertips before he realized he'd called on his power.

"Who are you? How do you know my name? Why are you trying to get rid of magic?" His voice was more shrill than he would have liked, but that guy seemed to know an awful lot about him, and Q still didn't know a single thing about him.

"Me? I'm no one. A tool sent to free the world from the stain of magic. I'm an interchangeable part merely created to bring about the end of an unjust society and restore the balance of power." He spoke in a casual tone, as if this was a typical day for him, but Quinn thought he noticed a slight quiver in the guy's voice.

"What do you mean?" Elena asked. "How is removing magic going to make the world more just?" She somehow managed to sound calm while addressing the guy. Q was still fixated on finding out who this guy was.

"Magic creates power for those who are unworthy. Magic is the tool of weak, feeble-minded, and evil people. It must be purged from this world so that peace and prosperity can prevail." His response was automatic, like he'd been hearing these words for cycles. He didn't say them with the conviction and belief of a zealot, but he stated them as if they were simply known truths.

"You're wrong." Elena's blunt statement stunned the guy for a moment. He studied her quizzically, and then he laughed. It was the laugh of condescension.

He continued to chuckle as he turned his back to them and started to collect the items from his altar and pack them away into a large sack. Quinn hadn't noticed before, but the guy had an entire cart behind him. Clearly, it had been used to bring all of these tools down into the cavern to complete whatever ritual he and Elena had nearly interrupted.

"You are either arrogant or naive. I'd say that it's likely both. You have a limited view of the world, Elena, and it has made you ignorant of the harm your mother causes." He spat the word mother at her, as though it were poison.

"Have you met my mother?" Elena asked cautiously.

"In a way, we all have." It was becoming rapidly, and irritatingly, obvious that they weren't going to get any straight answers from this guy.

"Listen, man, I don't know how you know us or why you're doing this, but you have to see that taking magic from this world will harm a lot of people. Nearly half the world has at least some magic in their blood. How do you think they will be affected if you take it all away?" Quinn wasn't sure the guy had a conscience, but appealing to him in such a way would at least buy them enough time for Lyra to find a way across the chasm and block his exit. Maybe Agon could make it across and incapacitate this guy with his lightning.

"Don't worry. Most will survive. They might feel weak or sickly for a few days, but only those who are more magical than human will die." He continued to load his cart, as though the idea of killing thousands of creatures was nothing.

"You can't kill innocent people just because they have magic! That's cruel and wrong. How can you be so heartless?" Elena's voice held a quiver of its own. A quick glance in her direction confirmed that she was near tears. Q wasn't sure if they were tears of sadness, fear, or rage. He could see the sparks flickering between her fingers.

"Trust me, *tyttö*, I'm saving the world from people like you. Like dear Quinn here. Like your mother. How many lives have you taken? How many lives will never be the same again simply for having crossed your blighted path?"

Elena flinched at his words, as though he had physically struck her. Quinn reacted, without thinking, throwing his hands up and hurling fire at the arrogant fool. He would have hit his target too, if not for the sudden stream of what appeared to be snow that shot from out of nowhere and extinguished his flames on impact.

"Thank you, Demoni," he spoke kindly to someone—or something—hidden from their view, then he turned back to face Q directly. "That, *veli*, is why I'm doing this. Magic is violent and pure evil. It must be removed from this world so that those who remain can finally find peace."

Demoni. What is a Demoni? Almost as soon as Q thought of the question, he found the answer.

A teal, lizard-like creature crawled out from behind the altar. Its tongue flicked the air like a snake, but it had the body of an elongated iguana. From where Q stood on the other side of the chasm, he couldn't quite judge the size of this creature. It was easily larger than Agon, but he felt confident in thinking that Lyra was bigger than it. The creature deftly climbed up the guy's back and made itself at home on his shoulders, much like Quinn had seen Agon do so many times with Elena. That was no ordinary lizard creature. That was a…

"You have a familiar." Accusation filled Elena's voice as she pointed angrily at the creature, sparks flying off the tips of her fingertips. "You, who claims to hate magic and wants to purge it from the world. You have a familiar. Which means you are a magical being. You will die in this purge, just like us."

"Yes. And it will be worth it to know I'm leaving this world a better, safer place for those who are meant to be in it. We, the three of us and all magical beings, are abominations. We shouldn't exist. I'm simply putting the world to rights." With that, he turned to leave.

Unfortunately for him, Lyra and Agon had managed to find a way across the chasm. Lyra bared her teeth and flicked fire across the tunnel the guy had intended to use as an escape route. Agon snuck up behind him and quickly wrapped himself around the guy's leg, zapping him into unconsciousness, along with the lizard on his shoulders. They both collapsed where they stood, a sickening crunch echoed throughout the cavern.

42
ROSKA

CROUCHING ON THE PACKED *earth floor, he cowered in the corner, curled protectively around his only friend in the world. He could hear the Brothers talking about him in the next room. After they had completed his weekly "maintenance" beating, they were relaxing by the fire, having dinner, and drinking the wine they fermented at the monastery.*

For as long as he could remember, he received regular punishment in an attempt to beat the magic out of him. It didn't work the way the monks had hoped. He still had his magic, but he no longer used it. He'd been found on the monastery steps one cool evening during the growing season and had been saved by the monks who raised him to be an obedient, faithful, and submissive boy. He attended daily prayer, in which they preached about the evils of his magic, the demonic nature of his familiar, and the abomination of his existence and the existence of all magical creatures. They explained that they couldn't save his soul, as it was already damned, but they could train him to remove the scourge of magic from the world, thereby liberating the good, clean people of the world and removing the devils from it.

Most nights, curled on the floor of his cellar room, the boy dreamed of a family. People who loved him and held him close, keeping him warm and protected and safe. Each morning, he would be roughly awakened from his dreams by the aggressive prodding, and oftentimes kicking, inflicted upon him by his caretakers. The monks were the only family he'd ever known, and he desperately wanted to feel the love and affection that they readily shared with each other. The monks treated each other as brothers, but the boy wasn't a brother. He was an abomination sent from the depths of the Pit, but he was a tool they honed into a weapon.

They told him daily that he wasn't worthy of love, as he did not possess a soul, and the soulless cannot love or be loved. The only way he could possibly be of any use and therefore earn a modicum of their kindness, was to serve. First, to serve the monastery, and ultimately to sacrifice his life in the pursuit of erasing all magic from the world.

He understood their words, and he trusted they were right because they were men of faith, and that meant they couldn't possibly be wrong. But how could he be a threat to them? He kept his doubts and his tears to himself and never voiced his skepticism to the Brothers. It would only result in more pain and suffering anyway.

He confided in Demoni, through their telepathic link, so that he never had to fear being overheard. He was fairly confident that the brothers didn't know just how deep his connection was with his familiar. They had eventually learned that hurting Demoni would cause him physical pain, or vice versa. It quickly became their favorite method of discipline. Demoni was much smaller than the boy, making her a much easier target for their rage and disdain. She also represented everything they hated in the world. She was a physical manifestation of his magic, and she was punished often, merely for existing.

Each morning, they would rouse him and put him to work in the vineyard until sunset. Then nightly prayers before he served their meal and ate what scraps he could find before curling up to sleep on the packed earth floor of his cellar room.

If he was very lucky, he would dream of a family at night. A brother and sister. A mother and father who cared for them. People who loved him.

He woke up on a packed earth floor and it took him several moments to realize he wasn't back in his old room at the monastery. He lay on his side in the cave still with his arms and legs bound. And voices argued around him.

"What are we going to do now? We can't just leave him here." Elena's voice wavered as she spoke, clearly uncomfortable with having a prisoner.

"We need to figure out what he knows and get him to undo whatever he did. Bring that massive cloud back and end the *turmio* before anyone gets seriously hurt or killed." Quinn sounded tense, bordering on aggressive.

"How do you propose we do that? Interrogate him?" The horror in Elena's voice almost made Roska chuckle.

"Well, that's how you learned to trust me when we first met."

Snarky, Quinn, but interrogation will get you nowhere. Roska had been through more torture in his training to become the catalyst for the *turmio* than either of these two children could devise.

"I can't keep apologizing for that, Q, and you know you would've done the same had our situations been reversed." Elena sounded exasperated, but there was a hint of righteousness in her voice. Like this was an argument they had often, and she knew she would win it again.

"I wouldn't have been in your situation in the first place. What kinda idiot sleeps on the side of the road in the Dark Woods?"

"I already explained that!"

"Can we postpone your bickering match for the moment and focus on the problem at hand?" The voice, Roska guessed it belonged to Lyra, sounded irritated. Clearly breaking up these spats had become a regular practice for their familiars.

"Yes, please. He'll be up soon, and I'd rather not find out what else he's capable of." Agon. The weasel.

He's worried about what I'm capable of? He found the thought truly laughable but didn't want them to notice he was conscious just yet, so he kept his eyes closed and his breathing steady. He could sense that Demoni was nearby and equally alert, but contained somehow. Likely in similar binds to that which held his arms and legs in place.

"What if we just talked to him? Explained all the people who will be hurt or killed and how badly that will affect the world as a whole. Then maybe he'd undo the *turmio* and we can all go home?"

Elena's innocence was adorable and pathetic. Her ignorance of the world and how it worked was practically palpable when she said stupid shyt like that. Still, Roska couldn't help but feel a small bit of warmth toward the girl and her seemingly endless optimism.

"You can't honestly think that will work. You're not that naive." Quinn, always the firm voice of reason, and so tactful too. "You already tried talking to him. He's a muxing zealot. You can't talk sense into a zealot any more than you could explain to the sun god that He should take the day off. He's deranged, El. No amount of pretty words can change that."

While Roska agreed with the sentiment of Quinn's statement, he took offense to being called a zealot and deranged. He wasn't deranged *or* a zealot! He was simply more informed about the behind-the-scenes workings of the world and the puppet masters who ran it, using their magic to get what they wanted.

"We have to try." Elena's voice was so guileless and hopeful.

Roska cringed at the sound of it.

If our situation had been reversed, she would not have survived a week with the Brothers.

"You're probably right." The barely contained rage in Quinn's voice surprised Roska.

Had he spoken those words aloud?

He slowly opened his eyes to find himself face to face with Quinn.

43
ELENA

"**Y**OU WERE SAYING? ABOUT how Elena wouldn't have survived a week with your brothers?" Q prodded their captive with the toe of his boot, poking the guy in his gut. Elena grabbed Quinn by the sleeve and pulled him away. She gave him a look that said *Knock it off. We aren't going to hurt him.*

"Not *my* brothers," he responded, but he didn't elaborate any further.

After a moment, Elena gasped. "Wait, do you mean *the* Brothers?"

The Brotherhood? Those murderous zealots Belladonna had told them about? The ones who had hunted and slaughtered hundreds, if not thousands of innocent women?

"Ah, you've heard of them. That will make this so much easier then." He struggled to sit upright, so Elena carefully flickered her fingers to loosen his magical binds, ever-so-slightly, to enable him to achieve a vertical position. She was impressed at how easy it was to do, now that she'd burned through all her emotional deadweight at Belladonna's cottage. She could feel magic all around her now. Floating just outside her field of vision, waiting to be called forth.

"Thank you, *tyttö*," he muttered begrudgingly, before continuing. "Yes, those brothers. The Brothers. They are the ones who trained me and sent me here, so you must see that my cause and my actions are just. This is for the betterment of all mankind."

Elena didn't respond. She stood over him, momentarily stunned by his words. Q was right, there would be no way to convince him that the *turmio* was wrong or that this wasn't the right way to solve the world's problems. He had been raised in a brutal and violent cult. How could her words convince this poor boy that "the betterment of mankind" was a phrase often thrown about by men who wanted to hurt, subjugate and control women? This wouldn't be something she could explain in a matter of moments. Or even days. He had been through cycles of, likely traumatic, brainwashing, where the Brotherhood turned him into their perfect weapon before they sent him on a suicide mission.

In her silence, she heard Quinn discussing something with Lyra and Agon in hushed tones behind her, but Elena had turned all of her attention on the boy before her. He didn't look much older than her, now that she had a moment to study his features. Young, yes, but his eyes reflected something of age and experience. Elena inferred, based on the tale Belladonna had told them, and the history lessons she'd received about the Brotherhood at Harbor Ridge, that they hadn't been kind to this boy. Based on the ferocity she'd seen in his brilliant eyes and the hint of striped scars she could see hiding under the collar of his threadbare shirt, he had endured far more abuse than any one person should ever have to live through.

There was something else about him though. The more Elena stared at his face, the more familiar and confusing it seemed. There was something about this boy that resonated deeply with her.

What is it? Agon, sensing the abrupt shift in her mood, climbed up her cloak and took his seat on her shoulders.

I'm not sure. There's something... familiar about him, but I can't place it.

You mean you think we've met him before? Maybe at Amelia's? I guess it's possible. Maybe he was a migrant work-er, Agon mused, but that didn't seem right to Elena. There was something deeper to her connection with this boy. She couldn't pinpoint it, yet, but she knew it was more than just a passing greeting during the planting or harvest seasons in Andover.

"What is your name?" She addressed the boy now, never having taken her eyes off him.

"Roska." He seemed to be studying her as well.

Perhaps he feels the connection as well?

"How do we undo the shyt you started?" Q's complete lack of tact wasn't going to accomplish any more than her kind words and arguments for peaceful coexistence. Elena glared at him again. He needed to calm down, or they weren't going to learn anything.

"It cannot be undone. Once released, nothing can stop the *turmio*." Roska's voice was calm, eerily calm, giving Elena chills.

"There has to be some way we can save everyone," she pleaded.

"Don't you understand? That's what I'm trying to do." Roska locked eyes with her, a fierce conviction in his words.

Out of the corner of her eye, Elena saw his familiar moving. She had been trapped under a root cage Elena had called forth the moment Agon had shocked them into unconsciousness. It wasn't a flawless spell, but it was strong enough to contain the familiar until she and Q figured out their next moves. Elena walked over to the creature. She was unlike anything Elena had ever seen before, but her visage struck yet another chord of familiarity in Elena's mind. She was a little bigger than Agon and covered in shimmering blue-green scales. She appeared to have stumps on her spine, as though she had wings at one point but they were removed for some reason.

Why would anyone do such a thing? But even as she thought the words, Elena knew the answer. Control. Dominance. Punishment.

At Harbor Ridge, the girls would use their familiars to assert dominance over their classmates. Their familiars would attack one another until the strongest one overtook the rest. It was brutal and always ended in blood and tears, but the instructors never stopped the fights. It was an open secret that these fights were studied by the guards, and the best fighters were often recruited to join the guard. Elena had never been allowed to fight. Her mother forbade it, under the claims that because Agon had magic of his own it was an unfair fight. However, since Agon's magic was strictly confidential information, the other girls tormented Elena when she refused to fight. They assumed she was weak and knew she'd lose, so she rebuffed any challenge.

That couldn't have been the case with Roska, though. The Brotherhood abhorred magic. Elena knew they wouldn't have been raising and training their own army of enchantresses. Which led Elena to only one conclusion.

"They cut off your wings," she said, her voice a horrified whisper. "How could they?"

"So I couldn't sneak out."

Elena jumped at the response. The familiar, a miniature dragon from what Elena could tell, hissed quietly. Her tongue flicked quickly in and out of her mouth. She studied Elena and Agon but said nothing more.

"What is your name?" Elena asked the dragon gently.

"Demoni."

"You named your familiar 'demon'?" Q asked Roska, incredulously.

"I didn't name her any more than I named myself. This is simply what we were called in the monastery. *Roska*, meaning garbage or trash, and *Demoni*, or demon. I didn't know what the words meant when I was a child and by the time I'd learned their true meanings, we had already accepted them as our names." His tone was so calm and matter-of-fact, he might have been talking about the weather rather than the emotional and mental abuse he'd clearly suffered as a child.

"That's terrible." The more she learned about these two, the more pity she felt for them.

44

QUINN

Q STEPPED AWAY FROM Roska and his demon, grabbing Elena by the elbow and pulling her from them roughly.

"Stop it. I know what you're feeling, and stop. We can't feel bad for them. They are trying to kill anything and everything with magic in the world. It sucks that they had such a shytty childhood, but so did we, and we aren't trying to kill the world because of it."

Elena blinked the tears from her eyes and wiped her cheeks dry with her cloak. Q could tell she was trying to steel herself against the emotional outrage that she felt for the guy.

"You're right. We need answers, not emotions."

Q scrutinized her face for a moment before releasing his hold on her arm. Then he turned back to Roska.

"What was that thing you set loose? That big, black cloud of nasty shyt?"

"That was the *turmio*," Roska replied, looking slightly irked as though he were stating the obvious. "The *turmio* is a living thing. You two really have no idea what's going on, do you?"

"We haven't had much time to study or research this shyt," Quinn snapped back.

"Can you tell us more about it?" Elena knelt before their prisoner and kept her tone gentle, but Q could see the anxiety bubbling just below the surface.

"There's no point. It's done. It can't be undone, so we might as well get out of this drafty, cold cave and find a nice warm meal. It won't be long now."

"What the hells is that supposed to mean?" Q had never been that good at containing his rage, and this little mux pushed all the right buttons to end up extra crispy.

"It means I've spent years studying prophecy and preparing for this moment. Whereas you two stumbled in literally at the last moment, knowing nothing, doing nothing, and still know nothing," Roska smirked at Q.

Proud. Was this little bastard actually muxing proud of himself?

Q felt the heat rising up his spine and down his arms. He took a couple of steps towards the guy but stopped short when he felt Elena's hand on his arm. She didn't say anything, just held his gaze for a moment before shaking her head and leading them both to the mouth of the cave.

"You told me talking won't change anything. We need to get out of here and figure out our next move." Her calm tone helped soothe Q's rage some, but he could still feel the fire burning just below the surface. He needed to let it loose, or he'd end up exploding again just like he had at Belladonna's. He nodded in agreement with her words, then turned away from her and walked back across a small lip of cave flooring at the base of the wall that served as a bridge across the chasm.

"Where are you going?" Elena tried to follow him, but Lyra jumped in the way.

"He needs a minute," she said curtly.

Once he was in the middle of the cavern—back on the far side of the chasm Roska had opened—Q raised his hands, and let go. The flames shot skyward, well cavern ceiling-ward, lighting up the entire room and raising the temperature in the dank cavern to an uncomfortably warm level. His flames raged for a few minutes, then faded away, and he crossed calmly back to Elena and Roska.

Roska had a look of pure shock—and possibly a little fear—plastered all over his face.

Quinn felt a little smug at the sight of Roska's countenance. "What? Never seen anyone shoot flames from their hands before? I thought you were some all-knowing, hyper-informed supervillain?"

Elena swatted Q's arm and shot him a threatening look that said *Don't be a jerk*, but Quinn just shrugged. He'd been a jerk for as long as he could remember. No reason to stop now.

"I've never seen magic before. Aside from Demoni's frost breath. I know about it and the evils it brings, but I've never seen any other magical beings, outside of books." Roska's voice was a hushed, awe-filled whisper.

"We need to get out of here. If we unbind your legs and release Demoni, would you be willing to help lead us out of this cave?" Elena used the same calming tone with Roska as she had with Q. It was impressively effective.

"Yes, I will lead you out. And then we will go our separate ways. Demoni and I have been planning for this day for as long as I can remember. We have things we'd like to do before we die." Roska's voice was equally calm. He seemed entirely unbothered by his imminent death.

Quinn pulled Elena away from Roska before she unbound him. "Are you sure about this? We don't know him. How can we be sure he isn't going to lead us into a trap or some shyt?"

Elena looked over his shoulder to Roska and shrugged. "I guess we can't know for sure, but I'm trusting my intuition. There's something about him that I can't quite place, but I know we need him, and I believe we can trust him."

Q wasn't one to question her intuition, not after seeing her be right so many times, so he shouldered his pack and turned back to face their captive. Lyra trotted over to the root cage that held Demoni and took up her self-appointed position of "familiar guard." Q knew she'd stick close to the little dragon for the entirety of their trek out of the cave.

"You will walk ahead of us, and your dragon will walk in the back with Lyra. You will not communicate with each other. We will roast you in a heartbeat if we see anything suspicious. Understood?" Quinn, channeling his inner Bossy Amelia, addressed Roska, looking him dead in the eyes.

"Yes, *veli*, I understand and accept your terms." Roska raised his hands, either as a sign of submission or in an attempt to wordlessly ask for help getting off the cavern floor with his hands and feet still invisibly bound.

Elena flicked her wrist and the binds on Roska's ankles released. He stood and offered his hands to her.

"No," Q said firmly. "The hands stay bound until we get out."

Roska shrugged and headed to his cart, still loaded down with all of the supplies he'd used for his ritual.

"What are you doing?" Quinn demanded; there was no way this guy thought they were going to let him have any of his magic potions and shyt.

"You can't really expect me to leave all of this here. The chalice alone is worth more than you've had in your whole life.

I'm taking these supplies because this is how we plan to live out the last few days of our life."

Q turned to Elena. He didn't know shyt about magic or the potions and ingredients in Roska's cart. He didn't want the guy to have access to poisons or weapons he could use to kill them in their sleep, and he didn't know how long they'd be traveling with him.

"I'll take the athame, potions, and ingredients. Q will carry the other jeweled tools. We will leave the cart. One less thing to slow us down," Elena replied firmly. "When we get out of here, we will return it all to you. Until then, you will remain unarmed."

45

BEATRICE

"**G**ODS, THERE IT GOES again. Another wave of new power, like the one we felt a couple of days ago."

The unknown irritated Madame LaBelle to no end, and the complete lack of communication with the investigators added to her stress. "This one feels different from the one a couple of weeks ago, but equally strong," she mused, as she glared out of her east-facing window, willing the source of these magical power surges to reveal itself.

"We should hear from the investigators any day now, Head-mistress," Marsali said, trying to console her. Sweet, innocent, naive Marsali. She sat at her regular spot at the table in Beatrice's office, her floppy-eared rabbit napping peacefully on the table beside her stack of admissions requests from prospective students. Beatrice knew she should tell the girl to stop worrying about new students and admissions when the whole world was ending, but in a rare moment of gentle kindness, she decided to let the young woman continue as if things were largely unchanged. After terrifying the girl into tears the day before, Beatrice felt a modicum of maternal desire to protect Marsali. The idea was laughable, even in her mind, but it was the truth. Despite her admittedly many failures as a mother, she felt compelled to buffer Marsali as best she could.

Beatrice spent the entirety of the last sixteen years distancing herself from the only blooded daughter she had. That pregnancy and birth had been so much harder than she'd ever imagined or expected, and she'd handled it very poorly. It didn't help that Elena and her damned familiar were so abnormal. Beatrice often told herself that if that damned creature had just been a normal weasel instead of a magical raju, she would have been able to see past the mess of their conception and birth to be a good mother for Elena.

Rationally though, she knew that wasn't true or fair. Elena didn't have any choice in the form her familiar took, or the magic he possessed. All of the circumstances surrounding Elena's conception, birth, and the days that followed were so far from the norm that Beatrice had tried to disconnect from it all. Disassociate. It meant that she had willingly driven a wedge between herself and her only daughter, but it was all she could think to do in an effort to protect herself.

These last few moons, after sending Elena away, Madame LaBelle had had time to think about how she'd treated her daughter and how she'd handled the whole pregnancy and the days that followed. Beatrice had many uncomfortable revelations about herself and the relationship she'd denied herself with her daughter.

"Headmistress," Marsali's voice carried a tone of apprehension. Madame LaBelle was shaken out of her thoughts, realizing by the girl's tone that she had probably been trying to get her attention for several minutes.

"Yes, Marsali, what is it?" Beatrice tried to keep her voice steady.

Marsali handed her a sealed missive. "We have word from the investigators, Headmistress."

Beatrice took the letter, taking care to conceal the shaking in her hands. "Thank you, Marsali. You are excused for the day."

Marsali said nothing, simply bowed, and collected her things before she scooped up her rabbit familiar and left the headmistress's office, closing the door firmly behind her.

Beatrice sat at her throne-like chair behind the desk and studied the wax seal of the letter she held. Zied rose from his regular spot on a massive pillow behind her desk to come to take a seat beside her, resting his head on her lap.

"You will have to open it eventually," he chided after several minutes had passed and she had yet to make a move to break the seal.

"I know what it will say."

"You can't possibly know for sure. Your fears are getting the best of you. We don't know anything for certain yet."

"Don't try to pacify me. We both know that won't work. We know what is happening and we know exactly who is at the center of it. With one surge, we could have deluded ourselves into believing it was just a coincidence, but two? No, we know who the investigators are following now, and there's nothing we can do to stop it. We missed our chance to protect her. To protect all of them. Now we're stuck on the precipice of an undeniable, unavoidable paradigm shift that will reshape the entire muxing world!"

"There's no need to shout," Zied grumbled, as he rubbed his head against the underside of her arm. He could feel the anxiety, bordering on terror, she was suffering through.

"You're right. I'm sorry." Beatrice exhaled a breath she didn't realize she had been holding and broke the seal on the missive.

> *Apologies, Headmistress. We were delayed with the witch. Possibly dosed with something, we can't be sure. Lost two days in her damned fog, but we are on the trail again. According to the locals, the only new people in town were a young man and woman, traveling with a fox and a blue weasel.*

Mux, Elena, Beatrice realized.

*Their trail seems to lead into the mountains. Will
keep you posted.*

The investigators had to have recognized the description of
the Headmistress' daughter, but they'd made no mention of
any of it in their missive. Good. It was safer that way, in case
their communications were intercepted.

Beatrice's hand shook as she let the missive fall to her desk.
Her eyes misted over as her heart raced in her chest.

"Goddess, it really is them. I didn't want to believe it. I kept
hoping that I was wrong. I just wanted to keep them safe.
Clearly, I was wrong."

46
QUINN

THE TREK THROUGH THE cave tunnels was slow and tedious. Q kept a close eye on Roska, following behind him and put himself between their captive and Elena. There was something about this guy that pulled at Q. Something that felt familiar and unsettling, and he was certain that Elena felt the same strange pull to Roska. She'd all but said it when they were negotiating their terms with their prisoner in the cavern.

They didn't speak much while they traveled, mostly because the tunnels on this side of the cave were very narrow, and they were forced to walk in a line, one directly behind the other. It limited their ability to communicate with each other, but it gave Q plenty of time to dwell on his feelings about Roska, the utter idiocy of his triggering the *turmio*, and their now seemingly unachievable goal of undoing the damned thing.

Muxing suicidal idiot. Damning us all because of his bigoted and ignorant beliefs.

You know it's not that simple.

Gods be damned. Lyra knew he wasn't actually talking to her. Why did she feel the need to interject?

Don't tell me you actually feel pity for this idiot? He's helping to annihilate the entire magical population. You know that includes you, Q countered.

Yes, of course, I know that.

Then what? You want me to feel bad for him because he grew up in a shytty, abusive environment? So did we, in case you forgot, and we aren't trying to kill off half of the world!

There's no need to shout. Even in his mind, Lyra's tone carried a hint of contempt.

Gods, he hated when she was so calm and patronizing. Which was probably why she used that tone with him so often.

Yes, we had a hard start in life, she continued, *and yes, his past doesn't justify his present behavior, but you might recall how long it took us to start trusting people again. And we were in that shyt hole for less than a decade. He has been with the Brotherhood since he was a baby. He doesn't know any better.*

He hated her tone, but even more, Q hated that Lyra made good points. He didn't even want to imagine what sort of person he would have grown up to become if he'd spent his whole childhood in that orphanage. Assuming they'd even survived this long there.

Q begrudgingly agreed to not fully hating the guy, but he wasn't about to trust him. Yeah, he might've been raised by insane zealots, but Roska had come into the cave, alone, and triggered the *turmio* all on his own. The Brotherhood hadn't been holding a knife to his throat, making him perform whatever ritual he and Elena had walked in on. He had made those choices all on his own.

Q was still stewing in his thoughts when he heard a noise ahead of them in the narrow passageway. He grabbed Roska roughly by the collar and pulled him back, then he held up a hand to warn Elena and the troupe of familiars to halt.

Voices. He heard voices not too far ahead of them. They were too muffled to determine if they were male or female, but it didn't matter to Q. Anyone else coming down these tunnels was suspect, as far as he was concerned.

Quinn looked around, searching for a place to hide or better yet a side-passage they could duck into and stay out of sight, but they had no such luck. The tunnel was narrow and cut cleanly. No place to hide. No way to disappear. They were muxed.

"Elena? We know it's you. We don't want to hurt you. We just came here to bring you home." A female voice shouted down the tunnel toward them. Quinn felt like it was vaguely familiar but he couldn't place where he'd heard it before.

"Home?" Elena whispered.

In the darkness of the tunnels, Q couldn't see her very well, but he could tell the word home was said with a hint of incredulity and disbelief. She had recognized the voice and she wasn't happy to hear from them.

"Come on, Elena. Your mother sent us to find you and bring you home. She's worried about you," a second female voice called out from ahead of them in the tunnel.

At this comment, Elena scoffed. "My mother is worried about me? That's the best you could come up with? You honestly expect me to believe that?!" she jeered at them. "We both know she has never once worried about me or given a spare thought to my well-being my entire life. Don't try to pull that shyt with me, Noelle."

"Come on, Elena. You know that's not fair," the first voice spoke again.

"I don't think so, Maddy." Elena was getting angry now, Q could see the lightning flickering under the skin of her hands, and there was a faint blue glow in her eyes. "You know what's unfair, Maddy? The way my mother isolated me. Making sure everyone knew I was her daughter and just how disappointed in that fact she was. And do you know what's *really* unfair?! Being kicked out of Harbor Ridge for no muxing reason and being forced out of my home." Elena spat the word "home" out as though it left a sour taste in her mouth. "You don't get to lecture me about what is fair or try to convince me that my mother misses me and wants me to come back. That school was never really my home, and she never wanted me there."

Elena's words were so full of hurt and disgust. It hurt Quinn to hear about her childhood and how cold her mother had been. He'd known it was a shytty situation at that school, but she never spoke about it. Q was struck with another overwhelming urge to protect her.

Roska was fidgeting with his hands, trying to wiggle out of his magical binds most likely, so Quinn pulled hard on his arm, hoping to disrupt his efforts and remind him who was in charge. Q was shocked to see a faint blue-green glow in Roska's eyes when he turned the prisoner around to face him.

"What the hells...?" Quinn jumped back at the sight of Roska's intense, glowing stare, but caught himself before he fell onto Elena. "What the hells are you doing?" Q hissed and roughly grabbed Roska by the collar. "Are you possessed? Why the hells are your eyes glowing? You're gonna give our position away!"

Q knew that their position wasn't exactly a secret, but a glowing beacon would just lead those women right to them.

"What are you talking about?" Roska whispered, sounding both irritated and slightly nervous.

"Your muxing eyes are glowing. Fix that shyt. We told you, no magic! No weapons. Knock it off before I knock you out." Q knew his words were harsh, but he also didn't want to get caught by these women.

Quinn had realized where he recognized their voices from. These were the investigators that Amelia had known and that they'd been running from for the last week. The investigators had caught up to them and now he and Elena were trapped.

"I'm not going anywhere with you, so you might as well leave. Tell my mother I don't need her, and I'm not coming back," Elena called down the tunnel. If she noticed Roska's glowing eyes, she didn't react.

Quinn knew it was an absurd idea, but he desperately hoped the investigators and their guards would take Elena at her word and just leave.

"We can't do that, girl." That was one of the guards. The one who had spoken so callously about neutralizing threats at Amelia's.

"Lillith, just go. I don't want to go back there and trust me, she doesn't want me there either." Lightning flashed off the tips of Elena's fingers, casting spooky shadows along the tunnel walls.

Well, I guess glowing eyes aren't our biggest concern anymore, Lyra's voice quipped in his head.

47

ELENA

NOTHING ABOUT THE DAY had gone according to plan. But that was just the story of her life, and Elena felt foolish for ever thinking that their attempts at averting a prophecy would be any different. Of course they would arrive too late and hide in the cave watching instead of actually stepping in to stop the damned ritual in the first place. Of course she'd feel some weird pull and attachment to the muxing boy who triggered the damned *turmio*. Of muxing course they would get trapped and caught by her mother's muxing investigators while escorting a prisoner through the world's most narrow cave tunnels. Of muxing course.

Goodness, when did I start swearing so much? Elena was baffled by her foul language, even if it had been only in her head.

I blame Quinn. I told you he'd be a bad influence on you. She chuckled at Agon's words in her mind. He was always quick to offer comedic relief in times of great stress. She loved him for that.

Elena could feel her emotions getting the better of her, she knew she should try and stop the power from building within her, but she was just so damned tired. Tired of fighting losing battles. Tired of trying to live up to her mother's expectations. Tired of always falling short and feeling like a failure. Tired of never being who she truly wanted to be. She'd spent the majority of the last sixteen cycles bending over backward to make her mother happy, only to be evicted on what should have been the most important day of her life. She was so sick and muxing tired of her damned mother coming in and ruining any sliver of happiness she managed to carve out for herself. She was done trying to make Madame LaBelle proud of her.

She heard some angry whispering from farther down the tunnel, where their would-be captors waited for them, but she couldn't understand their words.

Elena turned to Quinn, hoping for some insight into how they should handle this, or an idea for escape. What she saw instead were glowing eyes. Blue-green eyes that seemed to be locked in a staring contest with red-orange glowing eyes.

Gods damn them all.

"Quinn! Roska!" she hissed at them, "Your eyes are glowing. What the hells is going on? How is that possible?"

"What do you mean my eyes are glowing? *His* eyes are glowing. And you've got lightning in yours." Quinn's voice was tight but quiet. Elena thought it was a wasted effort since her mother's investigators likely knew they were together, but she didn't say anything.

"Shyt, we need to get out of here and figure out what is happening to us." She turned to Roska. "Could this be a part of your ritual? Or a reaction to the *turmio*?"

Roska said nothing, merely shrugged, but he kept his eyes locked on hers, as though he were trying to read her mind.

"Any ideas on how to get out of here? We can't go back the way we came, so going forward is the only option. Are you planning on fighting our way out of here?" There was skepticism in Q's voice, but Elena couldn't think of a better option.

"I think that's our only choice. I don't like it, and honestly, I don't like our chances here. Those are my mother's best guards and investigators, but staying here isn't a viable option either." Elena didn't want to hurt the girls. They were a few cycles older than she was, so they never had any classes together, but Maddy and Noelle had always been kind toward her. Lillith and Seph were a package deal and very quick to violence, which meant they were very adept at fighting. Elena wasn't confident that they could best those enchantresses in a direct assault, but maybe if they sprung a sneak attack...

"Listen, I have an idea. I know this is going to sound risky, but I need you both to trust me. Q, I know you're not gonna like this, but I'm going to release the binds on Roska." Elena lifted her hands to absolve the magic holding his wrists together, but Quinn quickly grabbed hold of her arms.

"No! You can't be serious! He'll turn on us the second we get free of those damned hunters."

"I don't think he will. Q, he's like us. I know you can feel it. Something is pulling the three of us together, and it's more than that prophecy. Even if you don't want to admit it, we're going to need him to get past those four. They are some of the most skilled enchantresses at my mother's disposal, and we need all the help we can get."

Elena watched Quinn internally debate the logic of her words, and she suspected Lyra was quietly chiming in as well, but ultimately, he let go of his hold on her, and she released the spell that bound Roska's hands.

48
ROSKA

R OSKA RUBBED HIS WRISTS, sore from the invisible binds that had held him. His eyes glowed. He didn't know how or why, and he had been silently hoping that Quinn was lying to him when he'd said it, but Demoni had confirmed it. Glowing. And based on the description, it sounded like the same color Demoni glowed whenever she used her frost powers.

Well, this is an unsettling development.

It shouldn't have been, knowing what he knew about magic and seeing what Quinn could do. Magic was very real and alluring, that's why so many fell victim to it. The power and beauty of evil was indescribably attractive, which was why it had to be avoided and extinguished.

"Demoni," Elena spoke to his dragon as though they were old friends. "I need you to try and cover the floor ahead of us with snow, but try to be subtle about it. Quinn, I need you to melt the snow so that it spreads water down the tunnel."

Without a word, Demoni hopped a few paces ahead, out of sight, but still within earshot. Roska heard the gentle flow of her snow.

Can you see anything? he thought to her. Any insights she could provide them would give them an advantage in their escape.

Not really. Four figures. Four familiars. A cat, a falcon-type bird, an owl of some kind, and a rabbit.

The falcon and owl could be trouble. If they were anything like their non-magical counterparts, they had excellent eyesight and would spot them immediately. Perhaps they already had.

The silence of the cave had become unbearable. Roska could no longer hear the enchantresses arguing amongst themselves, which worried him. Had they stopped arguing because they'd settled on a plan of action and were putting it into motion? Were they all about to be attacked in this cramped tunnel? He prayed that Elena's plan worked quickly and gave them a chance to get out of the tunnels.

"Are you still out there?" Elena called out to the women blocking their escape route. She kept her voice loud but steady, as Quinn side-stepped around her and used his fiery hands to melt Demoni's snowdrift.

"We aren't leaving without you, Elena. We're under orders," the grumpy one said.

"I'll make a deal with you. I will go peacefully with you if you promise to leave my companions alone. They aren't a part of any of this, and we all know how my dear mother feels about the opposite sex."

"We have no quarrel with your boys, Elena. We just need you to come with us. We would love to keep this peaceful." Maddy, one of the nicer ones, responded this time. Roska could hear the optimism in her words. She really did hope to end this encounter peacefully. Fool.

"Fine. I will come with you." Elena stepped forward, walking through the thin layer of icy water that had spread throughout the tunnel before them. She took slow, deliberate steps, glancing back over her shoulder, then she knelt to the ground, as though she'd dropped something on the cave floor and Roska shielded his eyes as he was suddenly blinded by a stunning blue light.

He heard four shrieks, followed by a series of loud thuds.

"Holy Mother, I can't believe that actually worked," Quinn chuckled triumphantly.

"Don't celebrate just yet," Elena said. "We still have to get past them and out of here without them waking up. Let's go!"

They quickly crept down the tunnel, trying not to splash too loudly in their recently weaponized puddle. Demoni had resumed her preferred perch on Roska's shoulders, despite Quinn's previous rule about keeping the two of them separate.

Roska was still being escorted between Elena and Quinn, but at least he was unbound, and Demoni was with him again.

When they reached the unconscious enchantresses, Elena stopped to check them all.

"They're still alive. Thank the goddess. I was so scared that I'd killed them all."

Roska saw her physically relax, releasing much of the tension that had been plaguing her.

"Great. Now zap them again to make sure they don't wake up any time soon and let's get the hells out of here." It was very obvious that Quinn didn't feel the same guilt about attacking these women as Elena felt.

She didn't reply, but she gave him a scathing look and promptly turned away, carefully stepping over the women. Agon, however, seemed to agree with Quinn because he quickly zapped the women before Elena could stop him and hopped over their bodies, moving to the head of their troupe as though nothing had happened.

"Agon! You didn't need to do that."

"Better safe than sorry," was his only reply as he slipped farther down the tunnel.

The rest of their journey through the tunnels was uneventful, and they managed to catch the last rays of sunlight as they emerged from the cave.

"We need to make camp before it gets too dark to see, but we can't stay this close to the cave." Quinn glanced back over his shoulder, anxious to get away from the dark abyss that lay open behind them. "We need to put as much space between us and them as we can. Where did you sleep on your trip to kick start the end of the world?"

Elena elbowed him but turned to Roska to hear the answer just the same.

"We made camp just beyond that bend," Roska said, gesturing up the path a bit. "I'll show you the way."

Quinn waved his arm as though to say "after you," and they set off on the rocky path that wound down the side of the mountains.

The sunlight faded quickly within the confines of the mountains, and it was nearly impossible to see when they finally reached the cluster of fir trees that had served as his bed the night before.

They opted out of making a fire, to avoid detection from the enchantresses that were likely already awake, or would be soon. Elena was kind enough to share some of their provisions, handing him a couple of hard biscuits, some cheese, and a skin of water.

Roska sat back, slightly away from his unexpected traveling companions, and wondered at the situation he found himself in.

These two had no idea who he was, no clue of his connection to them, and they'd just witnessed him complete the ritual that will essentially kill them, and yet they were still being kind to him. Sure, Quinn was being a bit of a jerk, and quite snarky, but he was still helping to keep him alive. Roska didn't even sense any bite in Quinn's words when he'd commented on Roska ending the world. They were treating him with relative respect. Not like a prisoner of war, as the Brotherhood had warned. Elena treated him with genuine care and concern. If she was a true example of real enchantresses in the world, then perhaps the Brotherhood had been wrong.

49

QUINN

QUINN HAD VOLUNTEERED TO take the first watch and let Elena get some sleep, but just like before, Lyra and Agon had borderline-bullied him into getting some sleep himself while they stood watch. There was an added challenge of having to keep an eye on Roska and Demoni now too, especially after Elena refused to use her magic ropes to tie him up again. Lyra had agreed to keep a lookout for the enchantress hunters, and Agon, with his lightning powers, would keep an eye on the snow dragon.

Lyra woke Q at first light and gave him the quick, uneventful report of the night before. No sign of enchantresses or their familiars. Roska slept all night with Demoni curled on his chest. No movement. No attempts to flee or cause any more trouble.

Elena woke slowly, stretching and calm, as though she were oblivious to their impending doom. Hells, she was downright perky!

"Good morning, boys. How did everyone sleep?" She dug around in one of the many endless pockets in her cloak before pulling out a handful of hard biscuits, dried meat, three apples, and a bunch of grapes.

"Grapes? You've had grapes in your pockets for days? How are they have they not been smashed into jam?" Q took the food she offered him, baffled by the cloak.

Elena just shrugged.

"Magic," she said, like that was the only explanation needed.

She handed Roska a biscuit and some meat, then offered some of the magic grapes to Demoni, who sniffed them for a moment, then graciously grasped the stem with her small, vicious-looking teeth and began making quick work of the purple fruit.

"So what are we gonna do?" Q shoved a handful of grapes in his mouth and glanced over at Roska. "How do we undo the shyt he started?"

"Technically, I didn't start anything. The *turmio* started long before I walked into that mountain. Long before we were even born."

"Yeah, I don't believe you, and I have literally no reason to trust you." Q felt the words to be true, but he was keenly aware that his voice didn't carry the same harshness and aggression that it had yesterday.

"Q," Elena admonished. "He helped us escape the investigators. I think that has earned him a modicum of trust."

"Why? He helped himself escape. That's not anything worth bragging about." Q shrugged. "It was just self-preservation. How do we know he won't turn on us the first chance he gets?"

Roska said nothing. Not denying the accusation or trying to make himself seem less suspicious. He simply took a bite of his biscuit and held Quinn's stare. Q couldn't tell if Roska was trying to challenge him or just study him.

"Where are we going?" he continued. "According to monk-boy here, we can't stop that cloud, but I'd be willing to bet someone out there disagrees."

"Do you wanna go back to Fàidh?" Elena asked between dainty bites of dried meat.

"Gods, no. He was absolutely useless. Not to mention clothes-less. I still haven't recovered from our last visit with that loon." Q brushed his hair back from his brow and looked up into the trees. "Maybe... mux, maybe we should go back to Belladonna."

Elena choked on her biscuit. "Really? I wanted to say that, but I thought you'd hate that idea."

Q rolled his shoulders, trying to break loose the tension that had been steadily building there since he first met the witch. He took a deep breath, studying the sunlight through the limbs and needles of their fir tree canopy. It was true, that woman grated on him to no end, and he was not looking forward to seeing her again, but she was also the only person with any real, comprehensible, information about the damned *turmio*.

"I just think she'll be the best option if we plan on stopping this shyt before it ruins the entire world."

Elena didn't say anything, but she was practically vibrating with excitement. Dammit. She was back to being perky. Giddy, even. Quinn took that to mean he'd made the right choice. The last time he'd seen her this happy was when he'd decided to move back in to Amelia's instead of coming to visit several times a week.

"That still doesn't help us with this fool," Quinn said, glaring slightly at Roska.

"Well, first, stop insulting him. That's petty and unnecessary," Elena chastised Q. She turned to Roska and continued. "Secondly, we are taking him with us. I mean, if you'd like to come, I think Belladonna could help us all, and I know she'd like to meet you and Demoni."

"I think we can spare a few days from our busy schedule. What do you think, Demoni?"

Roska's dry humor irritated Quinn. His flippant attitude made it nearly impossible for Q to trust the guy, and he couldn't figure out why Elena cared. Or trusted him. Or took pity on him. Whatever it was that was driving her to be kind and muxing friendly with him. He was essentially killing them all, and she was acting like he was a lost puppy.

Demoni said nothing, simply nodded to Roska and Elena.

"It's settled then!" Elena jumped up from her seat on the rocky mountainside, dusting off her trousers and throwing her cloak around her shoulders. "We should make it back to her fog late tomorrow. Maybe she'll meet us at the boundary and escort us through again. I hope so. I really don't want to know what horrible feelings and memories that barrier of hers would pull out of me."

Quinn said nothing. He was already stewing in his own dread at their impending visit with the witch. He just hoped she would be able to help them and they could move on from her—and ideally leave Roska behind—quickly.

50
ROSKA

WHY ARE WE STAYING with them? We don't need to see this witch or help them stop the turmio. *We are done. We're supposed to be able to enjoy ourselves now. Or have you forgotten our plan already?*

He hadn't forgotten, and Demoni knew it. Roska knew exactly what they had been planning to do because they'd been planning it for years.

Survive the Brotherhood: check

Find the cavern in the Dragon's Teeth and complete the ritual to release the *turmio*: check

Spend whatever time they had left selling off the ritual items and living like royalty until the *turmio* came for them.

But now that he was with Elena and Quinn, he felt differently. He'd always known they would be there in the cavern with him, but he'd never expected to feel this magnetic pull to be with them. To stay with them. Roska knew, *knew* in his bones, that he belonged with them. Demoni knew it too, but all of her side-glances and cautious wariness of Quinn and Lyra let Roska know that while she might feel the same pull he felt to be with these two and their familiars, she didn't trust the boy or his fox in the slightest. Quinn had ensured that they knew the feeling was mutual.

Elena, though. Elena could sense that they were connected. She didn't know yet how or why, but she clearly trusted her intuition and wasn't going to let them just walk away without at least trying to understand them a bit more. Not that Roska thought she would hold them hostage.

You mean more than she already has? Demoni queried.

Yes, that's what I meant. She only had us contained before because she was scared and didn't know what to do. She let us go as soon as she felt our connection.

Maybe, she conceded, *but you know as well as I do that they will both flip out when they find out the whole truth about us.*

It was Roska's turn to concede the point. He glanced at Quinn and Elena where they stood a few paces from him, making plans for how best to travel while being pursued, their backs to him. Yes, they would likely both be very upset, and probably angry, when they learned why the three of them were all tied together and their connection to this prophecy, but Roska was fairly confident that their potential rage wouldn't be aimed at him. At least not completely.

Is that confidence you're feeling? Demoni prodded, *or blind hope and naivety?*

Why can't it be a bit of both? he retorted with a smirk. Both seemed more accurate.

Once they'd finished eating their breakfast, Quinn directed both Roska and Elena to cover their tracks so that the enchantresses wouldn't be able to tell that they'd rested in the small clump of trees overnight. The hope, Roska assumed, was to mislead their hunters into believing that they were much farther away, driving the enchantresses to move quickly, ahead of them, and give them a chance to reach this witch without incident. It was well into the morning by the time they started on the path down the mountainside.

Well, not "on" the path, because Quinn argued that they would be easier to track if they stuck to the rough road. So they traveled through the woods about a dozen paces in from the road itself. They had to stop every so often so Quinn could backtrack and hide their trail. Roska thought it was a bit excessive, but he had also never been a hunter or tracker, and he'd certainly never been chased by angry enchantresses before, so he held his tongue. If Quinn wanted to take extra precautions, who was Roska to tell him no?

They traveled to the far side of the mountain range, opposite from where Roska and Demoni had first entered, and found the cave. It seemed this side of the mountains was far rougher with considerably less greenery and a much harder-to-find path. The journey became increasingly difficult, despite their downhill mobility, simply because there was no real road to follow. Quinn led the way through the jagged rocks and guided them as carefully as possible along the slippery pebbles that littered their path.

No one said anything while they hiked. Either because trekking through an untamed mountainside was exhausting and required all of their mental focus, or because they didn't know what to say.

At least, those were Roska's reasons for keeping quiet. His time with the Brotherhood hadn't prepared him for such arduous and rigorous physical activity. Truth be told, Roska believed that the Brothers intentionally kept him from most physical tasks to keep him weak and therefore compliant. It would be much harder to maintain power over a boy when that boy could fight back.

Roska had been away from the Brotherhood for nearly a full week now, and he was starting to notice things about the outside world that were unlike anything they'd ever taught him.

Many of the townspeople that he'd met on his way to the mountain had been quite friendly, unlike the warnings the Brotherhood had literally beaten into him about the cruelty and boundless hatred that filled the world. They raised him to trust no one but them and cautioned him that anyone outside of the monastery would try to hurt him and manipulate him into doing their bidding. And above all, they taught him that magic corrupted all that it touched and was to be feared above all else.

From what little Roska had seen so far, that all seemed rather paradoxical to what the world was really like. Admittedly, Roska's "real-world experience" was very limited, but he felt confident in thinking that the Brotherhood's views were inaccurate, at best, and outright lies at worst.

He didn't want to believe that they'd lied to him about everything, but he was starting to wonder what was truth and what was fiction.

51
ELENA

IN ALL OF HER years at Harbor Ridge, Elena had struggled to learn even the simplest of spells and incantations. She was not adept at transmogrifacation. She was the worst student in all of her potions and chemistry courses. Elena was once laughed out of the room in her magineering class last cycle, but she had perfected trusting her intuition and following her heart. Elena had always seen that as her niche, her specialty. Seeing someone and being able to intuitively read them and understand their motives. It made her highly unlikeable at school simply because she could see through all the girls and their bullshyt, and she never got caught up in their ridiculous drama. All of the girls were trained to manipulate and conspire throughout their time at Harbor Ridge, but Elena never wanted to participate and thus was shunned for her refusal to play their conniving games and cater to their exploitation of others. However, since leaving that damned school Elena had found that her intuition was her best and strongest ally.

Elena felt confident in her choice to keep Roska unbound and encourage him to travel with them to see Belladonna. She knew that despite his actions, he was someone they needed to learn more about and grow to trust. He reminded her so much of herself when she'd first been forced to leave Harbor Ridge. Confused, ill-informed, lost, and homesick. Even though the home she missed was a fiction—Harbor Ridge may have been where she grew up, it never truly felt like home—Elena was fairly sure that Roska was having similar revelations now that he was away from the Brotherhood and able to really think for himself.

How could he possibly feel safe and maintain his allegiance to those abusive bastards now that he was away from them and able to breathe? Now that he was out in the world and free of their control?

You know it's not that simple. She bristled at Agon's thoughts. *It's never that simple. Roska spent his entire life with those men. They are the only family he's ever known, and he won't give them up that easily. They may have abused and tortured him for most of his life, but they also raised him, kept him safe from the outside world, fed him, clothed him, etc. He will feel an obligation to them, if nothing else. We can't convince him to cut ties just because we know it's the best choice.*

Elena didn't respond. She knew Agon made valid points, but she desperately needed to believe that she and Quinn could turn Roska around, set him on the right path, and maybe even convince him to help them end the *turmio* before anyone died.

Just don't get your hopes too high, ok? Agon nuzzled her ear with his warm, wet nose. *We never would have left Harbor Ridge if we hadn't been forced out, and that place was incredibly toxic. Just because you know something is bad for you, doesn't mean you're willing to let it go.*

The sun was well below the horizon by the time they made it out of the mountains and back on the path that had led Q and Elena into the Dragon's Teeth just two days prior. Two days. It felt like a million cycles since they first stepped foot in those ominously named peaks, and yet the reality of it was that they'd only left Belladonna four days prior. This whole world-ending, heart-racing experience had started less than a week prior, when Elena's mother's investigators came searching for her back at Amelia's.

"We'll make camp in the same spot by the creek tonight, then follow the water back to the main road through Nexton. With any luck, we'll make it back to the Dark Woods before dusk tomorrow and Belladonna's the next day."

Q led the way, with Lyra bringing up the end of their little troupe, using her tail to wipe away most of their tracks and hide their movements from the investigators. Elena wasn't sure any of that would really help, since these were her mother's best, and they were quite skilled at tracking and finding those who didn't want to be found, but she hoped their efforts weren't in vain.

"Do you think they're following us?" Roska asked.

Elena thought she might have heard a hint of nervousness in his tone, but he seemed to be hiding it well, so she answered as gently as she could.

"Yes, I'm certain that they are. But try not to worry; they aren't after you. Those women are from my mother's school. Their job is to find undiscovered enchantresses and bring them to Harbor Ridge to complete their magical education. They're after me. I imagine they're a bit... annoyed at how we left them, but they don't know about Q, Lyra, Demoni or you yet, and I'm hoping to keep it that way."

"How can you be so sure that they don't know about Demoni's magic? Or Quinn and Lyra?"

Quinn scoffed at this question. "Because enchantresses think men are useless, except when it comes to breeding. They aren't looking to have a baby with either of us—" He gestured to himself and Roska "—so they aren't paying any attention to us. We mean nothing to them. For now anyway."

Elena rolled her eyes at Q and his bluntness, but turned back to Roska as they continued down the dirt road for a few more paces before veering off into the tall, grassy meadow towards the sounds of the creek. "While I don't agree with his explanation, Q is largely correct. The investigators won't notice any of you, unless you make yourself known as a threat. If they catch up to us, we may be able to use that to our advantage." She said the last part aloud, but was mostly talking to herself.

"So you want us to be your secret weapons?" Roska asked, amusement mixed with incredulity in his voice.

"More like the aces up her sleeves," Quinn replied.

"No, Q, I don't like that one. It makes me sound like a cheater. I don't like yours either, Roska. You aren't weapons. You are my friends." Elena eyed him hopefully. Maybe if she called him her friend enough, he'd start to believe it and thus make it so. He said nothing, but held her stare for a moment, and she saw the hint of a smile cross his lips before he turned away.

"All right, I'll gather firewood. Roska, you refill the water-skins. Elena, can you make the stew again? The one from the last time we slept here? It was delicious." Q handed her his pack with the pot and cooking supplies. His words made her smile and filled her with a warmth and pride she rarely felt before.

"How can I deny such a sweet request? I'll add some extra herbs to keep us safe and throw in a dash of mint for good luck. We could definitely use it."

"Wait, you're going to spell our food?!" Roska, who had been walking toward the creek, turned around abruptly, clearly appalled by the idea.

"It's not like she's going to poison us, dummy. It's just a little magic to help us undo the shyt storm you started."

Roska opened his mouth, presumably to respond with something equally snarky when Elena exhaled an exaggerated—but fully warranted—sigh of frustration. "Will you two please just *try* to get along for a few minutes? Yes," she said to Roska, "I am adding some herbs to the meal that have magical properties, but if you are uncomfortable with that, then I will only add it to my bowl and Q's. You don't have to have any. If you could please take these to the creek, regardless of what herbs I use, I will need fresh water to make the stew." She handed him the empty waterskins from her magically voluminous cloak pockets. Once he was out of earshot, she unleashed her ire on Quinn, "You need to knock it off. Yes, he unleashed the *turmio*. Yes, that is a bad thing. And yes, we will be fighting to undo it and re-seal that monstrous cloud thing back in the cavern, but you need to stop being such a jerk about it. We've all made bad choices because of our upbringing. We need to learn to trust each other. It's going to take all three of us to fix this."

She hadn't meant to say that last part aloud. She wasn't sure how she knew it, and she was certain that Quinn would require more explanation, so she wasn't at all surprised when he tried to press her for more information.

"I don't know how I know it. I just do. There is something about him that I can't put into words. A sort of," she paused as she struggled to verbalize her feelings. "A sameness; an undeniable similarity to me, to us. I cannot and will not ignore. I felt the same thing when I first met you, and I know you know what I'm talking about."

Q avoided her eyes, drawing a small circle in the sandy dirt with his well-worn leather shoe, before responding.

"Yeah, I do. I don't like it, but there is something about this guy that feels frustratingly familiar. Like I've met him somewhere, but I can't quite place him. It's been buggin' the hells outta me since we met him."

Elena grabbed his hand and waited until he looked up at her. "I know it's unsettling, but that feeling is your intuition. Trust it. We don't know enough about him yet to make a fair judgment. We need to try to get him to open up. Maybe he knows how to stop the *turmio* or maybe he knows where to look to find out. Regardless, he knows more about it than anyone else, so we need to work with him." She squeezed his hand when she said "with" to emphasize it.

He pulled her into a one-armed hug, resting his chin on the top of her head. "Fine, El. I'll play nice. I don't trust him, but I'll stop making digs at him. For now."

"Thank you," she muttered into his chest.

Quinn planted a soft kiss on her forehead, then disappeared with Lyra into the high grass in search of kindling for their fire.

52

QUINN

T HEY ATE DINNER IN peaceful silence before heading into the makeshift shelter. Roska had abstained from El's magical ingredients, which Q thought was ridiculous, but in an effort to reign in his snark, he said nothing. Elena had thrown her magic cloak over the tops of the stone semi-circle, making a tent-like roof to protect them from the frosty winds and threat of storms thundering in the distance. Q decided he would never not be impressed by the magic infused into her cloak. The moment she'd tossed it over the top of the stones, it settled cleanly into place, shimmered, and proceeded to change color, blending in perfectly with the stones and surrounding high grass. From the road, no one would even know they were there; it was the perfect camouflage. He wasn't entirely confident that it would fool the enchantresses hunting them, but he was certain it would at least slow them down.

The stone circle was a bit tight for three people, but Q refused to leave Elena alone with Roska. Sure, he'd agreed to give the guy a chance, but he wasn't an idiot and he refused to put

348

Elena in unnecessary risk. Instead, Quinn positioned himself between Elena and Roska, keeping Roska at the entrance to their temporary home. At this point, he didn't feel the need to keep Roska around, so Q wasn't worried about whether or not Roska might sneak away in the night.

In fact, Quinn kinda hoped he would. Save them all a lot of trouble and headaches.

Unfortunately for Q, when he awoke the next morning—just before dawn thanks to Lyra—Roska was still there. Sleeping like a child, curled around Demoni as though he were trying to protect her from the world.

Q hated the feeling of understanding that he had at seeing them positioned in such a way. That was the same way he and Lyra had slept every night during their time at the orphanage and for several cycles after. Q was starting to get the impression that the longer Roska hung around, the more Q would start to identify and ultimately sympathize with him. That thought irritated him to no end. He liked it better when things were black and white. It was easier to think of Roska as the enemy, not someone with whom he shared a similar, traumatic back-story.

Q quietly stepped around Roska and Demoni. He needed to piss, stretch his legs, and clear his mind. He silently asked Lyra to stay with Elena to keep an eye on Roska before he headed down to the stream.

As he knelt by the cool rushing water, Q thought he heard something rustle in the grass behind him. He froze. Someone or something was watching him. Stalking him. He didn't want to tip his hand just yet, so he pretended as though he hadn't noticed them. Splashing some water on his face with one hand, while stealthily collecting his heat and power in the other. Listening intently, he was able to determine that the creature watching him was behind him and slightly south of his position. Whatever it was, it was big.

Q had to be careful. The grass surrounding them was dry and brittle. Apparently, the storm from the night before had decided to miss them entirely, and if he decided to throw his flames at the would-be attacker, he might set the whole field ablaze. He'd grown confident in his ability to control his fire, but not *that* confident.

Lyra, something is here. Q hoped that by alerting her, she would be able to warn the others. He didn't like not being there to protect Elena from whatever was stalking him, but having Lyra there was the next best thing.

I hear it. It sounds like multiple somethings, she replied.

The cry of a falcon echoed overhead. Q glanced up to track it, recognizing the creature a moment too late. Before he could shout a warning to Elena, Q was tackled by the creature that had been stalking him in the grass. The ocelot lunged at him, its front claws barely contained as it pinned him to the ground.

Quinn tried to throw the beast off and was quickly frozen in place by the shot of an arrow narrowly missing his thigh.

"My next shot will not miss, boy."

He recognized that voice. It was the investigator who nearly started an armed battle in the middle of Amelia's dining hall. Lillith. Q remained frozen, opting out of starting a fire fight just yet as he strained to hear what was happening with Elena. He couldn't make out much of the words being exchanged, but he could hear grunting, arguing, and the scuffle of a fight.

The ocelot had moved to a seated position on his chest. Claws still mostly contained, but making it clear that if he made any sudden movements, they wouldn't remain that way. They stayed that way for several tense moments until he heard the falcon's cry again. It must have signified an "all clear" to the blonde with the bow because she recalled her familiar and invited Q to stand. She kept her arrow trained on him as she gestured for him to walk, leading her back to their campsite.

Elena's hands were bound behind her back. Agon was in a small cage, shaking with rage and a vibrant, brilliant blue glow pulsated along his spine. Lyra was hogtied, lying on the ground beside Agon's cage, smoke rising faintly from her tail and a string of rope bound around her muzzle. Roska had a bloody nose and was bound in the same manner as Elena. Demoni was in a small cage of her own, but surprisingly calm about it.

Quinn had a distant thought that Demoni might have spent the majority of her life in a cage and was therefore used to the confined space.

"Q! You're bleeding!" Elena cried out. He looked down at his shirt to see that he was in fact, bleeding through eight small holes in the front of his shirt.

"Damn," he muttered. "This was my favorite shirt."

"Shut up, boy," the blonde said as she shoved him over to stand beside Roska. One of the twins used her magic to bind Q's hands behind his back as well.

"It didn't have to be this way, Elena," the other twin spoke with a heavy sadness. "We just wanted to take you home, back to Harbor Ridge and the life you loved. If your mother had known how powerful you are, she never would have let you go."

"Let me go?" Elena replied incredulously. "She didn't *let* me do anything. She kicked me out. She *told* me to go. She didn't want me there, and I have no interest in going back."

"I cannot believe your mother would do such a thing. She loves you. You are her only daughter. All mothers love their children."

Now it was Quinn's turn to scoff. "You can't be serious with that shyt. Not all mothers love their kids. Hells, some mothers see their kids as miserable little shyts, inconveniences that mux up their grand plans. From everything Elena has told me about her mother, that woman doesn't deserve another second of Elena's time."

Without warning, a hand struck across his face, knocking him to the ground and splitting his lip.

"You will not speak of the Headmistress in such a way, boy. You are unworthy to speak her name, much less besmirch her reputation."

Q spat out blood and glared up at the ginger enchantress who had struck him. "I'm not besmirching anyone. Just stating facts. If you're unhappy with the truth, take that up with your head bitch. Sorry," he spat blood at her feet, "headmistress."

His snark rewarded him with a swift kick to the ribs that left him coughing and struggling to sit upright.

"Seph, what the hells is wrong with you?!" Elena shrieked

"Your boy needs to be taught some humility," she replied coolly and positioned herself for a follow-up kick, but one of the twins stepped in front of her, blocking her aim and shielding Quinn from another blow.

"Seph, this isn't how we do things." Her words were quiet but firm.

"Maybe this isn't how you do things, Maddy," the reply came as an angry hiss. "But this is how we get things done. We've never had any complaints before." She added with a wink to the blonde who smirked in response.

"Elena, please," Maddy pleaded, "just come with us willingly. We don't want to hurt you or your boys. We are just following orders."

"Isn't that the same excuse people always use when they are caught in the act of committing atrocities?" Roska's voice was gruff and sounded odd in Quinn's ears. Although that could have been because his ears were still ringing from that slap.

Seph took an aggressive step toward him, but Maddy blocked her access again.

"Enough." Lillith's tone was harsh and authoritative. "We don't need your consent to complete our mission. We don't even need you to be conscious. We have our orders, and we will obey them."

Before Quinn had a chance to fully process her words, she waved her hand, muttering under her breath, and his world went black.

53

BEATRICE

A COUPLE OF DAYS had passed since her last missive from
the investigators hunting her daughter. In their note,
they informed her that they had captured Elena after an al-
tercation in the Dragon's Teeth mountains and were bringing
her home, along with her two "problematic" traveling companions.

Two.

Beatrice hadn't taken a full breath since receiving that message.

That message had forced her to confront truths about her
life and her past that were too much for her to bear. She had
spent so much time and energy trying to deny the truth or
convince herself that she'd misinterpreted the prophecy all
those cycles ago. Now though, there was no denying it. The
prophecy was coming true right before her eyes, and there was
nothing she could do to stop it. Hells, the prophecy was currently unconscious and being carried back to her front door,
expected to arrive any day.

Not for the first time, Beatrice wished she'd never met that damned trickster man. Never bedded him. Never gotten pregnant. If only she'd gone to a different tavern, or a different town. If she'd been a bit more experienced in the art of deception, then perhaps she would have noticed the flaws in his disguise. Assuming there were flaws in his disguise. He was a demi-god after all. It was possible that there was nothing she could have done to avoid that particular encounter. That was a common refrain she told herself hundreds of times over the years. She had no way of knowing who he truly was, and was therefore not responsible for the ramifications of that night.

She regretted becoming a mother because it meant that she was the reason the world was losing its magic, and she was responsible for all the death that would follow. If only she'd stayed home that night. This all could have been avoided.

"You know that's not how prophecy works. This was destined to happen, and there's nothing you could have done to change the outcome."

"Do you mean for that to make me feel better, Zied? Because we both know it won't. Save your breath." His logical attitude was entirely unwelcome in her emotional state.

He nudged her thigh with his large, wet nose and chuffed. His attempts at offering comfort and reassurance. She'd spent the days since that dreaded first missive, identifying Elena and

Agon as the source of that new power, sitting at her desk, wracking her mind to determine how best to proceed.

Things were coming to a head that she'd never intended to see the light of day. She was ill-prepared for this situation. If she hadn't spent all those cycles in denial, desperately and foolishly trying to ignore the prophecy and all that it entailed, then maybe she would be in a better position to explain her actions and choices to Elena, to all of them. They all deserved an explanation.

54
ELENA

ELENA AWOKE WITH A start in a silent, dark room. It took her several moments to realize where she was: on the hard, cold floor of the testing room she'd spent so many hours in before being abruptly booted from her home. She was back at Harbor Ridge, despite her vehement protests. At least this time she wasn't alone. Q and Roska lay in heaps on either side of her, groaning as they awoke and tried to sit upright while still being bound. She was surprised to see Agon, Lyra, and Demoni laying on the floor in front of their respective partners. Either her mother didn't realize what Demoni and Lyra were to Roska and Quinn, or she didn't deem them a threat. Knowing her mother and her incredible arrogance, Elena was pretty confident that she recognized them as familiars and simply considered them to be too weak to pose a viable threat.

Elena said nothing as she studied the room. It was dark with no sunlight shining through from the windows on all sides of the room, not even a hint of the sun's warm rays on either horizon. No candles had been lit, so she had to assume it was just after dusk and the maintenance staff hadn't come through to light them yet.

"Where the hells are we?" Quinn grumbled to her left.

"Harbor Ridge."

"Into the belly of the beast." Roska's flat tone betrayed his anxiety at being brought into the school that he had likely been raised to believe was the source of all evil.

"That description seems a bit harsh, young man, especially considering you don't actually know us. What makes you so sure you're the hero in this story? In this place, your so-called home is the cause of much of our strife and the site of our greatest enemy." Madame LaBelle entered through a hidden doorway behind a tapestry on the eastern wall. There were hundreds of hidden passages and secret doors throughout the school that were used almost exclusively by the headmistress in order to limit her time in the public eye and enable her to move around the school without being overburdened by her students. Walking a few steps behind Madame LaBelle as she made her way to the chair at the dais along the north wall, was her massive and intimidating familiar, Zied. Seph and Lilith along with two of the headmistress's special guards, flanked the chair and kept a close eye on their prisoners.

Sorry, "guests," Elena corrected her own thoughts sarcastically. "Why are we here, Mother? You made it very clear the last time I saw you that you wanted nothing to do with me."

"I made it clear that you didn't have the magical aptitude to maintain a position at Harbor Ridge. This school is, after all, a place for the best and most promising enchantresses in Waverly. When I sent you away, that was true. Even you must admit you were quite an abysmal student."

Her mother's bluntness felt like a slap across her already bruised and beaten ego. Before she could respond, Quinn was on his feet and taking aggressive steps toward her mother.

Madame Labelle flicked her wrist at him with an air of annoyance. "Sit down, boy. I don't have time for your rage at the moment. We have more pressing issues." Q seemed to be struggling to speak and he looked as though he was walking through quicksand.

"Mother! Release him! He's not going to harm you, and you're hurting him!" Elena cried out. She struggled to undo the magic that bound him. "Q, please, just stop fighting her. She'll stop when you calm down. Please." Her voice was strained.

"Take him to the cellars. I will deal with him later." Madame LaBelle waved a dismissive hand towards Q, but Elena stepped in front of him, blocking him from Madame LaBelle's sight. She raised her hands in his defense, as sparks of lightning arced between her fingertips. The magical binds that had held her hands behind her back were gone. Elena wasn't sure how that had happened, but she was pretty confident that her mother hadn't released her.

"You will not be taking him anywhere." Her voice was calm, but firm, and filled with a powerful rage she'd never felt before. Agon had jumped from his spot on the ground at Elena's feet to perch protectively on Q's shoulders. Lyra stood beside Elena, teeth bared with a flame at the ready on the tip of her tail.

"You arrogant, foolish child," her mother practically shouted at her. "You would choose this boy over your own mother? I created you! He's just a man. They are easily replaced and only useful for one thing." The rage in her voice was palpable, but there was a hint of something else there too. Fear?

"You might be my blood, but he is my family. More so than you have ever been," Elena shot back.

"Ah, the irony of that sentiment. I'm surprised you never told her," Roska spoke with the passive arrogance of someone who knew something he shouldn't. Elena wasn't sure who he was addressing at first until she saw the fury in her mother's eyes turn to him.

"You have no idea what you're talking about, boy." There was venom in her words as she spoke to him. "Seph, get him out of here. Take him to the prisons by the guardhouse. I don't want him anywhere near the girls."

"Why is that, Mother? What is it about this boy that bothers you so much?" Elena's inquiry was met with a glare from her mother followed by a loud guffaw from Roska.

"Because, dear *tyttö*, she's afraid I'll reveal the truth behind all the lies she's been telling for the last seventeen cycles."

Elena shifted her gaze from her mother, to Roska, then slowly back to her mother. Seventeen cycles. Elena was sixteen cycles old now, but if she did the math correctly, it had been almost exactly seventeen cycles since her conception. What lie had her mother been keeping all of her life? She felt as though someone had dropped a bucket of freezing water over her head. She wasn't sure how she knew, but she was certain this secret had to do with her "unusual" birth and the powers she and Agon shared.

"Seph, now!" Madame LaBelle nearly screeched.

Roska knew things she didn't want him to share, but even the guards were intrigued and unmoving. Giving Roska a chance to demolish Elena's whole world.

55

ROSKA

"**Y**OU SEE, *TYTTÖ*, SEVENTEEN cycles ago, almost to the day—"

"Stop talking, boy!" Madame LaBelle shrieked with barely contained fury and fear.

Elena raised her hand toward the woman, blue lightning flashed across her fingertips and pulsated up her exposed arms.

"Mother, do not say another word," Elena commanded.

Roska was momentarily stunned as he watched the clearly furious headmistress freeze, as though the words were literally stuck in her throat. Her hands flew to her neck and her eyes popped wide.

One of the guards moved to take a step toward Elena, but Quinn, having somehow been released from the spells that bound him, raised his own hands in a defensive posture. His hands were on fire. At the sight of him, the four guards all froze, looks of shock, awe, and terror passed across each of their faces.

"It's quite a sight to behold, isn't it?" Roska asked the guards, knowing they wouldn't respond. They were too astounded to put together a coherent thought. Roska took this moment of distraction to test his own binds. They had vanished as well. He had no idea how magic worked, but he had to assume that Elena had managed to release the magic that bound them when she cast her own magic on the headmistress.

He nodded a quick thanks to Quinn and continued. "When I was a young boy, the Brotherhood told me about a prophecy that heralded the end of magic and the rebirth of the world, free from the stains of evil that magic attracts. They taught me that I was the first and only FrostBorn child, and it was my soul's purpose to release the *turmio* and rid the world of evil."

Elena and Quinn both turned to him with looks of shock and confusion on their respective faces, but neither said a word. They were waiting to hear his whole story. Roska held their stares respectively for a moment but glanced down to pick up Demoni. She coiled up his arm as he continued his tale.

"As I got older, they revealed more and more of the prophecy to me, explaining that I was one piece of a three-part puzzle that would change the world forever. I was the product of evil, they told me, but I wasn't alone. I took comfort in knowing that somewhere in the world, the rest of my puzzle was waiting for me to join them and finally find peace.

"A few moons ago, I felt a strange surge of power pass through me. Like a monster waking up from a long hibernation, I felt the strength of it grow within me, and I was compelled to leave the monastery. The Brothers told me that it was time for me to know the whole truth of my history and my future.

"They told me about an enchantress, the most powerful and talented enchantress the world had ever known. This woman in all of her arrogance had ventured out into a small hamlet with the intention of deceiving a man and conceiving his child. What this arrogant enchantress didn't realize was that the man she picked wasn't a random farmer as she had been led to believe. He was a rare magical creature himself, hiding in plain sight, lying in wait for her arrival.

"He was the last of his kind, a demi-god of untold age, and the most powerful creature on this planet. Their coupling set into motion a long-forgotten prophecy when the enchantress beget not one, not two, but three magical children at once. It was the first time such a pregnancy had ever existed, and it will likely be the only pregnancy of its kind to ever occur again."

Roska paused, letting his words sink in and waiting to see the realization cross their faces. Agon slipped down from Quinn's shoulders to run up the back of Elena's leg and settle around her neck. Lyra kept her fierce gaze on the guards but edged closer to Quinn.

Elena, who had still been staring angrily at Madame LaBelle, slowly paled and turned to face Quinn and then Roska.

"Three. Three babies," she uttered. Her voice barely above a whisper.

Roska nodded solemnly.

"You're... FrostBorn?" Quinn asked as he turned his perplexed face toward Roska and away from the guards. The flames on his hands dimmed but didn't fade.

"Yes, *veli*, I am."

"I'm FlameBorn. Elena is StormBorn. That's what the witch said." Roska could see the gears turning in Quinn's head as he processed Roska's revelations.

"Are you saying...?" Elena led but didn't seem to want to vocalize the words.

"Yes, my dear *tyttö*, we are the children of the prophecy. I am your brother. Quinn is your brother. You are our sister. Madame LaBelle bore the three of us in her womb and separated us at the first possible second, forcing us to grow up alone, isolated, ignorant of our powers, and scared."

"I have brothers." Elena's voice was raw. Her skin had gone white as the sheets Roska used to clean at the monastery.

"I have siblings?" Quinn was less shocked and more confused.

The three of them shared a long look, and then Elena turned on her—*their*—mother.

"I have brothers?!" The rage in her voice shook the windows. Lightning flew from the tips of Elena's fingers and left scorch marks on the stone walls and ceiling.

Madame LaBelle collapsed in her chair, head in hands, her white lion almost seemed to cower behind the chair.

The flames on Quinn's hands roared to life, raising the temperature of the otherwise chilled room to an uncomfortably warm degree.

Roska, finally feeling free to release the rage that had been building within him his whole life, raised his own hands and felt a well rise up in his chest, rising higher and higher until it crested and poured out of his hands like a busted dam. Ice shot from his palms in a great rush, filling the room with snow that quickly melted thanks to Quinn's fire, ultimately soaking them all.

Elena quickly put her lightning away, as she had the control to do that and presumably didn't want to electrify everyone by mixing her powers with those of her brothers. Roska felt as though he were drowning in his powers. He'd never felt this release before, and he had no idea how to stop it. The more ice and snow that poured from him, the more terrified he became. He squeezed his eyes shut and tried desperately to put a seal back on the well that had exploded within him.

He felt warm hands on his face and shoulders. Slowly, Roska opened his eyes to see Elena and Quinn holding him. Neither of them said a word as the ice continued to cascade from his opened palms. With a gentleness that Roska didn't realize Quinn possessed, he felt Quinn's hands enclose his left hand. Elena's hands left his face and enclosed around his right hand. Despite the ice still flowing, Roska could feel the warmth seeping in from their hands as their powers mingled with his.

They stood like that for moments, or eons, Roska wasn't sure. The moment they all connected and their powers intertwined, the world stood still.

When the ice eased and the lightning and flame dissipated, they remained standing together in the middle of the room. Elena released a hand from Roska's and took Quinn's hand in her own. As they closed the circle with their contact, a pulse of power surged through them and spread from them like an earthquake, shaking the building around them and shattering every single pane of glass in the castle.

Acknowledgments

First and foremost, I want to thank my husband for his unending support. None of this would have been possible without him. He has always cheered me on—quietly because he's not a very vocal man—and encouraged me to keep going, especially when my anxiety gets the better of me and I start doubting every single thing I do.

I'm so grateful to my parents for their support (and free babysitting) while I try to create a world and raise a couple of tiny humans at the same time.

My friends, Kayla, Melissa, Lena, and Tonya, have been so amazing and supportive through this whole process. Helping me find the right words when my brain would crap out. Talking through plot twists and the creation of new characters. Honestly, this whole book would have been a mess without them.

To the friends I've made "in the biz" over the last few months. Kerrie, Vanessa, Arielle, Alina, Cynthia, and Julia, thank you all for keeping me sane through this crazy process, answering all of my incessant questions, and being so supportive. My favorite thing about the Bookstagram and Booktok universes is just how open, helpful, and supportive these communities really are. Arguably, these women are my competition, and in any other field, they would likely not want to share their trade "secrets" or offer advice to help me succeed, but this is not a normal job. Writing books can feel like a very isolated and lonely world, but these women have helped me grow in my confidence and supported me while I fought to navigate the rough waters of indie publishing. It would have been a much more challenging experience without them and I am forever grateful.

Lastly, I want to thank you, dear reader, for spending your precious time and money with me in the world that I created. None of this would be worth a damn without you.

About Author

2021

Mallory is a wife to the most wonderful man and a stay-at-home mom to two young boys. She spends her days homeschooling and full-time parenting. Her nights—and any free time she manages to carve out during the day—are spent reading and writing.

In 2018, Mallory decided that she would finally write a book of her own. Three and a half years later, squeezing in writing sessions every chance she could get—in coffee shops while her husband was home with their boys, at the dining room table between snacks and meals, in the middle of the night on her phone—Mallory finally managed to complete her goal!

Sometimes it takes a long time for our dreams to become a reality, but if you keep moving forward, you will get there. It might take [years] longer than you expected, but you can do it!